Finding OUR FOREVER

LAURA RILEY

Finding Our Forever
A Second Chance Romance
Copyright © 2020 by Laura Williams

Published by
Laura Williams
www.authorlaurariley.com

Cover Artist: Steamy Designs
Photographer: Wander Aguiar
Model: Dane D
Editor: RJ Locksley

Library of Congress Cataloging-in-Publication Data
Finding Our Forever – 1st ed
ISBN-13: 9798734717158

Prologue

Lizzie

The waters are a little muddied as to when our journey began. I've loved you as far back as I can remember, maybe before consciousness took hold and memories formed everlasting imprints in my mind.

My earliest memory of you is when you threw a water balloon in my face. It was meant for my older brother, but he ducked out of the way. I was five, and you were fourteen. I remember how you scooped me up when I cried. Holding me close, you dried my cheeks with your t-shirt. That's what I remember—that's the moment our journey began.

You see, moments are like stepping stones. They form unique paths. Once started these paths cannot be erased, nor can you stop the journey, no matter how hard you fight it.

This, Seth Stevens, is the stepping stone path to us.

Finding our forever.

Chapter One

Lizzie

"—and Lizzie, in a few hours you'll have kissed your prince and be living your happily ever after." Chelsea sighs dramatically as she clasps the pink-dusted makeup brush to her chest. She stands like she's holding an Oscar for the speech she just delivered about true love and fate.

I snort out a laugh. If only life were that simple. One thing I love about my friend is her optimism. But what's the harm in dreaming, right?

When I don't reply, she snaps out of her reverie and continues to add the finishing touches to my makeup.

It's a typical Saturday evening with my girlfriends, sisters Chelsea and Amber. We're glamming ourselves up in their photography shop in preparation for a girls' night out. The 'closed' sign hangs on the door so that we have the place to ourselves.

Chelsea steps back. "Word has it that Seth Stevens is officially back on the market."

Like I didn't know.

Her crystal-blue eyes are like saucers as she tries to read my expression. I liken myself to a book that is half open. My hope is that I can keep an air of mystery while at the same time giving only snippets of myself away. But who am I kidding? The spine is bent back, and all my pages are open for all to see.

My mouth drops open as I feign surprise. "Back on the market, really? I had no idea."

With her hands on her hips, she looks me up and down. "Mm-hmm. Really, Lizzie." Sarcasm twists her expression.

"I call bullshit," Amber hollers from the back of the shop, the sound of her stiletto shoes echoing as she tidies away her photography equipment.

I flip her the finger, which I know she'd flip back if it wasn't for the camera and tripod she's carrying.

She's right to call me on my bullshit. There isn't much about Seth I don't know. My brother works with him and occasionally I get snippets of information. I rake through our conversations, weeding out the unimportant stuff. I plant the seeds of knowledge and let them grow into endless possibilities in my mind.

When I returned home from uni a year ago, Seth was all I thought about. Something about being back home and geographically closer to him made him less of a fantasy and more of a possibility, more of a reality. Cornwall isn't a big place; I was sure to bump into him, right?

I played out our first conversation a million times in my mind—what I'd say to him, what he'd say to me in return, the way he'd look at me. I am a firm believer that if I ask enough times Fate will answer my call. So far she hasn't, but I'm not giving up.

But since I've been back, the days have turned into weeks and the weeks into months. I no longer play out my stupid fantasies in my mind. I no longer look for him.

However, tonight I'm flipping Fate the finger and taking matters into my own hands. Seth is out tonight and so am I. I'm going to make damn sure that our paths cross.

Chelsea spins me around on my stool so that I'm facing the long wall-mounted mirror. She bends down and presses her cheek against mine. "Well, what do you think?"

Wow. "I look... different."

I don't normally make this much of an effort on a night out, but this evening I'm letting Chelsea doll me up. I don't want Seth to look at me, I want him to stare. I want interest to claw at his resolve until he has no option other than to talk to me.

Amber's reflection joins Chelsea's as she stands at her side. "Yes, it looks like you're actually wearing makeup. The plain Jane schoolteacher look is getting old. Goodbye, Miss Boring. Hello, Miss Sex-ay."

I hold out my arms. "Well, I can't very well teach a class of thirty teenagers dressed to the nines, can I?"

Amber squeezes her boobs together, showing off her ample cleavage. "Why not? I think a few more kids would choose to take art if you did. Think of it like this, you'd be doing it for the good of your students."

I roll my eyes so dramatically that Chelsea yells at me because her carefully-placed false eyelash strip detaches from my eyelid.

"Hold still," she demands while gluing it back into place. My eyes have been heavily made up. I have three different shades of brown shadow on my lids. I feel like an

3

Egyptian queen with the combo of eyeshadow, liner, and long sweeping lashes.

Amber gives me a lopsided grin. "You know, my clothes look pretty good on you."

"Do you think so?" I glance down at the gold sequinned halter-neck top and black skinny jeans I'm wearing. They're so tight they feel like a second skin. I usually dress down, whereas Amber always dresses to impress. Tonight, I'm stepping out of my comfort zone and into her shoes, literally. Black stilettos with a six-inch heel.

Amber looks me up and down. "You look hot. I'd do you."

I don't feel comfortable in my own skin, especially when I'm out with Chelsea and Amber. The sisters are beautiful, with porcelain skin, crystal-blue eyes, and flowing blonde hair. Their flawless looks are enough to intimidate the most self-assured.

Chelsea stands with one hand on her hip and the other holding the curling irons. "Want me to style your hair?"

I beam up at her reflection. I read on a Facebook poll that guys find curly hair sexier than straight. I don't believe everything I read, but tonight, if I can do anything to make myself more appealing, I will. Right down to the dark red lipstick and matching nails I'm wearing.

Once we're ready, we call for a taxi. The company informs us that they'll be at least forty minutes, leaving us no other option but to finish another bottle of bubbly while we wait. A little bit of liquid courage is certainly called for tonight because, without it, I'll never get up the courage to approach Seth. I'll sit and watch him from afar, like I usually do.

By the time we've shared a bottle of bubbly and taken

a dozen selfies, the taxi driver honks his horn outside. We exit the shop, laughing like a bunch of teenagers going to prom.

Amber and Chelsea both opted for knee-length black dresses this evening, and their long blonde hair falls in soft curls down their backs. I don't know if them matching was intentional, but it certainly makes me feel like the odd one out, like an ugly duckling besides two elegant swans.

We cram into the backseat of the taxi. The driver stares a bit too long at us through his rear-view mirror. At traffic lights he adjusts his mirror downward, making no secret that he's staring at our cleavages. Chelsea doesn't notice his wandering eyes as she twirls her hair and pops her gum.

Feeling uncomfortable, I pull out my compact mirror from my clutch bag and peer at my face. Amber imitates a blowjob—something she often does to make men feel awkward. But her lewd gesture does nothing to dissuade our driver.

Amber averts her attention to her phone. "They're in the Golden Kite," she announces.

I close my compact mirror. "And how do you know?"

Amber grins smugly. "That's for me to know."

Chelsea waggles her eyebrows. "She totally stalks Rick on social media."

I've not been formally introduced to Rick, but Chelsea said he messaged Amber on social media, and the pair met up a few weeks ago.

Amber clucks her tongue. "Excuse you, have you seen Roderick lately? Hashtag #sorrynotsorry."

She definitely spends way too much time on Instagram.

The taxi drops us off outside the club. Amber pays the fare.

The Golden Kite is one of the town's oldest night-clubs. The exterior is rendered white, and a golden embossed kite is printed next to the double-door entrance. It isn't the most upmarket place in town, its clientele mostly in their thirties and older. Amber, Chelsea and I are in our mid-twenties, so there's no doubt in my mind that we'll be among the youngest partygoers here.

It's not surprising that there isn't a long queue of people waiting to get in. But I'm more than happy to slum it knowing Seth is inside.

"IDs, ladies," the bouncer says in a bored voice.

After we make our way in, we leave our jackets at the front desk, where a lady hands us a numbered ticket. Now that we're inside, we make our way up a narrow flight of stairs. My heart starts beating a little faster. What if he's really here? Then what do I do?

I've not seen Seth since I was eighteen, and I've often wondered how life has treated him. Will he be broader than I remember, taller? Will he have more facial hair? I remember years ago he started growing a beard. He was gorgeous then and I doubt he will have changed.

The music hits us as soon as we enter. Strobe lighting bounces around the room, making it harder to make out faces.

"Come on," Amber says as she grabs my hand and pulls me toward a corner booth.

While Amber and Chelsea browse the cocktail menu, I scan the room. And that's when I see him—Seth Stevens is sitting at the bar with a pint in his hand. Oh, my God, he's even better-looking than I remember. His dark brown hair is a little longer maybe, and a small section falls forward, covering his brow. Every so often, he attempts to push it back into place. His face hasn't changed, but he has matured and he has a trim beard. His body is more toned than I remember. He has defined biceps with a tribal tattoo that wasn't there before. He's wearing a tight-fitting black t-shirt and a pair of well-worn jeans.

"Screaming Orgasm, Sex on the Beach, Slippery Nipple, or Frozen Pink Panties?" Amber asks.

"Yes to all," I say with a sigh. "I'm sorry, what?"

Blonde curls dance as she shakes her head. "Cocktails. I'm reading out the list."

All the cocktails have a sexual reference. I'm not a prude by any stretch of the imagination, but I just don't think that way. Amber often calls me Sandy—as in the Olivia Newton-John character from *Grease*. The boring, cardigan-wearing wallflower. But not tonight. Tonight, I'm the hot, carefree version and all I'm missing is her black leather catsuit.

"Oh, my God, girls, look." An arm shoots in front of my face as Amber points toward Seth and the two men at his side. "There's Rick."

While my friends swoon over him, I spare him a quick glance before returning my gaze to Seth. "He's not my type."

Chelsea's mouth falls open. "What? Tall, dark and handsome isn't your type? Are you mad?"

Amber grabs my arm. "There's Seth."

I glance down, inspecting my painted nails. "Seth? I can't say I noticed him."

She gives me a knowing look. "Let's go order the drinks."

Seth's sitting at the bar, so if I walk up there to order drinks, he'll surely see me. If he speaks to me, what will I say? "No, you guys go ahead. I'm just going to—"

"Just going to what? Sit here gawking at him?"

Sounds good to me.

Amber doesn't give me time to reply. She grabs my hand and pulls me toward the bar, purposely leading me to where Seth and his friends are sitting. He's just feet away from me now. All I need to do is reach my hand out and I could touch him. My cheeks heat, butterflies dance in my stomach, and I inwardly rehearse our introduction.

"Thank me later," Amber hollers over the music.

Frowning, I turn to her. "Thank you for what?"

With a mischievous grin, she shoves me straight into Seth.

Tripping over my heels, I grab onto his t-shirt to steady myself. "Oh, my God, I'm so sorry!"

I take a second to compose myself. Still holding his t-shirt, I take a deep breath in. His scent is woodsy and masculine, with a hint of tobacco. Abruptly, I release him.

He turns and nods briefly. "No problem," he says before returning to his conversation with Rick and another man.

He didn't even recognize me. Did he even look at me? My heart sinks.

"Fucking seriously?" Amber says. "What do we have to do to get him to notice you, push you onto his dick?"

I swat her arm. "Shh, they'll hear you."

"Doubt it, but they'll hear this."

"Hear wh—"

She presses her index finger against my lips as the last few chords of the song play out. She waits for the small break between songs before waving her hand at the bartender. "I want three Screaming Orgasms."

As three heads turn our way, Amber smiles triumphantly.

Rick's eyes go wide as his gaze travels up and down Amber's body. Recognition sparks in his gaze. He jumps up from his bar stool. "Need me to help you with that?"

She blushes. "Sure. If you're man enough for the job."

"Three Screaming Orgasms. No problem. I'll carry them to your table."

Amber turns to Seth and the other guy. "Aren't you gentlemen going to offer to help?"

Crossing his arms over his chest, Seth examines Amber with fading interest. "Nah. I'm sure Rick's got this."

Seth hasn't looked at me once. Through me, yes. I may as well be bloody invisible. I spent hours getting dolled up, and for what? I'm kidding myself. Maybe he's not over his ex. Maybe he's not interested in anything tonight other than a drink with his friends.

Dejected, I follow Amber and Rick to our booth. Rick joins us for a short while, and Amber and Chelsea cling on his every word. I attempt to listen but instead find myself watching Seth and the other guy down a couple of shots and order more beers.

"I'm sorry, Lizzie. I seem to have drunk your Orgasm." Rick draws his lower lip between his teeth. "Can I get you another?"

"No, I'm good," I say.

"Hey, aren't you Cole's little sister?"

I don't recognise him. I don't recall my brother ever mentioning someone named Rick.

He extends his hand to me. "I'm one of your brother's business partners. Roderick Raffety."

I shake his hand.

Roderick Raffety. He must go by the name Rick now. Yes, I recall Cole talking about him. Seth, Cole, and Roderick own a construction company and I remember Rick hanging around with my brother and Seth at school. Rick would turn up at our house at all hours of the night and morning. He was what one would call a loose cannon. He was good-looking then too, but I only had eyes for Seth.

"It's lovely to see you again after all this time," I say. "My brother talks about you all the time." That's a lie. All Cole talks about is Cole, and occasionally Seth.

Rick stands. "I'd better head back to Seth and Dave, or they'll think I've abandoned them. Ladies, it's been lovely to meet you all. Maybe I'll come join you later." He winks at Amber before heading back to his friends.

"Bring your friend, and the bald one," Chelsea calls after him.

Amber snorts with laughter. "'And the bald one?' You've said some stupid shit, Chelse, but that—"

"I stood right in front of Seth," I blurt out, flopping back in the booth, "and he didn't even notice me."

An arm snakes around my shoulder. "Girlfriend, the night is young," Amber says. "Get some drinks inside you and then get your ass up on that dance floor. Make sure you dance where he can't miss you."

"And then what?"

"Then cast your invisible line and reel him in."

Somehow I doubt it's going to be that simple. The guy didn't pay one speck of attention to me. This whole evening is turning out to be a disaster.

Chapter Two

Seth

Tonight, I'm celebrating my divorce in the very club where I met my ex-wife. Talk about irony.

Up until now I've avoided eye contact with anyone other than my two friends sitting to my right. Apart from the blonde, no girl has attempted to talk to me. Every time I see a blonde, all I see is my ex-wife staring back. Anna hurt me pretty fucking bad.

Just as I'm about to order another shot, the DJ blasts the next tune. It's not just any song he's playing. It's the same track that was playing when I first laid eyes on my ex. She was wearing a leopard-print skin-tight dress, and boy did she look like she owned the dance floor. I have a sinking feeling in the pit of my stomach telling me that if I turn around, she'll be there. I glance at the dance floor, scanning the people dancing, and my eyes go wide.

When did she get here?

Not Anna, but someone else. Someone I haven't seen in years.

Lizzie Crowley?

Rick's eyes burn into me. "I hope you're not looking at who I think you are." His voice is laced with accusation as he hollers over the loud music.

I don't answer. I don't need to. On the dance floor I see only her, Elizabeth Crowley. What's she doing here? Didn't she move to London after uni? Maybe she's just visiting.

"Yo." Rick waves his hand in front of my face. "Put your damn tongue back in your mouth." He downs his pint. "We're leaving. Now."

Listen to your friend, Seth. Stop staring at Lizzie's ass and get yours out of here.

But I don't listen to Rick, and I don't listen to the voice of reason in my head. Instead, I swig my beer, set the empty glass down, and make my way across the dance floor. To *her*.

The music is blaring, and strobe lights bounce off her body, highlighting every delicious curve. Her eyes are closed, her arms in the air as she sways from side to side. Wearing a pair of tight-fitting jeans and a sequinned halter top, she's lit up like a damn Christmas tree, and I've always been a sucker for Christmas.

I make no secret of the fact that I'm watching her, and that I like what I see. I join her on the dance floor and tower over her petite body. Her shoulder-length brown hair falls in spirals to her shoulders. Her face is the shape of a heart, her nose small, yet slightly upturned at the tip. Her perfect Cupid's bow lips are painted fuck-me red.

Suddenly, her eyes open and recognition sparks in her gaze. She smiles right at me. Fuck! When did Cole's baby sister turn into a beautiful, sexy woman?

"Lizzie Crowley!" I shout over the music. "Last time I saw you, you were at secondary school, and you were this tall." I hover my hand in the air, estimating her height that last time I saw her. The fact that my hand is in line with her breasts hasn't escaped my notice. Her breasts are a perfect handful.

She attempts to stand taller, puffing out her chest in the process. "I'm all grown up now."

Stepping back, I allow my gaze to slowly rove over her body... a body she's grown into. I'm a bit drunk and the part of my brain that's supposed to help me reason isn't working very well right now, so I'm openly staring.

"You certainly are," I say. "Definitely all grown up."

She swats my arm, and if I'm not mistaken, she's blushing.

My ex, Anna, never blushed. She loved compliments. She was gorgeous, and she knew it. Beneath all her layers of foundation, fake tan, and hair extensions, she had an ugly soul.

I shake my head, removing my focus from Lizzie's tits to her caramel-brown eyes. "It's been a long time."

She smiles. "Not that long. You saw me about two hours ago at the bar and completely ignored me."

I run my hand over my beard, I honestly don't recall seeing her at the bar, only Blondie and her lame attempt to get our attention. I was too wrapped up in bad memories to pay attention to the present. But I'm paying attention now.

"Want to dance?" I ask her.

She motions from me to her. "We are dancing."

Well, shit, she's right. In this moment I don't feel like the guy whose divorce was made official today. I don't feel like the guy who has to work a sixty-hour week to make ends meet. I'm thirty-three years old, newly single, and ready to mingle. I laugh.

Single and ready to fucking mingle?

God, I'm so drunk.

My sister, Darcy, was the one who insisted I go out tonight. She said I needed it, and she was right. I also needed the six pints and three shots. But more importantly, I need to get laid. Lizzie, however, is one girl who is strictly off limits. Her brother, my best friend—Cole—would kill me if I so much as touched her.

I work my finger up and down the strap of her halter-neck top and notice it's tied at the back of her neck. I imagine how easy it would be to tug on that little ribbon and watch the straps fall one at a time. I can see she's not wearing a bra underneath from the lack of straps and the way her nipples pebble under the thin fabric.

Stop thinking about her tits, douchebag.

As I glance around the bar, Rick and Dave are nowhere to be seen. No doubt they've moved on to another club. That's loyalty for you, but people aren't loyal, and I learnt that the hard way.

My gaze returns to Lizzie. "You're not here alone, are you? Where are your friends?"

She points behind me, at a booth in the corner. I turn to see two busty blondes, one of them being the blonde from earlier. Lo and behold, Rick and Dave are perched at their sides. The guys are the same age as me, and I'm guessing the girls are around the same age as Lizzie. It kinda makes me feel less awkward about the age gap.

I'm not doing anything wrong, I remind myself. *It's just one dance.*

Dave and Rick join us on the dance floor, along with

the two blondes. Lizzie's friends each flash me a glance and then waste no time grinding against my friends. Or rather grinding against Rick, while Dave attempts to join in. It's comical to watch. Dave isn't bad-looking, but Rick is a show-stealer. He's built like a tank, tall and muscular from all the hours he puts in at the gym. His dark hair has been sleeked back and secured in a manbun. He's no stranger to the dance floor—his moves are smooth.

Before long, one dance turns into two, and two into a dozen. Rick buys our group a fishbowl—a humongous glass bowl filled to the brim with spirits and cranberry juice. The sober members of the group get tipsy, and the drunk get louder. We're having a great night. I make small talk with the girls, Amber and Chelsea, but I know I'm standoffish with them. I can't help it. The more I drink, the more they remind me of my ex.

By two am the music is quieter and the songs begin to slow as we approach closing time. Dave makes out with a redhead to my left, while Rick and the blondes are no-where to be seen. The space between me and Lizzie gets smaller and smaller, our bodies grinding together. She gazes up at me with expectation and without thinking I lean down, capturing her chin, and brush my lips against hers. It's so quick it doesn't even qualify as a real kiss… just a brief brush of skin against skin. Just a tiny taste. Not enough to count. Not enough to get me in trouble with her brother. Or at least I hope not. My thoughts in that moment are far from innocent. I'm picturing what I'd like to do to her. She's far too drunk, though. Even I'm too drunk.

So stop touching her already.

I put some much-needed space between us and shove my hands in my pockets. "I need air."

Confusion skates over her features. Without a word I take her hand, grab my jacket from the bar stool, and lead her down a flight of stairs and out back to the beer garden. It's a small bricked area with minimal lighting. A few people linger, puffing on cigarettes or chatting on mobile phones. I think there are more people loitering, but dim lighting conceals them from view.

Lizzie and I sit on a small wooden bench underneath a wall-mounted light that flickers on and off every few seconds. The fresh air is sobering. I look to Lizzie, who's shivering. I slip off my jacket and drape it over her shoulders. Her makeup has faded from earlier, her mascara has smudged under her eyes, her fuck-me red lipstick now resides on the glasses of wine she was drinking from. She looks younger now, and the arm I was about to place around her stays in my lap.

We're alone, and for the first time in a long time I'm lost for words. Lizzie sits in total silence; I get the impression that she's waiting for me to talk. I guess I could ask her what she's been up to. "So, what have you been doing with yourself?"

Lizzie shrugs. "You know, a little bit of this, a little bit of that." She smiles awkwardly. "I'm a schoolteacher. I teach art at the local high school."

I pass her a sideward glance. "You always used to write my name in clouds."

They were hearts, not clouds, but I won't embarrass her. She was a cute kid, but so annoying. One day every annoying kid grows up, and Lizzie turned out to be one fine woman.

She begins fumbling with her phone, and finally tilts the screen in my direction. "Here, let's swap mobile numbers."

I can see she's still keen. I stare at the screen for a beat. I haven't given a girl my mobile number since Anna. Reluctantly I take the phone from her and start typing in my number. What's the harm in texting?

"There you go." I pass her back the phone. I'm itching to put my arm around her, be close to someone. I need something to do with my hands, so I pull a pack of cigarettes from my pocket and light up.

Lizzie doesn't move away, but instead rests her head against my arm.

We sit in silence and I can see her toying with the material of my jacket. "Eighteen," she says out of nowhere.

I frown, not following. "Eighteen?"

"I was eighteen when I last saw you."

How can I forget? If the truth be told, I haven't. I was twenty-seven. Lizzie dropped in where we were working one day. She'd brought sandwiches for Cole, but he'd driven out to grab lunch, so she'd missed him. She offered the sandwiches to me, and I was only too happy to accept. We spent my lunch hour talking in the front seat of my work van, laughing and eating and having a great time. The thought of kissing her then crossed my mind, but I just couldn't do it. She'd just turned eighteen, and besides, she was my best friend's baby sister. When I looked at her, I imagined Cole's reaction to the two of us together. There was a spark between us even then, and after tonight, I can definitely say there's an even stronger one now.

Lizzie always has been and always will be an itch that I can't and won't scratch. Damn it, I should never have danced with her tonight.

She's waiting for me to respond, but I don't. Instead I put out the cigarette against the side of the bench.

I look down when she places her hand on my knee. It's a perfectly innocent gesture on her part, but I can't help imagining her hand skimming higher up my thigh to my crotch. I'm so hard right now it's all I can think about.

"Do you want to do this again sometime?" she says. "We could all meet up again."

I know I can't let this go any farther, so I decide to let her down gently. "No, I don't think it's a good idea."

She scrunches up her face. "Why?"

"Because I'm not going to get myself involved with another female ever again. You're trouble, all of you." I need to remember that not every woman is Anna, but it's hard. My heart took a beating, and I fear it'll never beat again.

I blow out, feeling I need to explain myself so she doesn't think I'm a complete tosser. "My divorce came through today. To be honest I'm not looking for anything serious. I was just hoping to get laid tonight. I've not had sex in a very long time, and—"

Wait, did I actually say that out loud?

She doesn't move for a second.

Maybe I thought it?

My jacket is strewn across the bench. Tears stream down her face.

Shit.

"I can't believe you'd think so little of me."

"Hold on, Lizzie, I didn't mean—"

My words are taken from me. I don't see her hand, but I feel the slap.

Without another word, she takes off. The two blondes appear out of nowhere and run after her. The clicking of their stiletto shoes on the concrete disappears with them, and I'm sitting alone, holding my cheek.

Clapping his hands, Rick steps out of the shadows. "Smooth, real smooth," he says, humour in his voice. "Let's round up Dave and head to mine for a nightcap."

I've not consumed nearly enough alcohol to call it a night. "I have a better idea."

Chapter Three

Lizzie

I've never felt so angry, so humiliated. The tears that fall from my eyes are tears of disappointment from years of hope gone up in flames. That's what I get for playing with Fate. Guess she didn't want Seth and I to meet for a reason.

We're queueing in the club's small reception area, waiting to pick up our jackets from the cloakroom. Chelsea's arm is wrapped tightly around my shoulders. My friends heard exactly what was said, and to say they're less than impressed is the understatement of the century.

Amber squeezes my hand. "You're better off without him."

I smile, wiping my nose with the back of my hand. She's right, I know she is. It's time to find someone else to obsess over. The truth is, I never knew Seth, not really. I fantasised over the idea of him. Tonight has made me question what is it about the man that made my knees buckle and my heart gallop. The reality is I've never looked for a relationship, never really put myself out there. I held back. Held back for what?

Amber hands our tickets in and retrieves our jackets. "What about we get some food and head home?"

I shake my head. "No, I don't want to go home, not yet."

Arms linked, we leave the club and glance around the town. People are jumping into taxis and leaving bars and clubs.

"Everything is closing, hun," Amber points out.

I nod towards the white-walled pub sitting on the corner of the street. "Not the Bull's Head."

"I thought it closed at two am?" Chelsea is correct, but my brother's on-off girlfriend Gail is the landlady. She'll ring the bell that hangs above the bar for last orders and host lock-ins for the regulars. They play drinking games till late morning. Gail can drink most men under the table.

I lead the way to the pub. People pass us as they exit and, as predicted, Gail stands at the bar ringing the bell.

"Last orders." Her voice is husky, her tone sharp. She smiles when she sees me and nods her head in the direction of the back room. "Cole's changing the barrel; he'll be out shortly."

I glance towards the door behind her and give her the thumbs up. We take a seat at the bar. My brother often helps her out on their busy nights. I think he worries about her safety sometimes, so he acts as her bodyguard, but he needn't bother. Gail is not a lady you mess with.

Smiling, she grabs three glasses, topping them up with vodka and orange juice. She pushes the glasses our way. "On the house."

I take a sip, enjoying the heat as it goes down. "Thank you."

She certainly knows how to pack a punch with the vodka. Gail single-handedly runs the roughest bar in Cornwall. The Bull's Head attracts bikers from across the county. They seem to have a mutual respect for Gail, who is also a biker. She's a petite lady in her mid-fifties. She has strawberry-blonde hair and the lightest green eyes. Her body is covered in ink, mainly bike memorabilia and skulls. I never understood why Cole always went for the more mature lady until he met Gail. Gail's hot. I always come in to talk to her on my nights out. It doesn't escape my attention that her black leather skirts are considerably shorter and her tops are skimpier when Cole's about.

Gail slaps the bar with her hands, making a drumroll sound. "Lock-in tonight, ladies?"

Amber downs her drink and slides it back to Gail for a top-up. "Yes, we aren't nearly as drunk as we want to be."

"I can solve that problem for you." Gail's eyes bypass me, and she waves. I turn. Oh, great. Seth and Rick are standing in the doorway. After our earlier conversation, Seth is the last person I want to see.

Maybe his words were a slip of the tongue, who knows. He didn't want to hold my hand. He only reluctantly gave me his mobile number. I could feel his resistance like barbed wire wrapping around my infatuation, stripping it back to mere interest.

Seth rubs the back of his neck. "We should go."

Rick takes a few more steps towards us, his eyes on Amber. "Nonsense."

"Oh, goodie." Amber claps her hands together, jumps

from her bar stool and runs over to Rick.

I fix my gaze on the back door.

Come on, Cole.

I know my brother and Seth have a mutual respect. Rightly so, they've been best friends since they were toddlers. Seth will feel awkward when he sees Cole and will surely leave.

The door to the backroom swings open and Cole appears. Like Gail, he's sporting biker attire, even though the only bike he's ridden has been a pedal bike. My brother's tall, a little over six five. His brown hair is cut short, and he has ocean-blue eyes. He nods in acknowledgement when he sees me.

"Yo, shitface," Rick calls, "you were meant to be meeting us in the Golden Kite."

Cole shrugs. "What can I say? My woman needed me." He wraps his arms around Gail. They stand and openly make out, her fingers clawing at his stomach.

"How long till closing time, baby?" he breathes into her mouth. He isn't one to shy away from public displays of affection. I personally never understood how you could share something so intimate with other people. Needless to say, Cole and I don't share the same sentiment. With the pub still half full, he reaches under her miniskirt.

"Get a room," someone calls from the bar, to which Gail flips them the finger. Her gold sovereign rings look like knuckledusters before she places her open palm on Cole's ass.

My cheeks heat up. I can't watch them, so quickly turn away, and of course look straight at Seth.

"Lizzie, I'm—"

I turn my back on him too. With nowhere else to

look, I peer down into my drink as an orange segment bobs up and down.

Cole finally tears himself from Gail's lips. "Everyone, it's time to fuck off and go home."

I look up. Red-faced, Cole unhooks a set of keys from Gail's waistband and tosses them in my direction. "Lock up when everyone leaves. We're just going to change a lightbulb."

Squealing, Gail runs for the back room, Cole running after her.

Chelsea huffs. "Why does it need both of them to change a lightbulb?"

I raise my eyebrows. "Seriously?"

I lock the door when all the punters have left. Amber is behind the bar, Rick's hand on hers as he shows her how to pull the 'perfect pint'. Chelsea is asleep in one of the booths. It's just me sitting at one end of the bar, Seth sitting at the other.

He's chewing on nuts from a crock bowl. I can see him attempting to make eye contact. I don't cave. My stare is fixed on the back room. It sounds like they're moving furniture back there. I heard Gail was into the kinky stuff, and from the noises I can hear, I believe it.

I cover my ears with my hands. I'd rather stick needles in my eyes than listen to them having sex.

"Put a song on the jukebox." I don't direct my request at anyone in particular, but Seth stands. He makes his way to the other side of the bar and flicks through the list of songs.

I shouldn't have hit him, but it upset me to think sex was all he wanted. He said he hadn't had sex in a long time, as though that was meant to make me feel better. I'm nobody's rebound.

Apart from my brother, Seth was the first boy to show me what it was like to feel protected. Hell, my parents were never around. Maybe that's the psychology behind my infatuation. He somehow resembled the father figure I was lacking growing up.

After selecting a song from the metal band The Crew Rebels, he retakes his seat and continues to eat the nuts.

"They're full of urine, you know," I blurt out.

The nuts scatter over the bar as he releases them. "Excuse me?"

"Everyone knows that you don't eat nuts from a bar. Men go to the toilet and don't wash their hands, then they eat from the bowl of nuts."

He gags. "Shit, you could have told me before I'd nearly finished them."

I smirk. I could have but chose not to.

Seth clicks his fingers in the air. "Hey, Rick, throw us something edible from behind the bar."

Amber turns, brushing her finger down on Rick's face. "What about my cherry?"

"Oh, my." Rick fans his face. "Have you got a curfew, little lady?"

She reaches into the bowl of cherries meant for cocktails and pops one into her mouth. "Nope."

Rick pulls his wallet from his trouser pocket and drops a twenty on the bar. "We're going to head off." He claims Amber's hand. "I think I have a lightbulb that needs changing too."

My mouth drops open as they exit the bar. Chelsea is a fantastic wingwoman. Not only is she asleep, she's snoring that loudly that you can hear her over the music. Then it hits me I'm on my own with Seth. All of a sudden, I feel very exposed.

Come on, Cole.

Seth slides behind the bar and checks over the bottles of spirits. "Drink?"

I circle my fingers around my glass. "I have legs, I can get my own." I turn and glance around the bar. I'm sure they had a bald guy tagging along with them in the Golden Kite. "Hey, where did the other guy disappear to?"

"Dave left with the redhead," Seth replies, whilst pouring himself a glass of whiskey.

"Looks like you're the only member from your little group who isn't getting laid tonight. Shame."

He covers his eyes with his hand, shaking his head. He looks embarrassed, and he should. "Will you let me at least try to explain?"

I shake my head. "There's nothing to say."

He opens his mouth to protest when Gail and Cole stumble out of the back room. Cole adjusts the waistband of his trousers. "Sorry about that, it was a really tricky light to put in."

Gail bites her lower lip. "Sure was, needed a good screw."

I place my hands over my ears. "I get the picture."

Cole high-fives Seth. Standing tall, my brother puffs out his chest. "Dude, I'm the man of this establishment, get your ass from behind my bar."

Seth holds up his hands. "I don't want to step on anyone's toes."

No, but you're happy to stomp all over my feelings, you jerk.

Seth sits at the bar stool at my side. Thick veins travel

the length of his forearm and bulge on his hands. I glance at his wedding finger and see the faint tan line where his ring used to be. It makes me question if he still wears it, if he's over his ex. I was way out of my depth tonight, assuming, hoping I'd find my forever. Instead I've been given a serving of reality, and it tastes bitter.

Gail slices a lemon whilst Cole grabs the salt shaker.

"Come on, fuckers, time to weed the men out from the boys," Cole says, lining up a row of spirits. Gail grabs a deck of cards from under the bar and we join them in a drinking game.

I'm going to be so hungover tomorrow.

Chapter Four

Seth

I wake to a pounding headache as last night's exploits come rushing back to me. Stupid! I can't believe how much I drank last night. What the hell was I thinking?

I crack open my eyes and see my five-year-old daughter lying at my side. Her brown hair is like a nest concealing her face. Brushing it aside, I see she's dribbling on the pillow. *Cute.* I scoop her into my arms, her little head resting in the crook of my arm. Her PJ bottoms are sodden and cold. This kid could sleep through a tsunami.

I got home late last night, four am to be precise. My sister was asleep on the settee, and Ellie was asleep in my bed. Seeing the state I'd arrived home in, Darcy said she'd sleep over so she could help me this morning. A hangover was certainly in the cards, and shit, I feel awful.

Last night is all a bit of a blur, and the less I remember the better. But it keeps coming back to me, piece by piece. What the hell was I thinking?

Cole's little sister?

Cole's *twenty-four-year-old* little sister?

God, I'm an idiot.

I carry Ellie to her own bedroom and lay her down in her princess bed. Once I've worked her wet PJs and underwear off, I dress her in clean pyjamas.

She opens one eye. "Hi, Daddy." She reaches for her stuffed Nemo and hugs it to her chest.

Tucking her in, I place a soft kiss on her forehead. "Go back to sleep," I whisper.

I make my way to the bathroom and have a quick shower. With a towel wrapped around my waist I return to my bedroom. I get dressed in a pair of grey sweatpants and a white t-shirt, then change the sheets on my bed, tossing the wet ones in the washing basket.

I grab my phone from my bedside cabinet and make my way to the kitchen, opening my text messages en route.

Cole: *Oi, lightweight, are you awake?*

Cole: *I need you to quote a job this afternoon, mate.*

Cole: *Nvm, I'm sending Rick.*

Cole: *Hello?*

Cole: *We have a job starting Monday.*

I don't read any more. In the kitchen, I blindly rummage through the medicine drawer while at the same time scrolling through my contacts. I click his name, deciding it'll be easier just to call.

He answers right away. "Morning, sleeping beauty."

I laugh, popping two painkillers. "Waiting by the phone for me, were you?"

"Something like that. Do you remember the house on Chestnut Avenue? The one that went up for auction?"

Sipping orange juice from the carton, I think back. Chestnut Avenue is near the beachfront. "The house that looked like it was still in the 1960's, had structural damage and was full of damp and mould? Yeah, I remember."

"That's the one. I bought it for Lizzie."

I nearly choke on OJ. "You bought your sister a house?"

"Yes and no. She needed somewhere to live, and I wanted a house for my pension. She's going to rent it from me, at a reduced rate of course. I got a team of lads in to fix all the structural damage. Rick and I have completed the work downstairs."

"You kept that quiet," I say, dropping a piece of brown bread into the toaster. I usually work with Rick, but the last few weeks I've been working alongside a subcontractor in a care home, whilst Rick and Cole worked on a secret project. Not secret any more.

"We need a push on the upstairs. Do you think—"

"No."

He laughs. "You don't even know what I'm going to ask you."

"Yes, I do. I've got real work to do and that doesn't include fixing your sister's house."

I'm being obtuse, but I don't want to face her, I can't face her.

"It's *my* house," he reminds me.

"And your sister will be living there."

"I don't know why you and Lizzie never got on. I could feel the tension between you both last night."

We got on fine in the Golden Kite. Until I opened my

big drunken mouth and ruined it. "I don't know, mate. She used to follow me around all the time and it got kind of annoying."

"I think you were her childhood crush. God knows why she liked your ugly ass. Rick I'd understand, but you?"

"Ha ha."

"She's a sweet kid," he says.

I cringe when he refers to her as a 'kid.' I rub my hand over the back of my neck and sigh. "Look, Cole, about her house—"

"Seth." His voice is harsh, and I know exactly what's coming. "I need the upstairs finished and the loft converted into a bedroom. It'll add value to the house when I eventually sell it. You and Rick are going to make it happen. Capiche?" He doesn't wait for an answer. "See you tomorrow," he says before ending the call.

Shit. Last night I laughed reason in the face. Today irony is laughing in mine.

Chapter Five

Seth

Monday morning soon came, and boy, does it feel awkward stepping onto the threshold of Lizzie's house with her brother and Rick by my side. We stop on her welcome mat, which is ironic seeing as I'm most definitely unwelcome.

The front door is painted bright orange of all colours. *Note to self: change the colour immediately.* Apart from the God-ugly door, the exterior of the house is pleasant. The whole house has been rendered and is painted light grey. It's a two-storey detached building, soon to be three storeys when the loft has been renovated.

Cole leans forwards, pressing the doorbell. I glance down at my watch. Six-thirty am. We don't usually start work this early, but we have the plasterboard, metal studs, fixings and loft insulation being dropped off any time after seven am. Cole wanted us set up and ready to start.

Cole clucks his tongue when Lizzie doesn't answer. He makes his way to the window and gazes in. The curtains are closed. "Shit, I hope she's up. I did tell her we'd be early today."

He presses the doorbell one final time. I can hear movement inside.

"Jeez, I'm coming, hold your horses," Lizzie calls as the front door swings open. "Morning." She yawns.

By the looks of it, I'd say she hasn't long got her ass out of bed. She's wearing a knee-length black cardigan; I'd bet she threw it on quickly and is wearing her PJs underneath. She's completely makeup-free. Her hair gives bedhead new meaning—it's sticking up in every possible direction. She must notice my scrutiny as she quickly brushes her fingers through the tangled mess to no avail. If anything, she's making it worse.

She steps aside. "Come in."

We walk into the hallway. I slip my shoes off, noticing the cream carpets.

"Bear with me, I need to get showered. I'll make you all a drink when I'm done."

Cole shoots me and Rick a stare. "Bathroom is out of bounds for the next five hours."

She punches his upper arm. "I do not take five hours to shower."

My gaze momentarily meets Lizzie's. She forces a smile before running up the stairs, I assume to the bathroom. I try not to think of Cole's sister naked in the shower but, being a red-blooded male who hasn't had sex for a long time, I can't pretend that the image doesn't flash in my mind.

I'm going straight to hell.

"Come, Seth, let me show you what makes this house special, the pièce de résistance." Cole doesn't wait for me to follow but runs up the first flight of stairs and straight on to the next.

I don't rush, especially at this time of the morning. I take a leisurely stroll to join him. My eyes go wide on reaching the loft room. Despite it needing a lot of work, I can see the potential. "Whoa, dude. This is pretty impressive."

"Sure is," Cole says, walking between the temporary floorboards that have been laid.

The room spans the entire length of the house. Natural light spills in from a large window that sits in the side apex.

Cole puffs his chest out. "The steel frame and the glass were imported from Denmark. I had to get a specialist to fit it."

I know it would have cost Cole a shit ton. I'm about to ask if it was worth the outlay, but that's until I take a look. The view is out of this world, an uninterrupted view of the ocean. I can only imagine the beautiful sunsets Lizzie will see from here.

I rub my hand over my beard. "Remind me how much you paid for this at auction?"

"Sixty thousand."

Not bad, he's snapped up a bargain. The property is in a sought-after neighbourhood. There has got to be a catch—subsidence, a restrictive covenant, extensive renovation works.

I know it's none of my business, but I'm going to ask anyway. "And how much are you expecting the renovations to cost?"

Cole's eyes shoot up and his lips move briefly as though he's working it out. "Around fifty thousand, and that includes labour."

"What's the catch?"

He smiles smugly. "No catch."

Shit. Once the renovations are completed, he'll easily triple his investment. Houses in this part of the country, big or small, carry a hefty price tag.

"Would anyone like a hot drink?" Lizzie shouts up. I can hear Rick talking to her on the second floor.

Cole and I both call down for a cup of tea with no sugar. I'm beginning to think that the other night's escapade is behind us, that is until Lizzie brings our drinks up. I take a sip of mine and it tastes as though I'm drinking pure sugar. After heaving, I can't help but smile to myself as it goes down.

Touché, Lizzie, touché.

Me and the guys spend the morning prepping the job. The material arrives at eight am. We carry the rolls of insulation to the loft, the plasterboards and metal to the second bedroom where we stack them against the wall.

Cole and Rick start work insulating the loft whilst I begin ripping the mouldy ceiling in Lizzie's room. It hasn't been artexed so it's unlikely that it contains asbestos, but I wear my PPE as a precaution.

Lizzie asks again if there's anything we need. There isn't. She politely excuses herself and spends the remainder of the morning sat in her back garden sunbathing. I may have noticed her from the bedroom window. By noticed, I mean ogled.

Someone clears their throat from behind. I jump, nearly falling off my stepladder, which incidentally is positioned in front of the window.

"Shit, Cole," I say, grabbing my chest. "You gave me

a damn heart attack."

Cole stands in the doorway; his red face is dripping with sweat. I do not envy him working in the loft room. We're experiencing the hottest August on record. I know I'm hot, but it must be like a furnace up there.

He juts his chin forward. "What do you see, Seth?"

I jump down from the ladder.

A cocky piece of shit.

I remove my goggles and mask and look him up and down. Is this a trick question? Did he see me checking his sister out?

He frowns when I don't answer, then motions around the room. "God's sake, Stevens, I must sound like a fucking parrot. What do you see?"

As requested, I give the room a once-over. The walls have been taken right back to the brick and old plasterboard is scattered around the floor. Wires are pulled from sockets and a few floorboards are up, exposing the brass water pipes below.

Wiping sweat from my brow, I answer him honestly. "I see a shithole."

He shakes his head. "Potential, I see potential." He marches around the room, his chest puffed out and his hands wedged in his pockets. "What do you think about us investing in houses like this, doing them up and renting them? We can build a portfolio and eventually sell them. I reckon we'd make a tidy profit."

Looking around the room, I rub my hand over my face.

Cole's brows rise. "Well?"

Seriously, he wants an answer now? He must know with any new business venture there are risks, risks I'm not in the position to take.

"Honestly, mate, I haven't got the money to outlay. It's not just that, we'd be landlords. Tenants can be a real pain in the ass."

The corners of his eyes crinkle. "Don't I know it."

"Hey." I toss a broken piece of plasterboard in his direction. "I'm the perfect tenant."

I've been renting my house from Cole for fifteen months. Anna left me with a seventy-thousand-pound credit card debt. Due to her online gambling addiction I had to sell our house to pay off her debt. My baby lost her mum and home in the space of a week.

What Ellie needs now more than ever is security, not me chasing dreams.

Since becoming a single dad, I've managed to save twelve thousand pounds and book my little girl a dream holiday to Disney World. With the six thousand pounds I have remaining my hope is that by the end of the year I will have enough saved to buy the house I'm renting. Cole has even offered to sell it to me for fifty thousand pounds below the asking price.

Cole rocks on his heels. "I've spoken to Rick about the business venture and he's up for it."

Of course Rick is up for it, he hasn't got kids or responsibilities other than getting his arse out of bed in the morning. Growing bored, I push my goggles up the bridge of my nose and clasp my stepladder.

"You don't have to invest any of your own money."

I stand statue-like. A free business venture? I'm interested to see where this is going. "Go on."

Cole sucks in a long breath. "There's an auction next Monday in Bristol. I want you to go. If something catches your eye, then bid on it. I'll pay your share, and when we sell up you can have the profit minus what I outlaid. Sixty-six percent of the risk is on my shoulders then, you can't lose. With the extra money, you can buy the house."

This could solve all my financial problems overnight. He has no idea how much easier it'll be to breathe. I make my way towards him. I feel a bro-hug is in order. "Cole—"

He waves his hand dismissively. "You're welcome."

I watch him leave and text my sister to tell her the news. My signal bar is crawling and the text refuses to send.

Endless possibilities fill my mind. Cole specified that I wasn't to decorate whilst renting, but the first thing I'm going to do when the house is mine is paint Ellie's bedroom.

I feel like I've got a spring in my step. I spend an hour rewiring the lights, feeding the cables through the joists. Every so often I return to the window to steal a glimpse at Lizzie. I've got to apologise to her for my behaviour. I jog down the stairs. "Taking a break," I call up to Rick and Cole, who are in the loft.

I pass through a narrow hallway. Knowing I haven't got a lot of time, I hurry through the kitchen and to the garden.

She's lying on a stripy blanket. Her face is turned away from me and she is resting her head on her arms. She's wearing a black strappy t-shirt and cute denim shorts that hug her ass, which I can't take my eyes off. I watch her for longer than is necessary.

"Either lotion my back or move. You're blocking the sun."

Great. Now I look like a stalker, casting a dark shadow over her. I step back. "I'm sorry. Er, about Saturday night, I was drunk and…"

Lizzie spins round, taking up a sitting position. Using her hand as a visor, she looks up at me. "I thought you were Cole."

I hold out my arms. "Nope, just me."

My eyes take a detour to her breasts, and it's there they stay. I've completely forgotten what it was I wanted to say.

So leave, stalker, and stop checking her out.

She looks at me expectantly. "Would you mind?"

Oh, great, now she thinks I'm a perv. "Sorry." Turning my back on her, I'm about to make a beeline for the house when she calls after me.

"Seth."

I turn back to face her. Sweet Jesus, I should have kept going and not looked back. She's holding her hair to the side, giving me the perfect view of her back and her neck. "I'm burning."

The lotion, right.

I grab the bottle from the ground and do as she requests. I squirt the white liquid into my hands, applying it to her back, rubbing it in in small circular motions.

Her skin feels so soft. Without thinking, I slide the thin strap of her t-shirt down, pressing slightly firmer.

"That feels good." She almost moans. Is she getting off on this?

Shit, I'm enjoying this way too much. "All done." I jump up, giving her shoulder a friendly pat.

"Wait," she calls after me.

Keep walking, keep walking.

"Yes?" My traitorous feet take me right to her, and I

sit at her side.

She looks down, picking at the frayed edge on the blanket. "I forgive you."

"For what?"

Wanting to stick my tongue in your mouth, staring at your ass and then your tits, and thinking of all the ways I'd like to fuck you?

"We'd both had too much to drink. I shouldn't have slapped you."

Instinctively, I rub my hand over my cheek. "It's okay. I was completely out of order. I shouldn't have said what I did. There was no excuse."

"It was a good night though," she muses.

"Yeah. I kinda needed it, you know."

Her eyes go wide. "No, I don't know."

I don't need a shoulder to cry on, or someone to listen whilst I vent. I'd rather keep some parts of my life hidden away.

Her hair is picked up by the soft breeze and all I can do is stare at her face. The more I sit staring at her, the more this feels like some kind of moment.

I can feel myself start to retreat. "I've got to go."

She reaches for my hand. "Please, stay. Just for a bit longer. It's been forever since I saw you, and seeing as we're both sober, it'd be nice to catch up."

She wants to pry, she means. That's all people do, ask me questions about my life, my ex, my daughter. Brick by brick, I've built a fortress around my heart, around my truths. No one will penetrate the bricks, or even rattle the foundations.

I shake my head. "I can't."

She frowns. "Why not?"

I pull my phone out of my pocket. "I've got to ring my sister, see how my daughter is."

"I've heard all about Ellie. How is she?"

"She's fine." My tone is more abrupt than I had intended.

Lizzie leans forwards. "I'd love to see a picture of her."

"Some other time. I've got to ring my sister." I jump up. Message after message flashes on the screen of my phone, texts from Darcy. Now I finally have signal.

Panic wraps its invisible fingers around my throat, squeezing. What if something's happened to Ellie?

Lizzie falls into insignificance.

I don't read any of the texts. Images of every awful scenario flash through my mind. My heart's racing. With shaky fingers, I scroll and click Darcy's name. It rings three times before she answers.

"Is Ellie okay?" I bark.

"Jesus, Seth, she's fine."

"What's the problem then?"

"If you calm down and stop shouting at me, I'll tell you."

I feel a hand on my arm from behind. It's Lizzie's. I pull from her embrace; all I can think about is Ellie. I'm extremely protective over her, I can't help it.

I scuff my foot on the floor. "Well—"

"Alice had an accident at work."

I let out a harsh breath. "And that affects me how?"

"I've got to cover some of her shifts."

I shake my head. "Your job is looking after Ellie. I pay you to have her."

"It's only for the next couple of weeks until they can

41

find cover. I've got to go in this afternoon."

"Seriously, Darce?" Blindly I feel around my work pouch. I'm making a mental note of what tools I've got on me and what I'll be leaving here. "Don't worry, I'll come home right away."

"You don't have to, I'm outside."

My hand falls to my side. "Outside where?"

She cuts the call. Does she mean she's outside Lizzie's house? Sure, she knows I'm working here, but it's not like my sister to turn up at one of my jobs.

Leaving Lizzie in the garden, I run back through the house and to the front door, which Cole is already opening. My sister and Ellie stand outside on the welcome mat.

Cole looks at me. "What is it, Bring Your Kid to Work Day? She can't stay."

I clench my fists. "I know that."

Ellie hides behind Darcy. Of course she does—she isn't good with new surroundings and strange faces. Although she's familiar with Cole and Rick, she isn't comfortable around them. Shit, she's only comfortable around me and my sisters, Imogen and Darcy.

I walk towards my little girl. My car keys jingle as I yank them from my trouser pocket. "I'm gonna get going, Cole."

"You can't."

Scowling, I face him. "What do you mean I can't?"

I know how Ellie gets with strange people, and I wouldn't get a sitter at such short notice. I can't, I won't do that to her.

He shrugs and attempts to look concerned. "We're on a deadline, two weeks to get this finished before our next job starts. Sorry, mate, but I need you here."

Mate? Mate? I feel like wringing his damn neck. "You said it yourself, she can't stay," I spit out. "So, Einstein, enlighten me, who's going to mind Ellie while I work?"

Cole's eyes move around the hall. He smiles and clears his throat. "Lizzie's off work for the school holidays. She can mind her."

Chapter Six

Lizzie

I'*ll look after his daughter, will I?*

I blow out my cheeks. Trust my brother to come up with such an ingenious idea. He talks as though me being off work means I have nothing better to do. Is he forgetting the work I do over the summer? I have several meetings with the head of the art department, my class displays to arrange, and not forgetting the supplies I need to order ready for September.

"Come on, Lizzie," Cole pleads, clasping his hands together as if praying. "You're a teacher. You work with kids every day."

I look at the little girl. She's dressed in a pink summer dress with a pink embroidered flamingo on the breast pocket. She has her father's blue eyes. Her mousy brown hair is totally wild—it doesn't look as though it's ever seen a brush. She's a pretty little thing, or she would be if she wasn't frowning.

I speak in a hushed voice that only my brother will

hear. "I work with teenagers, Cole. I'd have no idea what to do with a child her age."

Cole's jaw ticks and he stares at me expectantly, like he's waiting for me to have some kind of epiphany and be totally fine with babysitting. Sure, I like little kids, but from afar. I don't feel comfortable looking after one.

"Just give her a bowl of popcorn and sit her in front of the TV."

Seth scrapes his hand through his hair. "Cole, it's not as easy as that. You know about Ellie's issues."

Ellie's issues?

Cole jerks his head in the direction of the stairs. "You're working upstairs. What do you think's going to happen to her? We have another job starting in a couple of weeks and I want this finished. All hands on deck."

I glance at Darcy. She's wearing a blue work tunic and matching trousers. Looks as though she's wearing scrubs. Like Seth, she's tall. She has short brown hair and hazel eyes that pingpong between Seth and Cole. She shakes her head. "As entertaining as this is. I'll let you boys argue this out between one another."

Without another word she gently nudges the little girl over the doorstep onto the hessian mat inside.

The little girl's face reddens, and for a moment it looks as though she's holding her breath. With teary eyes she runs to Seth and buries her head into his work trousers, her hair adhering to the thick blue material.

Cole's nostrils flare. "I can't stand here all day arguing. I have work to do. Just let Lizzie watch her today."

Seth glowers at me, his good looks devoured by a scowl. "Whatever," he snaps, aiming his frustration at me. "I will finish the boarding and then I'm off. I'll be taking

Ellie home."

The intensity of his stare is getting too much. I glance out of the front door and see Darcy removing a child's booster seat from her car. She offers me an apologetic smile before she places the seat on the driveway, in front of Seth's work van.

I look back in the hallway. Cole's already left. I can hear him hammering loudly upstairs.

I'm standing, my arms folded, as Seth pries his little girl from him, one finger at a time.

"Ellie's not like other little girls, Lizzie, she has… she has some issues." His voice is little more than a whisper, as though he doesn't want Ellie to overhear him talking about her.

There goes that word again. "What do you mean?"

Shaking his head, he bends down on one knee, brushing hair behind the little girl's ears. "Sweetheart, it'll just be for a little while, I promise. You can have some ice cream when we get home. What do you say?"

As pissed as I am right now, it warms my heart to see the way he looks into his daughter's eyes. Their stare remains unbroken and he waits for her to reply. After long drawn-out seconds he stands. He looks at me one final time before storming up the stairs.

I'm standing in the hall, alone with this young girl. I teach kids for a living; how hard can this be? "Come on, Ellie." I hold my hand out, expecting her to take it, but she takes a step away from me. I take a step towards her and wrap my fingers around her wrist. She stiffens at my touch.

I crouch down, plastering a smile on my face. "I haven't got ice cream or popcorn, but I have cookies." My voice is unnaturally high-pitched and sounds like I've been sucking on a helium balloon.

No reply. No wonder.

Try not to sound like Minnie Mouse this time, Lizzie.

I clear my throat. "I've got paints in the cupboard. How about we paint your daddy a picture? We can sit in the garden if you like, there's a table and chairs out there."

Much better. Less like Minnie Mouse and more like me. Ellie glances up the stairs and back to the floor.

"Come on, sweetie."

She drops her shoulders and drags her feet as I guide her out of the hallway and into the lounge.

"Do you want to paint?"

She shakes her head.

I glance around the room. It's not exactly kid-friendly. I don't have anything apart from my art supplies that would occupy her. I suck in my lower lip. What does a child her age like to do? I don't even know how old she is. Seven, eight? I glance down and realise the whole time I've been lost in my thoughts she's been staring at a blank TV. I glance around and spot the remote control on the arm of my settee. "How about I put the TV on and we find a cartoon?"

She shakes her head, this time with more certainty. I get the feeling she doesn't like me. I open my mouth to suggest making cakes when she tears her wrist from my grasp and runs out of the room. I trip over my feet, then rush after her, but by the time I make it into the hallway she's already halfway up the stairs.

"Daddy!" she screams, sheer panic in her voice.

She makes it all the way up the stairs and to my bedroom before I catch up with her. Seth is balancing on a pair of stepladders. Rick, a few feet away, stands on stilts. Together they're nailing a length of white plasterboard to the ceiling's wooden joists.

Looking up, I can't help but admire Seth's broad chest and muscular arms. He turns his head and instead of a smile, I get another scowl.

"Ellie, can you go downstairs, please, sweetheart?" he says sweetly, yet sternly. His jaw ticks before his eyes narrow. "Lizzie, can you get her out of here?"

Ellie's lower lip quivers, and she steps away when I attempt to take her hand. Blowing out my cheeks, I wrap my hands around her shoulders.

"Come on," I say, leading her out onto the landing, and together we walk down the stairs.

I don't ask what she wants to do, instead guide her into the kitchen. I pour her a glass of orange juice and scatter a couple of cookies on a plate. Picking her up, I place her on a ladder-backed chair next to the breakfast bar. I sit opposite.

Humming to myself, I cross and uncross my legs. I try not to stare at her, so sporadically check social media on my phone. Realising I've been looking at my screen for the past five minutes, I glance up, giving the little girl my undivided attention. Her head is bowed. The juice I poured for her is untouched. The cookies I laid out for her still lie on the plate. The only things nearing Ellie's mouth are her fingers, which she chews.

I teach kids for a living, and yet I'm at a loss as what to do with this one.

I scroll to Amber's name in my contact list. She has a young daughter, she'll know what I should do.

Me: *Help.*

Little dots appear under my text. I can see she's typing back.

Amber: *What's up?*

Me: *I've got to babysit Seth's daughter.*

Amber: *Playing Mummy already?*

Me: *Ha. Ha. She hates me. I have no idea what to do with her.*

Amber: *How old is she?*

Me: *The hell should I know?*

I glance at Ellie. Although she's tall, facially I don't think she's as old as I first thought.

Me: *Around the same age as Freja, maybe older.*

Amber's name appears on my screen. She's calling me. I turn my back to Ellie and accept the call.

"Stop overthinking it, Lizzie. Take her to the park or the beach, kids love anything like that."

I sigh, toying with a lock of hair. "I don't think anything will work."

"Sure it will. I could always drop by with Freja. Ask Ellie if she'd like a little friend to play with—"

Turning, I glance towards the chair where I sat her. Damn it, she's gone.

"Amber, I've got to go." I hang up and run to my bedroom. Ellie is sitting in the corner of the room, her legs pulled tightly to her chest.

Rick and Seth are standing by the window. Rick drinks from a silver flask whilst Seth drums his fingers on the sill.

Seth exhales loudly. "I'm sorry you've been put in this position, I really am. If your brother wasn't offering me the opportunity of a lifetime, I'd be out of here." With his arm outstretched he motions around the room. "She can't stay. Floorboards are up, nails and wires everywhere, it's an accident waiting to happen." He looks at his daughter. "Ellie. The quicker you do as you're told, the quicker we can go home." His voice is firm and authoritative.

She hugs her knees, as if making a barrier to keep everyone away. Seth strides towards her and lifts her to her feet. His expression softens as he manoeuvres her towards me.

Downstairs is a stalemate. I try everything, even resorting to singing nursery rhymes and using a wooden spoon and a saucepan as percussion. Still she sits silently.

I manage to get her to sit down on the settee in the lounge. I fetch the drink and cookies from the kitchen, placing them on the coffee table where they sit untouched. After turning on the TV, I switch it to a kids' channel. I make sure to sit on the easy chair near the door. There's no way she will get past me again.

What the hell do I do when the programme finishes? Not that she's watching it, but it beats sitting with only the sound of hammering and sawing from upstairs.

As a last resort I ring Amber. "Please rescue me. Bring Freja round. Maybe a little friend to play with is what Ellie needs."

"Sure, but I can't stay long. I've got to pop into town to speak to a lady about exhibiting some of my photos."

"No problem."

"Give me half an hour."

The bell rings after ten minutes. I run to the door to let them in.

"Hey," Amber says, giving me a hug.

"Hey, yourself." I smile. She has no idea how happy I am to see her.

Amber's wearing a light blue summer dress that matches the colour of her eyes. I squint, noticing the peculiar way her hair is moving.

"Boo," Freja yells, jumping out of her mum's locks.

I jump back, holding my hand over my heart for effect. "You scared me."

"Coz I was invincible."

"Invisible," Amber corrects.

"You certainly were." I laugh.

We make our way to the lounge. Freja is carrying a plastic carrier bag behind her back. I reach forward and the bag rustles between my fingers. "What have you got there?"

She turns, placing her finger to her lips. "Shhh. It's a surprise."

"Oh, okay," I whisper.

Amber reaches the lounge door first. She strolls inside and kneels directly in front of Ellie. "I'm Amber, and this is Freja. She's brought some goodies from home that you can both play with."

Freja places her little hand on her hip. "Mummy, it was a surprise."

Amber beckons Freja, who without question sits next

to Ellie on the carpet and empties out the bag. Puzzle boxes, dolls, crayons and two colouring books lie in front of them.

Freja waves the book in the air, the pages flapping open. "I'm going to colour."

For the next five minutes, Amber continually tries to engage with Ellie, whose face remains sullen, her body statue-like.

"Finished," Freja declares, flicking through the pages. Her idea of finished is random scribbles and more blank page than colour. She holds the book up for us to see. "Look, Mummy, a fishy."

Ellie rocks forwards, leaning on her hands, and peers at the picture. Freja smiles at Ellie and briefly Ellie smiles back. I inch forward, which causes the floorboard to creak. Ellie's eyes meet mine for a beat. Like a feral cat looking for escape, she runs and jumps onto the settee and curls up into a tight ball.

Freja colours for another ten minutes. I keep hoping that Ellie will join in, but she doesn't.

Amber sits on the arm of the settee, stroking Ellie's hair. She possesses that motherly instinct that just doesn't come naturally to me, maybe because I haven't got a child of my own. Maybe it's because my own mum didn't have a maternal bone in her body.

I've got to try harder.

I follow Amber's eyes as she glances at the screen of her phone. "Is that the time? I've got to run. It was lovely to meet you, Ellie."

"It was nice to meet you," Freja says, whilst bundling her toys into the plastic bag.

I stand. "I'll see you out."

When we reach the front door Amber gives me a hug. I guess it's a group hug as one of Freja's arms wraps around my thighs.

"What am I doing wrong?" I ask into Amber's hair.

She pulls away, offering me a sympathetic grin. "You're trying too hard, that's what. You're an art teacher, why don't you get her to paint with you?"

"That's the first thing I suggested we do."

She raises a brow. "Exactly my point. You suggested it. You need to make her think it was her idea."

"But how?"

She winks. "You're a smart girl, figure it out."

Figure it out? Figure out what?

Keys jingle in Amber's hands. I can see she's in a hurry to leave. I open the front door and move aside for them to pass. "Thank you both for coming."

Amber's lips curve up into a smile. "Any time."

Freja skips behind her mum. Amber opens the car door and straps Freja into her car seat.

I stand silently waving them off. Hearing footsteps behind me, I turn. Ellie's grabbed the banister and is attempting to bolt up the stairs.

I lunge forwards. "Not so fast." I capture her under the arms and pick her up. I carry her back to the hall. "It's okay, sweetie. Your daddy will be done soon, and—"

She panics. Her arms and legs dart everywhere. I'm about to set her down when she lets out the most ear-piercing scream I've ever heard.

Footsteps boom onto the landing.

"What the hell?" Seth yells. My heart races as he descends the stairs three at a time. On reaching me, he grabs Ellie from my arms, like he's somehow protecting her against me. With his little girl wedged under his arm, he storms out of the house. "I knew this was a bad idea!"

I run out onto the drive. "Wait up. Let me explain."

He doesn't acknowledge me. He unlocks his van, one-handedly opens the door and tosses the booster seat in. He gently sets the little girl in the seat and straps her in.

He slams the door, his eyes locking on mine. "Your brother's an idiot." He wrenches open the driver's side door and jumps in.

"What's going on?" Cole says, standing behind me as Seth's van reverses off the drive.

I shove him. "Seth was right. You are an idiot."

He spreads his arms wide. "What did I do?"

"You're telling me you didn't hear her?"

Cole leans forwards, looking both ways at the rows of houses. "Yeah. I think the whole street heard."

My eyes tear up. I feel like a complete failure.

Being the protective big brother, he grabs me in a bear hug. "I'm sorry, Lizzie. I thought she'd be okay, what with Seth upstairs. I'm sure she'll be better tomorrow."

I stiffen in his embrace. "Tomorrow? Are you crazy? No way in hell will he leave his daughter in my care again."

"Leave it with me, sis. I'll talk to Seth later when he's calmed down."

"Wait till he's calmed down? What about me?"

Cole takes my shoulders in his hands. "I'm on a deadline with this job. I can get a team of subcontractors in, but they can't start till Wednesday. If his sister can't watch the kid, could you mind her for just one more day?"

Chapter Seven

Seth

With the engine still running, we sit at the drive-through. Ellie bites into a burger.

"Nice, Ellie?"

She nods. "Daddy, I said no pickle."

She pulls the pickle from her burger and dangles it in my direction. The joys of parenthood—eating shit your kids won't. As much as I tell her to try new foods, pickles are the exception. Leading by example, I pop it into my mouth and try not to heave as I swallow. I can feel my face contort.

With widening eyes, she looks at me for my verdict.

"That tasted like a slug. You made your daddy eat a slug."

She guffaws. "That's gross."

"That's gross?" I repeat. "Is that all you have to say for yourself?" I launch over the seat, grab her and squeeze her sides and thighs.

She bursts into a fit of laughter. "Don't tickle me!"

she yells, her little hands flapping around as she attempts to push me away.

I love seeing her like this, happy and laughing. It broke my heart earlier seeing her so upset at Lizzie's. I just had to get her out of there. I can't imagine how Lizzie felt. I never should have put her or Ellie in that position.

Feeling like a total prick, I shoot Darcy a quick text to see if she'd mind putting Ellie to bed this evening. There's someone I owe another apology to.

I park at the end of Chestnut Avenue. It's a little after nine pm and Rick and Cole are only just leaving. Cole wasn't kidding when he said we're on a deadline.

I purposely parked out of the way so the guys won't pass me on their way home. The last thing I need is Cole thinking something is going on with me and his sister. After-hours visits usually mean one thing.

When only Lizzie's car is on the drive, I unbuckle my seatbelt and jump out of my van. I take slow, measured steps, going over in my mind what I want to say to her.

Stop stalling.

Taking a deep breath, I press my finger on the doorbell.

I can hear footsteps from inside. The door flings open. "Did you forget somethi—" Lizzie frowns the moment our eyes meet. "If you've come to make me feel any worse than I already do, you're wasting your time."

I place my foot in the door, preventing her from slamming it in my face. She applies pressure, but I don't budge. "Can you just hear me out, please? All I want is five minutes of your time."

The pressure on my foot is gone, and the door slowly opens. She disappears into a door to the right.

Time to eat some humble pie.

I kick off my shoes and follow her into the lounge. The room is unbelievably tidy, which is something I'm not accustomed to since having a child. All the walls are magnolia, except for a red feature wall. The room's upholstery is also red and a selection of canvas-style paintings hang on the walls.

Lizzie sits on a small easy chair next to the door. I sit on the settee.

"Drink?" She taps her foot on the floor.

I'd love a tea, but I know she's only asking out of politeness. I won't overstay my welcome any more than I already am. "Thanks, but no. I'm recovering from the sugar overdose from earlier."

Needless to say, the joke isn't well received. She folds her arms tightly across her chest. "Just say your piece, *please*."

Rubbing my fingers over my beard, I clear my throat. "The thing is—"

Breathe. This is unavoidable.

"The thing is," I repeat, "I may need you to babysit Ellie for a few days this week. Maybe next week. Darcy's boss is still working through cover hours, but it looks like her hours will be sporadic, meaning she'll have to drop Ellie off in the mornings or early afternoons. It depends which shifts she gets."

With jerky movements, Lizzie shakes her head. "I'm sorry, Seth. I'd love to help you, I really would. But no."

Why are women so damn awkward? I don't act shocked; deep down I knew what the answer would be before I asked the question.

Her stare pingpongs from me to the door. I know she won't ask me to leave. She'd rather drop little hints and hope I pick up on them. I choose ignorance on this occasion and stay seated.

I steeple my fingers on my lap. "I can't afford the bills if I don't work."

Her expression softens and, uncrossing her arms, she leans forward in her seat.

Okay, now I have her attention I need to lay it out. I let out a harsh breath. "My ex-wife…"

She raises her hand. "You don't have to go into detail. It's really none of my business."

I don't argue. She's right. Snippets of my life with that woman I keep locked away in the recesses of my mind. There are only so many times in one's life you can be kicked down. Eventually you just don't get back up.

Lizzie's chest rises and falls before she finally speaks. "I'll look after Ellie whilst you're working. But I'm not going to lie, in my time teaching, I've never felt so lost, so out of my depth as I did babysitting Ellie today. I tried everything and nothing worked. I felt like a complete failure."

Welcome to my world.

"I'm sorry, Lizzie. I should have told you about Ellie's issues…" I try to carry on, but instead sit in silence gathering my thoughts. The smartass who said 'a problem shared is a problem halved' is a complete moron. Bowing my head, I rub my hands over my eyes, like not seeing makes it less of an admission.

Here goes.

"Ellie developed separation anxiety when her mum left."

Each word, each syllable feels like a razor blade, tearing my dignity to shreds. What I've done in one short sentence is prove what a crappy dad I am. I know it, now Lizzie does too.

I glance up. Pity clouds Lizzie's features, but she doesn't break eye contact.

"I'm so sorry, Seth. You should have told me."

I should have, but didn't because I didn't want her damn sympathy. Telling people, especially strangers, about Ellie's condition is something I'm not comfortable doing, and I don't think I ever will be.

"Is she better at school with her teachers and peers?"

Lizzie just had to go there. If she didn't doubt my ability as a dad before, she sure as shit will now. "Ellie isn't at school yet and I pulled her out of nursery last year."

Her eyebrows furrow. "How old is she?"

"She's five. She was due to start school last September, but her birthday is in August, which meant she would have been one of the youngest. I was given the choice to send her or hold her back a year."

"So you held her back?"

I sit in silence and wait, wait whilst Lizzie judges me, wait for her verdict. I'm waiting for her to tell me I failed Ellie. Tell me I'm not capable of bringing my own daughter up. I can feel myself tensing, the emotion like a volcano bubbling up in the pit of my stomach and I'm about to explode.

"She wasn't ready," I bark, my voice that loud I'm

sure her neighbours heard.

Lizzie's eyes widen. I shocked her with my outburst. Shit, I've shocked myself. I didn't realise how much I've kept pent up until now. She doesn't reply. Try as I might, I can't push down the feelings of inadequacy.

I can see it on her face. She's judging me. She's no different to anyone else.

"Go on, say it. Say *I* wasn't ready to send her." I pound my fist against my chest. "Say that I've held her back, that the way she is is my fault."

Lizzie stands and walks towards me. "Seth, I wasn't going to—"

"It's not my fault," I holler.

God, I love that little girl so much that it hurts. I question everything, from her diet, to her sleeping patterns, what she watches on the TV—the list is endless.

"Seth, stop it this second. Do you hear me?" Lizzie's voice is harsh.

I reach up and take her hand in mine, pulling her onto my lap. Is it wrong to want, to crave physical contact? She's not judging me, she's not criticising me, she's listening.

Feeling like I owe her an explanation, I continue. "Ellie's mum walked out a little over a year ago. There were no signs that she was unhappy. She just left. The only thing she left was the divorce papers. She hasn't been in touch to see Ellie, to ask how she's getting on. Nothing. It's as though she just erased our little girl from her life. To put the cherry on top of the cake, Anna left me with a debt I couldn't pay and we lost our home."

Lizzie's body stiffens in my embrace. My embrace. I'm fucking hugging her.

"Oh, my God, Seth, I'm so sorry. Poor Ellie. She must have been heartbroken."

"I thought she was okay, you know. It started gradually. The bedwetting, night terrors. She wouldn't sleep in her own bed, so I let her sleep with me. She would wake up constantly to check I was still there. She was becoming more and more detached at nursery. She'd get so worked up about going that she was making herself sick. I couldn't bear to see her so upset, so I pulled her out. Darcy cut her hours down at work to help out. I just feel that if I'd been a better husband, a better dad, none of this would have happened. My little girl is broken. She's breaking more and more every day and I don't know how to fix her." My eyes are stinging so much from the pain and torment I've held behind them for so long. "I've got to be strong for Ellie."

"You've got to be strong for you too. Your mental health is as important, Seth. You're a good dad."

You're a good dad. Her words echo in my head.

I pull her into me and hold her close. I hold her tightly to my chest. I feel untethered from the guilt I've been harbouring. Validated. Released. Accepted. For the first time in a long time, I don't feel like a failure.

"Thank you," I breathe into her neck.

"Any time." She gasps for air, squirming in my embrace. "Now, if you don't mind, could you let me go? I can't breathe."

I laugh. "Sorry." I let her go and she stands. Her face is flushed red. "Can we forget this ever happened?" I say, pointing from me to her.

She nods. "Already forgotten."

Without another word she rearranges her t-shirt. From the lounge we go into the kitchen. It's a large rectangular room that overlooks the back garden. The kitchen units as well as the breakfast bar are bright red. *She must really like the colour.* The kitchen's only redeeming feature is the black granite worktop.

We sit drinking tea, chatting about the house. She tells me about the team of builders who, along with Cole, fixed the house's structural damage. She tells me they located the source that was causing the damp and that was fixed, and shortly after mould was ripped from the walls. She says she's sleeping on the sofa bed in the lounge until her bedroom is ready, and that the loft conversion is to be her art room.

After my cup of tea, the conversation returns to Ellie.

"How about I spend my lunch hour with you both tomorrow? That may help her anxiety," I suggest.

Lizzie rubs the top of her arm. "We could certainly try. I can't promise anything, Seth, other than I'll try my best with her."

"That's all anyone could ask."

"If at any time you undermine me, then I can't babysit. If she's crying or screaming, I will sort it."

I nod, knowing how much it'll break my heart to hear Ellie get so worked up. I've got to put that to the back of my mind. Seeing my baby's face when I take her to Disney World will be worth the sacrifice. Not only our holiday, I've got to get enough money saved to buy our house.

Lizzie clicks her fingers in front of my face, forcing me to refocus on her. "No good cop, bad cop. We're on the same team, okay?"

She holds her fist out in the air. Leaning forwards, we fistbump. I know that nothing can happen between us, and yet… I smile at her, I mean I really smile. My eyes soften at my new friend, my ally.

I form a fist and gently nudge her cheek to the side. "You're all right, Lizzie."

Returning my gesture, she replies, "You're not too bad yourself."

I stare at her for long seconds as her face transforms from smiles to seriousness. I snap us out of the moment. "Now let's discuss the plan of action for Ellie."

Chapter Eight

Lizzie

It feels nice calling the shots and being a little more in control after the disaster earlier. With Seth fully on board, I feel more confident about looking after Ellie. Now, how to make her feel more at ease with me?

I glance at him. He's leaning against the kitchen worktop, drinking another cup of tea. A cup of tea that hasn't had five teaspoons of sugar tossed in.

He eyes me suspiciously. "What put that stupid grin on your face?"

I deliver an incredulous stare, feigning innocence. "Nothing at all. I was just thinking of ways to make Ellie feel more at ease here."

He stands taller. "Go on, I'm listening."

Feeling somewhat on the spot, I say the first thing that pops in my head. "How about you bring a few toys from home?"

Seth nods. "That's a great idea."

"And if you could let me know the sorts of things she

likes on the TV—"

"*Nemo, The Little Mermaid.* She loves anything relating to fish and the ocean."

I look him up and down. Ironic that the two films he mentioned feature a strong single father role. I don't know how Seth could even doubt his ability as a father—it's clear to see how much that little girl adores him.

Seth glances down at his watch. "Shit, Darcy's got to leave for work soon."

After placing his cup in the sink, I follow him to the front door. He sits on the stairs, pulling his shoes on.

"Where does she work?"

"She cleans at the hospital. She works ten-thirty pm till twelve-thirty am Monday through to Thursday. Her main job is looking after Ellie. Her boss said they'll increase her hours at the hospital when Ellie goes to school."

"That's really good of them. Not a lot of workplaces are that flexible."

Seth shrugs. "Well, it's not like she needs the job or the money. Her husband Dwight is a neurosurgeon there. He asked nicely that they gave her flexible hours, and they were only too happy to oblige. Problem is, when they ask her to cover shifts, she doesn't know how to tell them no."

"She doesn't like to let people down, that's a good trait to have."

He gets to his feet and stands looking down at me. The moment of politeness passes, and we're heading towards awkward.

Either kiss me or say something.

"I'm glad we had this talk," he says, holding his fist out to me. We fistbump. Twice in one night.

Fantastic.

We've officially entered the friendzone.

Seth turns up at eight am the following morning. Winking at me, he nudges Ellie into the hall and walks in holding a large wooden box. Without a word he takes said box into the lounge and places it next to the settee.

"Is it okay here?" he says, pointing to the toy box.

I raise an eyebrow.

He merely shrugs. "What? We spoke about this last night. It was you who suggested I brought a few things to make her feel more at home."

By 'a few things' I envisioned he was going to bring a few items, not her toy box. The lid won't close over the mountain of toys beneath. I like to be minimalistic, and the thought of all these toys strewn across my floor is bothering me.

I give him a thumbs up. "To be honest, I thought you'd bring the entire contents of her room, bed and all. But I see you opted for being minimalistic and only brought this one, albeit massive, toy box with you. It's totally fine."

Now it's Seth who raises an eyebrow. "You know, sarcasm is the lowest form of wit."

"But the highest form of intelligence," I fire back.

Seth attempts to flatten some of the toys inside so he can put the lid down. He fails.

I smile at the little girl who stands in the lounge doorway. Needless to say, my smile is not returned. As well as a frown, Ellie is wearing the cutest blue and white sailor dress.

Seth motions for her to join us. Dragging her feet, she does as requested.

I consider this to be a massive step for Ellie. Though the moment is gone when the front door opens and slams shut. Deep in conversation, Rick and Cole proceed to make their way up the stairs.

"Today, Papa Bear," Cole calls.

Ellie jumps, diving into Seth's arms. With her head buried in his chest, he flips Cole the finger.

I wag my index finger from side to side. "I'll tell him you did that."

"You do that," he says, a mischievous glint in his eyes. He releases Ellie and squeezes her little hands. "Remember what Daddy said. If you're a good girl then we'll go out for lunch. Okay?"

My heart melts at how devoted he is to her. Seth alone in a bar is hot, but single dad Seth brooding over his little girl, that's every woman's fantasy.

I gaze out of the window. Beautiful pastel-blue sky and not a single cloud in sight. "What about the beach? Perfect weather for it."

Seth holds out his arms, as if making a statement. He's wearing a tatty pair of work trousers and a paint-stained t-shirt. "I didn't bring a change of clothes."

That's a big fat no then. Seth must pick up on my disappointment, as he hasn't stopped staring at me. "We passed a park on the way here, didn't we, baby?"

Ellie's face lights up. I'm sure mine does too. Who doesn't love the park?

"What a fantastic idea. Does Daddy want me to push him on the swings?" I say, winking at Seth.

Ellie laughs, burying her face in his t-shirt. He looks down, ruffling her hair. "Why are you laughing? Is Daddy's butt too big to fit on the swings?"

She squeals as he begins prodding her sides.

He flashes me a glance. "I really should get to work. Any problems, just shout. I'm talking to Lizzie, by the way, little miss, you filled your week's quota of shouting yesterday."

I laugh, but the sound that came out of her mouth yesterday, that godawful scream will haunt me till the day I die.

He kisses Ellie on the head. Then he turns and hurries up the stairs.

As Seth suggested, I try a different approach today. Instead of fussing over Ellie, I sit on the settee in the lounge. My book is open, and I occasionally turn the page. I'm not reading, I'm watching her. When she looks up, I look down, burying my head in my novel. I want to suss her out before I decide the best way to approach her.

Unlike yesterday, the hours pass smoothly. She watches *Finding Nemo* and *The Little Mermaid*. She even hums along to some of the songs.

I'd love to take credit for her change of attitude today. However, to her I'm no more than a bystander. Seth's promise of our lunch date does the trick. I think it helps that he shouts down every half an hour. "Three and a half hours until we go to the park… three hours…" And so forth. She visibly relaxes when she hears his voice.

We while the hours away until finally Seth calls down, "Park time."

I close my book and make my way to the hall. Ellie is already there waiting. She's even put her little shoes on.

"Great job," I say, even though they're on the wrong feet.

Seth bounds down the stairs and it's as though he reads my mind. He hits his palm over his forehead. "Wrong feet, the buckle needs to be on the outside."

She smiles triumphantly as he crouches and switches her shoes over.

Clever girl. She has him where every little girl should have her daddy, wrapped around her little finger.

"What does my little girl want for lunch?"

Ellie rubs her stomach. "A pizza."

"A pizza?" He leans forward, tickling her neck. Her shoulders scrunch and she giggles. The sullen look I know has been replaced by the sweetest smile. Her large blue eyes are focused solely on her dad.

Seth stands, rolling his neck from side to side. "Come on, time's ticking."

Rather than Seth driving, we decide to walk to the park. We stop at a small grocery shop en route and buy a selection of snacks and sandwiches for lunch.

With a carrier bag in one hand and Ellie's hand in the other, Seth swings the gate to the park open.

Ellie points. "Monkey bars."

Seth passes me the bag before lifting Ellie high in the air so she can hold onto the metal bars. Holding her thighs, he walks beneath so she can swing from one to another.

After placing her feet on the ground, Seth jogs towards the swings, calling over his shoulder, "I'm going to beat you."

Ellie is soon running behind, her little legs doing everything they can to catch up. "Wait for me, Daddy."

Not wanting to be left behind, I jog after them.

Seth begins running in slow motion, allowing Ellie to overtake. "No, she's just too fast."

Laughing, she grabs the metal chain in her hands. "Beat you, I beat you."

"Maybe, but I can go higher," he teases. Sitting on the adjacent swing, he kicks off the ground. "Told you Daddy's butt wasn't too big."

I can't help glance at his muscular arms. They're flexing and tensing as he holds the chains. His tattoo looks even sexier in the afternoon sun.

"You're cheating," Ellie says, trying hard to match her dad's pace.

Instinctively I step forwards. "Would you like me to push you, sweetie?"

She hears me, but doesn't answer. She's determined to do it on her own. I just stand watching them swinging side by side. The shrill squeals leaving Ellie's mouth warm my insides.

I can see the trust she has for Seth, the love in both of their eyes. There's another swing besides Ellie, but I can't swing with them. They're a unit, their own exclusive club that no one else will be allowed to join. It makes me kind of sad. I wonder what it'd be like to be granted momentary access, to be part of their club.

"Come on," Ellie yells.

I jump, jolted from my reverie. Ellie's running to the slide, Seth on her heels. I know I need to be more approachable, fun-loving. Hoping it'll gain me some brownie points with the little girl, I skip my way over. The bag rattles as I do. I'm conscious about what I must look like, but Ellie looks at me. She doesn't smile, but curiosity skates across her features, which in my book is better than a frown.

I stop at Seth's side. His lips make a thin line and I know he's trying not to laugh. He looks me up and down. "Finally decided to join us?"

I stand taller. "Yep."

"Nice skipping by the way."

"Thanks."

He juts his chin in Ellie's direction. "See, she's a different kid when she's with me."

"I can see that." I gaze at the tall steps she is climbing. She's so much more confident when he's around. Shaking my head, I can feel anger rising in my gut. "Anna hasn't the slightest idea what she's lost."

He blows out. "Or the damage she's caused. All I can hope is that in time Ellie will start to trust people. I know this won't be easy after she was let down by the one person she needed the most."

I realise I've lifted my hand from my side and run my fingers softly down Seth's arm. He doesn't pull his arm away, nor do I move my hand. With my hand now resting on his arm we stand together as Ellie takes a couple more turns on the slide.

Our contact is finally broken when Seth reaches down into his pocket and pulls out his phone. I'm tempted to place my hand on his arm again, but I have to remind myself that he isn't mine. They aren't my family.

He doesn't like you in that way.

"Shit, is that the time?" he says, so only I can hear. He reaches for my hand—

Oh, God, it's happening—and takes the carrier bag out of my hold.

Sigh.

Holding the bag up, he rattles it in the air.

"Picnic time," Ellie chants.

We find a small, shaded area under a horse chestnut tree where we sit cross-legged.

"Here," Seth says, handing out sandwiches and bottles of lemonade.

We sit as a few more families arrive with their children. Ellie's shoulders hunch over and she stops talking. She shuffles along the grass so she's sitting closer to her dad.

Seth continues to eat. He hasn't noticed. I figure he's used to her anxiety. He's glancing down at his phone and, without a word, he swipes his finger across the screen. He stands, takes a couple of steps away and leans his elbow against the tree. "Cole." Seth takes the phone from his ear, looking at the screen for a beat before placing it back to his ear. "No, I did not know it was that late."

I glance at my watch. It's one-thirty pm. We've been an hour and a half, not the hour he's allocated for lunch.

"Thanks for being so understanding." There's a short silence. I have no idea what Cole's saying, but Seth is nodding. He ends the call and retakes his seat beside me. "I'll take two hours for lunch, and whatever work isn't done I will stay behind and finish off."

"Sure."

I was so busy watching Seth that I completely forgot about Ellie. She's bent over picking dandelions and blowing their seed heads into the wind. I edge forward, thinking maybe I could join her, but Seth rests his hand on my knee.

"Leave her," he says under his breath. "It's just so nice seeing her happy and not looking for me."

I nod and edge back. His hand remains on my knee and whilst he watches Ellie, I watch his hand. I wonder how it'd feel to lace my fingers with his. To sit back and lean my head against his chest. To have him want me as much as I want him.

"Darcy finishes work at four o'clock. She'll pick Ellie up and take her home. I'll stay at yours until six pm, if that's okay?"

The idea sends gooseflesh crawling its way up my arms. Rick and Cole are finishing at normal time today—they'll be out of my hair at five o'clock—which means I'll have Seth to myself for a whole hour. I give him a side-ward glance. "That sounds good to me."

Seth loses track of time and finishes work at seven pm. We chat over a cup of tea. Our conversation is focused on Ellie.

I take a sip from my mug. "Beach tomorrow?"

Seth's gaze lowers to the floor and he shakes his head. "I don't know. I've kinda put off going to the beach since…"

I lower my mug and raise my brows when he doesn't continue. "Since?"

He lets out a long breath, and I can see the turmoil in his expression. "It was the last place we went with her mum. I'm worried it'll stir some negative memories, and she'll only associate the beach with her mum leaving."

I get what he's saying, but that's no reason to stop going to the beach. "I think it's time to make new memories."

"I think you're right."

We finish our drinks and he leaves. As soon as I close the door I pick up the phone and call Amber. It goes to voice mail. "Amber, it's me, call me when you get this message. I need your help planning tomorrow."

The second I cut off the voice message, my phone rings.

"Lizzie?" It's Amber.

I walk to the lounge, sit on the settee and watch as Seth's van reverses off my drive.

"Amber, I need your help…"

Chapter Nine

Lizzie

I've only seen Ellie wear dresses, but today she's wearing a pair of shorts and a bright lemon t-shirt with a smiley face on the front. One face is happy, now to get the other to follow suit.

"An hour till we go to the beach," Seth yells down.

Leaving Ellie watching the TV, I close the book I'm reading and hurry into the kitchen. I stayed up late last night thinking about the advice Amber had given me. I know I can't give the child a paint brush and expect her to paint a picture, I have to be cleverer than that.

My eyes rove over the breakfast bar. One freehand sketch of Nemo, a plastic bowl full of mosaic-like paper tiles, and two glue sticks. By the time we leave for the beach I am going to have a mosaic picture of Nemo, which Ellie will have helped me complete.

I bundle the items into my arms and hurry into the lounge, purposely tripping myself up near where Ellie is sitting. The orange squares fall like confetti around us. The cardboard picture has landed in front of the child, the glue sticks inches away.

Perfection.

She watches me closely for my reaction. Now to perform for my audience.

I rub my elbow and examine the skin. "Ouch."

Ellie's eyes are wide as she too looks to see if I'm hurt.

I slap my forehead. "I'm so clumsy." I point to the picture. "I'll just spread glue here and stick the pieces of paper here. Darn, the bowl is empty."

I try not to smile as Ellie gathers a few pieces of the orange paper and places them next to the picture. I don't thank her. She has to join in without realising what she's doing.

I grab one of the glue sticks and pull off the lid. Time for the demo. "It's really simple. All I have to do is cover a small area with glue and stick the squares on." After spreading glue on Nemo's head, I do just that.

Phase two of my plan.

"Oh, darn. I left the other colours in the kitchen."

After standing and brushing myself down. I walk slowly to the kitchen to retrieve the other bowls. I make a point of rattling a few pots and pans about. Then, as slowly as I entered, I make my way back to the lounge.

Ellie is sitting on the carpet, gluing the pieces of paper squares to Nemo. Without making eye contact I sit next to her, placing the bowl with black paper squares between us.

We sit in silence, sticking paper squares to the picture whilst, ironically, *Finding Nemo* plays on the TV. She doesn't look up at the screen once. I have her undivided attention.

Seth makes his way down the stairs. "Beach time, baby."

Ellie doesn't move. She sits looking down at our mosaic. In my periphery I can see her glancing at me. When I look at her, she looks away. Against my better judgement, I reach over to her, brushing hair out of her eyes. She doesn't flinch, instead her gaze stays fixed on my hand. I don't have one maternal bone in my body, but all I want to do at this moment is hold her in my arms and tell her everything will be okay. I don't do this, instead softly stroking her cheek with my index finger.

She clears her throat, I assume to speak, but she says nothing.

I wait for a beat and finally break the silence. "Is there something you want to ask me?"

"Can I keep it?" Her voice is little more than a whisper.

"Of course you can, sweetie. I'll leave it here to dry, and you can take it home with you later."

I envision her hugging me and saying thank you. She doesn't. Instead she offers me a small smile.

Poker-faced, Seth stands in the open doorway.

"Ellie, Daddy's here," I say, getting to my feet.

Seth's quiet as we get our shoes on, and even quieter when we get into his work van. Ellie and I wait for him to join us. I prepared a packed lunch which, amongst other things, Seth is trying to ram into a black rucksack. He holds it up triumphantly when the zipper is finally closed.

The van dips as he climbs in to join us. "Finally," he says, tossing me the bag.

I've never really looked at his profile before. His face

is a mix of angles and sharp edges, his skin bronzed from the sun. My gaze moves down to his broad shoulders. His arms appear even more muscular in the white t-shirt he's changed into for the beach.

Ellie leans forwards, blocking my view. Her car seat is in the middle, and, reaching between us, he grabs her seat belt and straps her in.

He sits taller in his seat as if switching to dad mode. "All aboard?"

I salute him. "Aye, aye, Captain."

Ellie's little legs begin swinging to and fro in her seat and she hums quietly to herself.

We reverse off the drive. It isn't long before we leave Chestnut Avenue behind. Seth heads for the long windy country lanes that take us to the beach. Houses are soon replaced by green leafy trees.

Once we pass the signpost for the beach, Seth parks on the street not far from the beachfront. I unbuckle my belt, open the door and slide out of my seat.

"Be back in a second," I say. Holding the hem of my dress, I run across the road and into a shop designed to look like a wooden beach hut. I pick up a bucket and spade and a selection of plastic sea creatures.

Jogging back to the van, I see Ellie leaning against the bonnet. I crouch down in front of her. "Here, a little something for you."

Our gaze meets momentarily as I hold the bag out for her. She looks away, so I pass the bag to Seth.

"Thanks, Daddy," she squeaks. The bag rattles as she snatches it from him. I like this side of her, the cheeky, disobedient side. Maybe because it's something I was too scared to be.

My parents were married to their work. They spent a majority of my early years overseas. In their absence I attended a private boarding school. I was the perfect child in the eyes of high society—that was until my parents retired, my grandparents passed away and Cole returned home. Those three events were pivotal and served as a domino effect leading me to where I am today.

"Now be a good girl and thank Lizzie," Seth says, lifting Ellie's chin. Ellie half-smiles then skips around her dad.

He looks at me, almost embarrassed. "I'm sorry, Lizzie."

I smile. "It's fine."

Seth slips an arm around my shoulders. "No, it's not fine. I will be having words with my daughter later. But for now, I'll say it for her. Thank you."

I can feel my face heat up and hope I'm not blushing. "Can't go to the beach without a good old bucket and spade, now can we?"

He doesn't answer, instead he gazes at his arm which is still draped around my shoulders. I smile away my disappointment as he withdraws his arm.

Crouching down, he mimics a runner about to start a race. "Last one on the sand is a rotten egg." The black rucksack bounces up and down on his back as he runs in front.

"Wait up," Ellie yells, panic in her voice. We run as fast as we can until our feet sink in the golden sand. It's a scorcher today. The air is hot and muggy. I thank God for the fat clouds in the sky that occasionally block the sun's overpowering heat.

Ellie pants with her hands on her hips as she follows

her dad's footsteps in the sand. *Cute.*

Seth isn't far in front; he stops when he finds a quiet spot for us to sit. The rucksack is open and he's laying the picnic blanket out.

Standing straight, he pulls the t-shirt over his head. Oh, my God, he's topless. His body is even better than I imagined—defined pecs, strong biceps.

He points to the blanket; Ellie sits whilst he coats her in sun lotion.

"What now, Daddy?"

Seth strokes his hand over his beard. "You remember the beach, don't you, sweetheart?"

She shakes her head. I swallow a lump in my throat. I remember Seth telling me the beach was the last place Ellie went with her mum. If she can't remember the beach, I wonder if she can remember the woman who brought her into the world.

He bends down and kicks his trainers off. "Shoes off, the sea has our name written all over it."

Ellie doesn't say anything, but she's squinting towards the water. I figure she's taken his words literally. She jumps up when Seth begins walking towards the sea.

Dodging between people, we amble to the water's edge where small waves creep towards our feet. Grabbing my and Ellie's hands, Seth yells, "One, two, three, jump."

The three of us jump over the waves. Seth smiles, but it doesn't reach his eyes. It's in this moment I can see he's happy, but he's mentally drained. I guess drained from the long workdays, and, dare I say, drained from having to switch into dad mode the second he's home. It must be so hard being a single parent. I feel the need to step in and lessen the burden, if only for a few short minutes.

I pull my hand free and begin to gallop. I can see Seth's growing amusement. Well, I've committed to looking like a complete tosser, may as well own it. "You know, when we were kids, me and my brother used to pretend the waves were white horses."

Seth bites back a grin. "You did?"

Ignoring his comment, I turn to Ellie. "Come on, ride with me. Giddy up, giddy up."

My hands extend as though I'm holding the reins of a horse. Ellie's mouth drops wide before transforming into a smile. Her eyes sparkle with interest, and her jumps become gallops. She's playing my game.

Seth stands like a statue; from his expression I'd say he's lost for words.

I swat his arm. "Want to play horsey?"

He deadpans, "Depends who's going to be riding me."

I stop galloping and gaze up into his eyes. "I'm sorry, what? I think I misheard you."

"You didn't," he says without humour. He waits a beat before wrapping his arm around my shoulder. "I'm messing with you."

He pulls me into him, my head pressed against his bare chest. As expected, his chest is firm, damp from sweat, salty from the spray of sea water, and Jesus, my body is reacting. Butterflies don't dance, they cartwheel in my stomach, and the electricity I feel from his touch travels right to my core.

"Can we get some shells, please, Daddy?"

I look up at Seth. *God, don't let me go, don't ever let me go.*

He releases me. My make-believe butterflies stop flying in an instant. Their wings, like my silly imaginings, turn to dust.

Still playing horsey, Ellie canters to the beach. We pluck shells of all shapes and sizes from the wet sand and drop them into her bucket. Little by little I can see her confidence grow. It's like watching a caged bird being released for the first time—she hovers between safety and freedom. I see a bird who desperately wants to be free, free from the restraints of anxiety. I'm sure she'll get there, and the little bird will spread her wings and fly.

Her tongue pokes out of her mouth as she examines the shells like they're diamonds. "Daddy, they're so pretty. I love the seaside."

Seth stalks up from behind me and squeezes my waist. His breath warms the side of my face. "Thank you," he whispers.

He's so close, so close I'm scared to move, scared to breathe. I turn my head and our noses almost touch. Touching is something we're doing a lot more of. Is it possible for our friendship to develop to the next level without either of us realising? Can touching one another become the norm? I decide to test out my theory. With his hands still on my waist, I cross my arms over my stomach and lace my fingers with his. "For what?"

He squeezes my fingers. "For somehow getting my daughter to stick paper to a fucking fish. For getting her to pretend to be a horse. For getting her to pick shells. For getting her to agree to come to the beach. You don't get it, do you? She's never opened up to anyone other than me and my sisters. As small and insignificant as it may sound, in Ellie's world, it's huge." He releases my waist and motions in her direction. "Just look at her. The last time I saw her this happy was when…"

He pauses for a beat, the words seemingly too hard to admit. His face is more drawn than seconds ago. I can feel his pain, like a fresh wound, raw and deep.

I squeeze his hand softly. "She's happy now, which is the main thing. Always look forward, Seth, never back. The past is quicksand, waiting to pull you down, don't let it."

He raises a brow. "Oh, yeah? When did you get all wise?"

I take a sharp breath in. "When I grew up, and I did."

I can see him ponder my words, and the added ambiguity. I know part of him will always see me as that little girl from all those years ago. I want him to open his eyes and see me as a woman.

We follow Ellie along the beach, Seth's index finger linked with mine. The beauty of it is he doesn't even realise. He's so engrossed watching his daughter pick shells that he didn't even flinch when my finger sought his out.

Ellie turns to face us. "I'm hungry, can we eat now?"

Seth looks at me and I nod. We each take one of Ellie's hands and make our way back to our picnic blanket. To the outside world we must look like a family, me the young mum, Seth the hot dad, and our daughter. For a moment I allow myself to stay in that fantasy, only letting go of it when we break apart.

Ellie runs to our picnic blanket and pulls out the lunch I prepared and packed earlier. Seth coats her with lotion again before we tuck into the food. As soon as she finishes eating, she scrambles onto the sand, dragging her bucket behind her. "I'm making a castle."

I'm about to join her when Seth takes hold of my arm. He waves the sun lotion bottle in the air. "Don't think you're getting away. Get your ass over here."

Seth pulls me back so I'm sitting between his legs. I tremble as he brushes my hair to the side. His warm creamy fingers circle my neck, working down my shoulders. I lean back and close my eyes.

Every muscle, every nerve ending tingles whenever he's near. I've got no idea how to make it stop, though deep down I don't want it to.

Chapter Ten

Seth

I don't know what the fuck has gotten into me today; I can't keep my hands off Lizzie. Every time she's close, I want her closer.

All I can see is her with my daughter. The two of them making that goddamn mosaic earlier. It was as though Lizzie drove over in her bulldozer and destroyed one of the walls I had built around my heart, leaving me open and vulnerable.

My heart feels heavy in my chest. It hurts, but in a good way. My daughter, my Ellie has finally opened up to someone. For a moment, it was like looking at Ellie and her mother, or rather where her mother should have been. It felt good having another person there, but Lizzie isn't Ellie's mum, she isn't my girlfriend and she never will be.

Lizzie's a friend, just a friend. Our relationship is one hundred—no, a million percent platonic. But then friends don't have an erection the size of the Eiffel Tower when the other friend is near.

Damn it.

I keep reminding myself that my body's reaction to her is perfectly normal. I'm a guy who hasn't had sex since forever. She's a beautiful young woman wearing a knee-length black dress that occasionally flies up a little when the wind blows.

Fuck.

Lizzie turns and takes the lotion from my hands. "Your turn."

There is no way I can have her touch me, not now. I'll come in my pants like a goddamn teenager.

I snatch the tube. "No. I'm good, I put plenty on earlier."

Her expressions dulls. "Oh, okay. In that case, I'll help Ellie with her sandcastle."

With my ass rooted to the spot, I sit and look at anything and everything that isn't Lizzie. The sea, the sand, the sky, everything that is nonsexual. By this point I can feel my back starting to burn under the thirty-degree heat. I reach for my t-shirt and pull it on.

My gaze falls on Ellie, who's building a sandcastle, and I steal a glance at Lizzie. She jumps up to retrieve a stick my daughter is pointing at, I presume to make a flag to put at the top of their fortress.

It's as though the gods are listening to the war raging in my mind, and on cue they blow with all their might. Sand blows in every direction. Ellie covers her eyes with her hands. Lizzie's little black number whooshes up. For a split second her red lacy knickers are on show. Lucky me, I get a front-row seat. The red lace fits snugly between the globes of her behind, and I picture how her ass would look with those lacy panties pulled all the way down. She grabs the hem of the dress and quickly pulls it down, covering up her modesty.

Two things I realise in this moment:

1) I really, really, really need to get laid.
2) I've got to put the brakes on with Lizzie. All this touchy-feely shit isn't good for my head, and it certainly isn't good for my dick.

I'm feeling...

Shit. I'm feeling things I shouldn't be feeling for her.

Another week. Another week and she'll be out of our lives for good. She's a client, nothing more, nothing less. It's about time I started acting like a professional. The saying is right, you can't mix business with pleasure.

Red-faced, Lizzie scampers over to me, sitting at my side. "Oh, my God. Did you see that?"

Yes, everyone on the whole fucking beach saw.

I frown, readjusting the waistband of my shorts. "See what?" I inch away, looking straight in front at the ocean. In my periphery I can see her yanking at her dress to get the limited material to cover her knees.

"Oh, nothing." She too stares out to the ocean, as though we're two people sitting together admiring the view, only we're not together. She reaches for my hand.

I look down. *What the hell is this?* I dig my fingers into the picnic blanket. I'd be a total dick to pull away, I'd be guilty of giving her mixed messages. It's clear we can't be friends, not the touchy-feely type anyway. I glance down at the watch I'm not wearing and jump up. "Is that the time? Come on, Ellie, time to go."

Ellie's little shoulders drop. Throwing her head back,

she starts kicking the sandcastle. "Noooooo."

"Daddy's got to get back to work."

When there's no visible trace that her sandcastle ever existed, she stands. "But Daddy," she whines.

With my back toward her I open the rucksack, tossing our things inside. "We're leaving." My voice is authoritative. She needs to know that when I say something, I mean it.

She begins to stamp her feet and protest, loudly. I refuse to succumb to her tantrum, so don't even acknowledge her until she's calmed down. I know people are staring, but to hell with them. I turn my back on Ellie and make my way to the van. It takes her exactly five seconds to stop whining before she runs to catch up. Her hand is in my hand before I know it and together we walk along the pavement.

Lizzie smiles and I look away. I don't intentionally give her the cold shoulder, but I purposely put space between us. She must feel the sudden chill in the atmosphere as she doesn't attempt to close the space, nor does she attempt to hold my hand.

I unlock my van and Lizzie slides in. Ellie hops in the driver's side and I fasten her belt.

"I've had a nice day," Lizzie says as I push the key into the ignition.

I slide the gear into first. "Yeah, me too."

Ellie bounces up and down in her booster. "Me three."

My back stings like a motherfucker as we make our way back to Lizzie's house. Every time I move, it feels as though my skin is tearing. By the time we pull up on her driveway I'm visibly shaking.

Lizzie looks over a few times, her face lined with concern. "Is everything okay?"

I take in a sharp breath. "I'm sorry, I think it's best I go home."

She wags her finger side to side, as though chastising me. "Cole won't be happy."

"Cole will be fine," I lie. I know I'll have to make the hours up.

She smiles impishly. "Should have let me put lotion on you when I offered." She pushes open the van door and slides out. She waits for a few seconds, scuffing her feet on the ground. "I guess I'll see you both tomorrow."

Ellie flaps her hands in the air. "Nemo!"

The corners of Lizzie's mouth turn up. "I'll be right back."

Lizzie returns moments later with the Nemo mosaic in her hands. "It's dry now." She glances at me. "Daddy might want to laminate it, it'll save the pieces falling off."

Ellie's eyes are fixated on the mosaic all the way home. I glance down every so often to see her running her finger over the coloured squares. Indicating left, I clear my throat. "Lizzie's nice, isn't she?"

"Yes."

"It was nice spending time with her today, wasn't it?"

"Yes."

"Do you think she's pretty?"

"Yes."

Her monosyllabic answers push me to ask her question after question. *Do you think she's pretty?* Sheesh. I really am clutching at straws to get Ellie to open up to me. I want to know how she feels. One of Ellie's issues is that she doesn't communicate her emotions well.

Indicating again, I pull into a side road and park next to a bus stop. I switch off my engine and look at my little girl. I brush my fingers through her hair.

"Talk to me." I tap her forehead. "Tell me what's going on in there."

No reply and she looks down.

I lift her chin. "Don't do this."

Parents often complain about their children talking too openly, saying embarrassing shit in public. God, what I'd give for Ellie to be like that. Sure, she talks to me and Darcy, but never about her mum, never about how she feels, what she wants from life. I feel as though I'm watching her tread water, one wrong move and she'll be lost forever. I just want something, anything from her.

"Talk to me." My tone is harsher than I had intended.

Her gaze meets mine. "I am talking, Daddy."

"Do you ever think of Mummy?"

"Yes."

"And?"

Silence. She just sits staring down at that bloody fish. I yank the mosaic from her hands. I hadn't anticipated her grip being quite so tight. She pulls one way and I pull the other. The thin card tears, each of us holding on to a broken piece.

Shit.

I glance down at the torn card. It's ruined, and no matter how I try to stick it back together it'll never be the same. "No, no, no. I'm so sorry."

Tears shimmer in her eyes. I know saying sorry isn't enough, I've got to wrap her in my arms and let her cry it out. I unbuckle her seat belt, and she kicks and punches me.

"I hate you, I hate you," she cries. "It's your fault Mummy left. I want to live with Mummy."

Her words hit my heart like a damn sledgehammer. The more I try to comfort her the more she lashes out. Her face is bright red and tears fall from her eyes. As much as it kills me, I lean back and give her the space she needs.

She cries for a little over five minutes. When she eventually calms down, she looks at the picture in her lap, her finger tracing over the frayed edge. That's when it hits me. I've got to stop trying to fix Ellie and start working with her. "I'm sorry, baby."

Sniffing, she climbs out of her seat and into my lap. She lassos her arms around my neck. I try not to flinch as her hands slap against my sunburnt back. I hold her close as she cries into my chest, really cries. No crocodile tears, no screaming blue murder, this is real. It feels as though she's released all that pent-up emotion and like a balloon she deflates until her whole body goes limp in my lap.

"Talk to me," I say softly, stroking her hair.

"Why did Mummy leave? Doesn't she love us any more?"

Finally.

"Of course she loves you, and I don't know why she left. Sometimes people make bad choices." I squeeze her tightly. "I will never leave you. Never. Do you hear me?"

Five, maybe ten minutes pass as we sit in complete silence.

"I love you, Daddy."

God, if only she knew how much I love her, how much I have sacrificed and will continue to sacrifice so that she's happy. "I love you, El."

She pulls away. I let her go. She slides off my lap and

jumps up into her booster seat. "I want to go home now."

I shuffle across, grab her seat belt and strap her in. I pass her my half of the picture and pull back into the main road. "I'll get some tape on it when we get home, it'll be as good as new, you'll see."

"It's okay, Daddy, we can both have half."

"Half each, eh?"

"Did you know half of ten is eight?" she says proudly.

I laugh aloud. "Close enough."

I know Darcy is keen to homeschool Ellie and has been trying to teach her the basic principles of maths. If Ellie's fractions are anything to go by then I'd say my sister is failing miserably.

I decide to test her knowledge. "Why half, why not a third?"

Hitting her head, she rolls her eyes. "Because there's two of us. That way we both have one half of the picture, and the other won't be sad."

I smile. What a sweet thing to say. "I'll never be sad because I have the best little girl in my life."

I pull into our street. Darcy's car is parked on the drive. Shit, I didn't tell her that I was leaving work early. I pull the handbrake up, turn off the engine and unbuckle Ellie's seatbelt.

"I like Lizzie," she says out of nowhere. "She's really nice to me, and she's pretty."

I swallow. "She is, isn't she?" I knew all of this to be true anyway, but I like that my daughter likes her.

We spend the remainder of the day creating our own mosaics. I attempt to draw Nemo and Dory whilst Ellie colours in pieces of paper and Darcy cuts them out. We make a good team, apart from sticking some of the colourful squares to the carpet, but hey, what good is a crafts day without a little mess?

By seven pm Ellie is asleep on the settee. I carry her upstairs and lay her in bed. Ten minutes later I can hear her running across the landing and into my bedroom, getting into my bed.

Darcy stares at me as we tidy up. I can feel the question burning on the top of her tongue, but she sits tight-lipped.

"Spit it out, sis, you've never been one for holding back."

"You're different."

The question I anticipated sounds a lot more like a statement. I don't know what she's insinuating, so spread my hands. "More good-looking?"

She throws a screwed-up piece of paper at my head. "You're spending a lot of time with that girl, Lizzie."

I nod. "For Ellie."

"Are you sure it's just for Ellie?"

"I'm sure."

Though am I sure? Work is a means to an end, but the last few days, I've looked forward to going. I've looked forward to seeing Lizzie.

Darcy looks past me at the clock. "I best get going." She slaps my back as she passes.

Immediately, I hunch forward. "Fuck's sake, Darce."

She looks at me with wide eyes. "What's wrong?"

I can't believe I'm going to ask this, but my back is screaming for some aloe vera gel. "Darce, do me a favour before you go."

"Sure."

Darcy leaves after applying a thick layer of after-sun lotion to my back. I retrieve my phone from the kitchen the moment her car pulls off the drive. Lizzie and I exchanged numbers on the night out. My finger hovers over her name. I call her.

She answers on the second ring. "Hello? Seth?"

I don't answer.

"Seth?"

I take a long breath in. "Sorry, Lizzie, I clicked on your name by mistake."

The truth is, I needed to hear her voice. I needed to call someone for a change who isn't one of the lads and isn't my sister. I feel like I need something, something for me. I'm just not sure what that something is. But I feel as though I'm closer to finding it when Lizzie's about.

Get a damn grip, Seth. What you need is a beer and to jerk off in the shower.

"Oh," Lizzie says. I can hear the disappointment in her voice, and wish there was more I could say. "That's okay. I'll see you tomorrow."

I creep upstairs and flick the light on to the bathroom. "See you tomorrow."

Chapter Eleven

Seth

I don't sleep well; my back feels as though it's on fire. I come downstairs early to catch up on some social media work for CSR's Cornwall Construction Ltd.

Ellie wakes up at five am and comes down to join me. I switch on the TV and we watch *Finding Nemo*. By seven am we move to the kitchen where I prepare breakfast.

Still wearing her PJs, Ellie spoons cereal into her mouth. Milk drips down her chin.

"Now remember, Aunty Darcy isn't working today, so you get to stay at home," I say while loading the dishwasher.

Ellie's shoulders drop and she clinks her spoon against the bowl as she eats.

I round the breakfast bar and sit at her side. "You like seeing Daddy at work, huh?"

She shrugs, circling her spoon in her bowl. "I guess."

"You guess?"

She takes a deep breath. "Well, the beach and the

park were good, but I liked making Nemo with Lizzie. I like fish. You promised I'd see fish at the beach. I looked in the sea, but you lied, there were no fish."

I laugh. "Oh, my God, Ellie. Breathe." My girl wants fish? I'll give her fish. "What about we go to the chippie when I finish work? I'll pick you up a battered cod."

She folds her arms, her eyes narrowing. "Daddy, that is not funny."

And just like that, my baby is a step closer to becoming a teenager.

"Okay, okay. What would you say to the aquarium?"

Squealing, she claps her hands. "Today?"

I shake my head. "You'll spend today with Aunty Darcy; we'll go over the weekend."

The doorbell chimes.

"Speaking of your aunty…" I kiss Ellie on the cheek and run into the hall. I let Darcy in at the same time as I run out.

"See you later," I call, shutting the door behind me.

I arrive at work at the same time as Cole and Rick. Cole presses the key fob, locking his Land Rover as I manually lock my beat-up old van.

A pink balloon floats above Cole's head. "Where's the party at?" I question, jumping up and giving the balloon a whack.

He grips the balloon for dear life. "Don't, Seth. It's Lizzie's birthday today, and her present is the balloon."

Shit, Lizzie's birthday, why didn't she tell me?

Because you're nothing to her, you tool.

I scrunch my nose up. "You brought your sister a balloon?"

Original.

"It'll make sense to her later, that's all I'm saying," he says, giving me a sharp nudge. "Now hands off the merchandise. This balloon cost me an awful lot of money."

Rick nods, as though they're in cahoots.

I motion them to carry on. "You go ahead. I've left my combi drill in the van," I lie. I walk around the side of my van and slide open the door, where I shoot Darcy a text.

Me: *It's Lizzie's birthday today.*

She doesn't reply right away, so I begin moving tools around in an attempt to look busy.

Darcy: *Do you want me to get some flowers from Ellie?*

Me: *Yes.*

Me: *No.*

Flowers fill a woman with expectation. I want a gift that'll say 'thank you', not 'I want to get in your pants'.

Darcy: *?*

Me: *Shit, Darce, I don't know, get Ellie to make her something.*

Darcy: *Like what?*

Me: *The hell should I know?*

Darcy: *Leave it with me, we'll come and drop it off later.*

My sister isn't working today, which means no Ellie. No Ellie means I can't spend the afternoon with Lizzie. My shoulders drop and I sigh heavily.

Get a grip. She's not your girlfriend.

I grab the drill, lock the van and make my way into the house. Lizzie is sitting on the settee in the lounge reading a book. She waves when she sees me.

I wave back. "Happy birthday."

She blushes. "Thanks."

There's so much more I could say, so much I want to say, but I don't. I can't stop thinking how good she was with Ellie at the beach yesterday and what a lovely day we all had. I stand staring at her for longer than I intended to.

"I best get to work." I turn and make my way to the loft room. It was Cole's great idea for us all to work together today. As spacious as the room is, the windows are a damn nuisance. The blinds haven't been fitted, so we're working in direct sunlight. Even with the skylight window open, it's like a furnace.

We have the arduous job of finishing the insulation. Rolls of rockwool have been laid out for the floor, and sheets of Celotex are stacked, ready for insulating the roof. It's amazing what three pairs of hands can achieve.

Cole's a brickie by trade. His forte is extensions. Rick is what I'd call a jack of all trades—he can plaster walls, tile, hang doors and lay floors. There's not a lot he can't put his hand to. On our own, our workmanship is pretty standard, but together we make an awesome team.

Sweat is pouring from us, and by eleven am, we're forced to take a break. Rick and I decide to get on with other jobs that need doing. Cole, however, is insistent that he wants to finish the insulation today. It's extremely ambitious of him, but I won't knock him for his determination.

Rick goes to the master bedroom and makes a start on the plastering. Cole mentions that Lizzie wants the colour of the front door changing, so I pop to the hardware shop to pick up a pot of white paint for that infernal orange door.

I don't fuck about when I get back, I open the paint pot and slap on the first coat. I hate painting, but it's another job on the list that needs ticking off.

With the first coat drying, I notice cars park up next to the house and next to the pavement opposite. People exit their vehicles and head this way.

"Walter, Edith." I nod as Cole and Lizzie's parents head onto the driveway. Edith is in her late sixties, Walter is in his eighties with his eyesight failing. She helps guide him to the house. I move aside so they can enter.

The two blondes from the nightclub are the next to arrive. One has a little girl around Ellie's age.

I point to the door. "It's just been painted."

The women walk past carefully, and of course the little girl sticks her finger right into the wet paint.

"Freja, that was naughty," her mum scolds.

Yes, Freja, that was naughty. I glare at the fingerprint mark, grab the brush and add a thin layer.

A lady wheeling a pushchair is the last to arrive. I suggest she enters the house from the side gate, which has been propped open with a bag of sand.

"All right, mate?" Cole is standing in the hall. His face is red and blotchy and he's wiping his head with a towel. "You can stop working now, we're having a little birthday lunch for Lizzie. You're welcome to join us."

"Sure, hold on." I place the brush in the paint tray and shoot Darcy a text, asking if she'd pop round with Ellie. Then, leaving the front door open, I follow the small party into the kitchen.

Lizzie has prepared a selection of finger foods on the breakfast bar and is plating up sandwiches when I enter. She looks so beautiful today. She's wearing a red polka-dot dress. Her hair is scraped up and a small hair piece is secured around her hair tie to give the illusion of a messy bun. It's sad I know that, but thanks to YouTube tutorials on hairstyling I know how to braid Ellie's hair. Granted, it may not be perfect, but it makes her happy, and that's all that matters.

I feel slightly underdressed in heavy blue trousers and a paint-mottled t-shirt, though I feel a little more at ease knowing Rick and Cole are also in their work clothes.

Lizzie stands the other side of the kitchen. It feels wrong standing this far away from her. We've been so close over the last few days, it's as though my place is by her side.

Lizzie hugs the guests in greeting and they hand her cards and gifts. She arranges them into a nice pile on the kitchen worktop.

Amber watches me as I watch Lizzie. I don't look back at Amber, instead stick a breadstick into my mouth and slowly make my way around the room.

Cole's balloon floats in the air. I can't miss it, it's bright pink and as big as a pumpkin. It's attached to a ladder-backed chair by a long pink string, a pink string that Cole is trying desperately to untie as Freja attempts to steal the balloon.

Once everyone is acquainted, the party moves out-doors. The garden is a nice size—the previous owner was an avid gardener and that shows with the landscaping and immaculately tended flower beds.

Holding a paper plate, I stand with Rick and Cole under a small gazebo. Our conversation is centred around the house and what works are left before completion.

Excusing himself, Rick heads to the kitchen for more food. It seems as though he's worked up quite the appetite. This will be his fourth helping.

Alone with Cole, I stand in complete silence. Lizzie is talking to her parents. The blondes are talking to the lady with the pushchair and cooing over her baby. Freja is playing with a bubble machine.

"You're spending a lot of time with my sister," Cole says. And there it is, the elephant in the room.

My body stiffens as I turn to face him. "Yes, with my daughter." My tone is harsh and defensive. I don't know why.

Cole smacks his hand on my sunburnt back. I clench my teeth together. Cole doesn't notice, carries on talking. "I know, mate. I'm sorry, I wasn't suggesting anything was going on. She's way too young for you."

Although there's humour in his voice, he's giving me a warning. His eyes burn into mine before he laughs. "I'm just fucking with you."

Thank God Rick rejoins us and the conversation is steered back to the house.

It isn't long before Lizzie's parents retrieve the gifts from the house for her to open. Chelsea and Amber run into the kitchen and bring out her cake, which is a unicorn of all things. Lizzie blows out the candles and we sing happy birthday. It's like a child's party, we all gather around and watch as she opens her cards and gifts. The blonde ladies have given her a voucher for their photography shop. Her parents have bought her a necklace. The lady with the baby has bought her a kettle.

Cole appears, the balloon in one hand, a card in the other. She kisses him on the cheek. "Thanks, Cole." She breaks the seal on the envelope and reaches inside, retrieving a Swiss Army knife. She frowns. "I wasn't planning on going camping any time soon."

Cole looks from the crowd to Lizzie, then points at the balloon.

With a mischievous glint in her eyes, she thrusts the knife into the balloon. The balloon pops and multicoloured confetti falls to the floor along with a silver key.

I lean forward and watch as she inspects the key. "I don't understand. This is the key to the front door."

He gives her an open-mouthed smile. "It's yours."

She shrugs. "What, the key?"

"The house, you idiot."

No one speaks. Mouths open wide.

Lizzie's whole face lights up. "You've giving me this house?"

"Sure am, sis."

Squealing, she jumps up into his arms and he spins her round. Everyone is smiling, and all I can do is stand with my arms crossed tightly in front of my chest and frown. He bought her a goddamn house. I don't know why it's bothering me so much, but it is.

The guests crowd around Cole, clapping him on the back like he's the messiah. Anyone would think he's just given her a three-hundred-grand house.

Oh, wait, he has!

How can anyone compete with that?

A little hand tugs at my trousers. "There's my girl." I lift Ellie off the ground and set her on my shoulders. I have to move away from the scene unfolding in front of my eyes, so walk a little way up the garden, where I spot Freja. "Hey, Ellie, want to pop some bubbles?"

She bounces up and down. "Yes."

Darcy joins me, and we stand and watch Ellie and Freja running together popping bubbles. The whole time Ellie is looking up, checking I'm still here.

I clench my teeth as red polka dots appear in my periphery.

"Oh, my God. That's adorable," Lizzie says. "That's a massive step forward for her."

I can feel my jaw tighten, and can't help the irritation that tugs at my nerves. "She has good days and bad. But then you wouldn't know that, you've barely known her five days, I've had her for five years. She takes one step forward and two back. She's only playing because I'm here watching her. It's not a step forward at all."

Lizzie's grin dissolves. I don't think she knows what to say. Forcing a smile, she excuses herself and goes to talk to her parents.

"Whoa, what's up your arse?" Darcy asks.

"None of your business."

"Well, I think that was incredibly rude of you."

She's right. I don't know why I'm so bloody worked up, but I can't shift it.

"Ellie," Darcy calls, pulling a card from a plastic bag. "Do you want to give Lizzie your gift?"

I don't look what's in the bag. I'm too embarrassed

to. Instead I snatch it off my sister. "No. She's not giving it to Lizzie."

"Giving what to Lizzie?" Amber asks, as she attempts to look over my shoulder. She's tiny, so she can't. She stands on her tiptoes, her head craned back, swaying side to side.

"The card I made her," Ellie says as she joins us.

Great, now my daughter bloody decides to talk.

Glaring at me, Amber reaches out her hand. "Come on, sweetheart, I'll take you."

Ellie takes Amber's hand then grabs mine. Great. Looks like we're all going. We make our way to Lizzie and I allow Ellie to pass her the bag.

Lizzie bends down. "Is that for me?"

Ellie smiles.

Lizzie opens the bag and peers inside. "Oh, my God, Ellie. I love it. Did you make this all by yourself?"

Ellie's nodding. Lizzie opens up a card with a picture of a fish on the front. The shells we collected from the beach are stuck onto its body. As if one cue, one shell falls off, followed by another. Noticing this, Lizzie carefully places it back in the bag. "I'm going to put this in a frame."

Ellie couldn't have made anything more perfect. But why do I feel so shitty right now?

I should be wishing Lizzie happy birthday, I should be chatting to her, but I'm the quietest I've ever been, and all I'm doing is counting down the hours till I can get out of here.

I should have told Darcy to buy the damn flowers.

Chapter Twelve

Lizzie

I can't help but wonder, did I do something wrong? Seth's been off with me all day and I cannot for the life of me work out what I did to upset him. We had such a lovely day together at the beach yesterday and the park the day before. It just doesn't make any sense.

It's three o'clock, and people are slowly starting to leave. My folks and Cole are the first to go, followed by my cousin Veronica with baby Grace. Seth disappeared some hours back—he said something about painting a door. Everyone else has been sitting in my garden, talking and drinking wine.

Amber and Chelsea swoon over Rick, honestly, they're like his harem. Darcy fetches some of Ellie's toys from the toy box in the lounge and the girls play happily in the grass.

Seth is right about one thing. Ellie will only play when he or his sister are around—the moment they leave her or stop watching her, she stops playing. I can see little moments when she opens up, but it doesn't take long before she disappears into herself.

I've made a real effort to strike up conversation with her today. She's smiled at me a few times but hasn't spoken to me as yet. It's like the last few days haven't happened, but as Seth said, one step forward and two back. He was right. Who am I to offer any kind of advice on his daughter? It must be so frustrating and heartbreaking for him.

"You never told me your brother was loaded," Amber pipes up.

Chelsea sighs. "If you had, I'd certainly have been a little nicer to him."

I pull up a chair and sit with my friends. "I didn't know he was. I mean, I knew he was doing all right for cash."

Clearing his throat, Rick joins in our conversation. "Your brother is like Jesus. He had the ability to turn water to wine, Cole has the ability to turn bricks into gold."

Has his business become that successful and I don't even know?

"How much gold?" I ask.

Rick wags his finger. "That is not for me to discuss."

Feeling somewhat smaller than I did moments ago, I pinch the imaginary zip on the corner of my mouth and zip it shut.

Our father gave Cole and I fifty thousand pounds on our twenty-first birthdays. Cole invested in his company, CSR's Cornwall Construction Ltd. The abbreviated CSR stood for Cole, Seth and Roderick. I believe Cole was the one who took all the financial risk, whilst the others were named shareholders. I know my brother calls the shots.

My money went toward my education and student accommodation. It was worth every penny; I love my job.

"How long until the house is done? You're having a housewarming party, right?" Amber's question sends a stabbing pain in my stomach. I know that when the work on the house is completed my time with Seth will come to an end, and although he blows more hot and cold than a sandstorm in the Arctic, I like spending time with him. I'll miss him and Ellie.

My eyes tear up. Quickly wiping them, I stand. "I'm going to run to the little girls' room."

I doubt anyone will even miss me. Darcy and the girls are playing happily amongst themselves. Rick reclines on my outdoor lounger, his arms extended on the back of the seat. If my friends were to sit any closer, they'd be in his lap. I wouldn't put it past Amber.

I run through the house and stop at the front door, the front door Seth was supposed to be painting, except he isn't there. He's propped against his work van, smoking. Running my hands down my dress, I approach him.

"The door looks good," I say, standing at his side.

Nodding, he exhales smoke into the air. "Looks a damn sight better than infernal orange." He turns his head so that he's facing away from me and continues to smoke.

Why is he being like this?

I place my hand on his forearm. "Did you want to join us out back?"

He pulls his arm from my hold. "Not really, no." He blows out more smoke.

What the hell's up with him? I want to shake him, like physically shake him and tell him to stop being this way. He's not being a jerk per se, but he's being weird.

107

"Ellie's playing nicely. She asked for you," I lie.

He gives me a sideward glance. "I won't keep my baby waiting."

He puts out his cigarette on the side of his van and makes his way through the house to the back garden. He walks past Rick and his harem, then sits on the grass beside his sister and the girls, his back toward me.

I place my hand on Ellie's shoulder. She doesn't tense at my touch, but rather looks at me with growing interest. "Hey, Ellie, Freja, would you like me to play with you?"

Freja shakes her head. "No, we don't have enough dolls."

She's right. Darcy, Freja, Elle and Seth each have a Barbie doll in their hand. There isn't another.

Crossing my arms, I look at Amber and Chelsea, who sit chatting to Rick. They're meant to be here to see me, and yet none of them give a damn whether I'm here or not.

I slip away into the lounge, grab my book from the coffee table and continue where I left off earlier.

I'm halfway into my chapter when a hand rests on my shoulder.

"Hi, Lizzie."

I smile up at Darcy. It's now I can see a resemblance between her and her brother. Her hair is slightly longer than Seth's—it's been sleeked back. She has a harsh look about her, and her face brings new meaning to resting bitch face. She's wearing a long black dress, which she straightens before sitting on the settee next to me. "It seems my niece has taken a liking to you."

"Hardly," I say, leaning my head in my hands.

"You seem to have made quite the impression on her over the last few days. She's talked about you all morning, and Ellie doesn't talk about anyone other than her dad."

Smiling, I sit taller. "That's nice to know."

Nice to know? Understatement, that's made my day. I am making a lasting impression on that little girl and it fills me with hope that one day she can live a normal life free from anxiety.

"Which is why"—Darcy breathes deeply—"I've managed to get out of some of the shifts I was meant to be working next week."

I turn to face her. "I'm sorry, what?"

"You only need to babysit her on Tuesday. Tomorrow and the rest of next week I can have her as normal."

I don't know why it bothers me so much, but I rearranged my own plans so that I could look after Ellie. "I don't understand, I thought I was going to babysit."

"We can't afford for her to get too attached to people who she won't see again, it's too confusing for her."

I frown, fumbling with the book in my lap. "But surely you can't stop her interacting with people? She's going to meet children at school who may leave to go to another school. You can't protect her forever."

Darcy taps her foot on the floor. "Okay, you're not understanding me." Her tone is derogatory and patronising. "I'm not concerned about her forming connections with other children, Lizzie, I'm concerned about her forming a connection to you."

My mouth falls open. "Me? Why? What have I done?"

Her expression hardens.

"There you are."

Both Darcy and I jump. Amber appears in the doorway.

"Get your ass outside. Chelsea's had a little bit too much to drink. She's trying to play kiss chase and is currently chasing Rick around the garden. It's fucking hilarious."

Darcy stands, placing her hand over her mouth. "Oh, my. Not the behaviour a child should witness. I think I'm going to take Ellie home now. It was lovely to see you again, Lizzie." She looks down her nose at Amber. "It was nice to meet you, Amber."

Amber snort-laughs. When Darcy is out of earshot she whispers, "That stuck-up cow has been giving us dirty looks all afternoon."

I don't argue with her. I saw the way Darcy glared at them. "I don't think it helped that you and Chelsea were trying to dry-hump Rick."

Amber's eyes go wide. "We were not."

Laughing, we head out to the garden.

With Darcy and Ellie gone, Freja asks Amber if she can watch cartoons in the house. Seth locks the now dry front door, and Amber checks on her every five minutes.

Chelsea holds up an empty wine bottle. "Hey, want to play spin the bottle?"

Amber laughs. "What are you, twelve?"

Winking at us, Chelsea nods her head towards Rick. "Come on, it'll be fun."

Rick folds his arms over his chest. "Fine."

Amber beckons. "Come on, Seth."

"I'm not playing."

Amber isn't one to take no for an answer. She runs over and grabs his hand. Shaking his head, he looks heavenward before finally giving in and joining our little circle. "God help me," he mumbles.

Chelsea claps her hands together. "Oh, goodie."

She spins the bottle, and of course, it lands on Rick.

"Truth or dare," she fires.

"Always dare, baby, no one will know my truths."

Chelsea's eyes go wide. "A man of mystery. I dig that." She takes a deep breath and runs her tongue over her lip. "I dare you to kiss me."

Amber tugs at her sister's arm. "You can't nominate yourself; you have to pick someone else."

"Oh, right." Chelsea glances around the group, her eyes fixing on mine. "I dare you to kiss Lizzie."

"Bitch," Amber berates, glaring at her sister.

My gaze shoots to Seth. His jaw is clenched, his arms folded. He watches every step Rick takes towards me. If looks could kill he'd be reading Rick's eulogy.

Rick reaches for me. I take his hands and he pulls me up to my feet. My heart is racing, not because of the adrenaline, but because I feel as though I'm being unfaithful to Seth, which is crazy because we're not together.

Maybe kissing someone else is exactly what I need to erase the idea of Seth from my mind.

Rick places his hand on my cheek, tilting my head so that I'm looking at him. It hasn't escaped my attention how gorgeous he is. His face is full, yet angular. Dark brown hair blows across his face and when pushed back touches the nape of his neck. I look straight at his lips, which he puckers. Closing my eyes, I lean forward. I feel the soft kiss he places on my forehead before he releases me.

"That's cheating," Chelsea scolds.

Rick shakes his head. "You said I had to kiss Lizzie, you did not specify where."

"On the lips!"

Rick wags his finger in the air. "I've done my dare, now it is my turn to spin the bottle." Rick retakes his seat. He takes the bottle in his hand and spins it. It lands on Amber. "Truth or dare?"

I zone out of the game and look at Seth. His eyes are on mine. Unblinking, he doesn't smile, nor does he look away. I wrap my arms around my waist, suddenly feeling very uncomfortable, exposed and vulnerable. It feels as though I don't need to play this game for Seth to know all my truths. It's as though he has the power to take them from me.

In my periphery I can see Chelsea doing a rather un-steady-looking handstand, followed by Amber and Rick slow-dancing. I kind of know where this game is going. Unsurprisingly, Amber and Chelsea both choose dare.

My attention is only brought back to the game when the bottle finally lands on Seth.

Amber taps her nail against the glass bottle. "Truth or dare?"

Dropping his shoulders, Seth sits back. "Truth."

"Boring," Chelsea scoffs. I gather she wasn't expect-ing anyone to choose truth.

Amber leans forward, her elbows on her knees. "What are your intentions towards our dear friend Lizzie?"

His face is stoic. "My intentions are purely platonic whilst I finish the work on the house."

"I smell bullshit," Amber pipes up, at which Seth stands.

"I'm going for a smoke."

Rick leans forward in his seat. "It's no good playing with a little boy, you need to play with the big boys who'll be up for a challenge. I will take Seth's turn. I choose dare. I will show Lizzie what it feels like to be kissed by a man."

Slowly, Rick manoeuvres himself out of his seat. With a confident stride he makes his way towards me. He leans down, scrunching the collar of my dress in his hand, pulling me to my feet. "I have one question. Tongue or no tongue?" He flashes me his tongue piercing, which he bites between his front teeth.

I fan my face with my hand, feeling very hot all of a sudden. Rick's gorgeous. I forget how to use my mouth. I forget how to talk. I forget how to kiss.

He reaches up and fists my hair. "Tongue it is, baby girl. Now pucker up, 'cos once you've kissed me, I'll ruin you for any other guy."

"I—I—"

"Put her down already, some of us have eaten," Seth barks out.

Rick tilts his chin in Seth's direction. "The way I see it, you wasted a perfectly good dare. So either you get your arse here and kiss her, or I will."

The grip Rick has on my hair is released. I don't see Seth approach, but feel his hold. I'm like a rag doll as he pulls me into him. I don't have time to think, I don't have time to breathe. His mouth captures my mouth. His beard is rough against my skin as his tongue pushes its way into my mouth. It's not a loving kiss—it's fierce, angry. His kiss is firm, his hold on me is tight, and I freakin' love it. My tongue stands its own ground as it prepares for battle with his. I tingle from my toes through to my core. Every emotion, every sensation is heightened. I forget our audience and the kiss slowly turns into something else. His grip loosens, his tongue doesn't seek war, but seeks out a partner with whom to dance.

Breathing heavily, he pulls away. His expression is completely unreadable.

"Now that, ladies and gentlemen, was a kiss." Rick claps his hands.

Seth flips him the finger. "You've had your show. Now, excuse me, I'm going home." He doesn't offer a goodbye. He turns his back on me and makes his way through the house.

"That was rude," Chelsea scoffs.

Rick steeples his fingers in his lap. "I will have words with Seth tomorrow."

Amber bounces on her heels. "I dare you to kiss me."

Rick raises a brow. "If you want a kiss that bad, all you have to do is ask."

Squealing, Amber jumps onto his lap. "Pucker up, big boy."

I draw my lower lip between my teeth. It feels swollen and hot. I swoon—that kiss, so firm and demanding. My heart's pounding in my chest, my head's telling me he left, he left me and didn't so much as look back.

Chapter Thirteen

Seth

Ellie chomps loudly on her cereal. "Are we taking Lizzie for pizza today?"

I choke on my toast. "I'm sorry?"

Ellie hits her hand on her forehead. "Are we taking Lizzie out for pizza today?"

I shoot a glance at Darcy, who with her back toward me is shaking her head. Ellie is sitting wide-eyed, awaiting my answer.

"Why would we take Lizzie out for pizza?"

She lets out an exasperated breath. "Because, Daddy, when it's my birthday, we always go out for pizza."

Darcy turns around, a glass of orange juice in hand, which she places in front of Ellie. "Lizzie has her own family she'll be going out to have pizza with."

I'm too lost for words to enter the conversation. Ellie wants us to go for pizza with Lizzie. Maybe Lizzie was right and she is making progress.

I can't stop thinking about our kiss yesterday. Why

did I kiss Lizzie?

Because you can't get her out of your head. Because you couldn't stand by and let Rick stick his tongue in her mouth.

"That would be nice, wouldn't it?" Darcy asks.

I've got no idea what she's asking me. Her fingers drum on the table, and she raises her eyebrows.

"Yes, it would." I've got no idea what I've agreed to.

Ellie's shoulders drop as Darcy jiggles from side to side in her seat.

"It's settled then," Darcy says, seemingly pleased with herself. "We'll all go for pizza tomorrow evening. Me, Uncle Dwight, and how about Aunty Imogen and Dan?"

Ellie shrugs. "But it's not your birthday."

"Don't be cheeky," Darcy snaps. "And besides, Lizzie's birthday was yesterday."

I raise my hand. "We'll talk about this later, okay? I've got to get to work."

I narrow my eyes at my sister. She knows she's crossed the line. Nobody raises their voice to my little girl. I give Ellie a quick kiss, grab my phone and keys from the breakfast bar and head for the door.

Cole isn't coming into work today. He called and said that he had to price another job. Apparently, he's looking at a plot of land being sold by a farmer. Land is gold, and Cole is already speaking to architects about building potential.

Being a man down and on a time limit, Cole had no other option but to contact the agency and call in six subcontractors. Six is far too many in my opinion, but if they help move the job along, I'm not going to argue. The quicker I get out of here and away from Lizzie, the better. It's becoming harder to be in her company. Unease is constantly tightening its grip around us, and I'd be lying if I said I know how to act around her.

I pick Rick up for work at nine am, an hour late.

When the cat's away and all.

I'm not trying to piss Cole off; I'm putting off work. I stop at the petrol station on the way to fill up my tank, wasting more time.

When we finally arrive at Lizzie's, the front door is propped open and she's nowhere to be seen. I can hear the clattering of plates from the kitchen. The polite thing to do would be go with Rick to say hello, but I don't. I head straight upstairs and get straight to work boarding the second bedroom. It doesn't take Rick long to join me upstairs. He works across the landing in the master bedroom, replacing floorboards in readiness for the carpet to be laid.

"Coffee break?" Rick hollers.

Scratching my head, I check my phone for the time. "No, it's too early." It doesn't matter what time it is, the answer would still have been no.

Footsteps cross the landing and Rick appears in the doorframe. "What got you rattled today?"

Pretending I don't see him, I continue nailing plasterboard to metal stud.

He folds his arms. "All I know is that you were fine yesterday, that is until Cole gave Lizzie this house. It's not a dick size contest. He's. Her. Fucking. Brother. Stop being a little bitch, suck it up and buy the girl some damn flowers already."

My nostrils flare. "I've got no idea what you're talking about."

"Oh, I think you do, not to mention the kiss. That shit was hot. It's obvious you're fucking."

"We are not."

He holds his hands up. "I pass no judgement, and I really don't care what you do with your dick or where you stick it. But when you're working, I need your mind on the job. Mistakes get made when your head ain't in it."

I ball my hands into fists. "I'm not fucking Lizzie."

"Don't even go there. That's just all kinds of nasty."

I throw the nail gun to the floor and pace towards him. My chest lines up with his, my face in his.

He squares up to me. "Look at you, getting all up in my face like a damn rooster, puffing your feathers out. Back the fuck off, or I'll—"

"You'll what?"

He shoves me. "Hit a nerve, haven't I? I'm not angry at you for having a crush on my little sister."

I shove his arm away. "She's *not* your little sister."

Rick places his hand over his heart. "We grew up together, man. You're my brother, Cole's my brother. Now if Cole's my brother, doesn't take a genius to work out what Lizzie is to me. She's my little sister, if she knows it or not."

I squint into his eyes, looking at his pupils. "Are you high?"

"No, I am not. Blood means shit. You guys are the family I never had. Now, as Lizzie's older brother, I have no problem with you and her getting it on. But Cole, he will be beyond pissed. He'll get over it, but he may not talk to you for the next decade."

I don't answer. This conversation is getting beyond weird. I step away and grab my nail gun.

"Why are you so angry? You like her, she likes you. As they say, the rest is history."

I snort. "Remind me when your last relationship was? How can you advise me on matters of the heart when you don't know the first thing about love?"

"Rick has a lot of love to give, it'd be unfair to give that to just one woman."

"Whatever." I turn my back to him and carry on working. I can hear him tapping his foot on the floor.

"I don't like her in that way," I spit out.

"I don't believe you. So here's what I'm going to do. I'm going to take a coffee break and tidy up your mediocre work. You are going to get out of my sight."

"And do what?"

"I don't fucking care. Run around the block. Get your damn nails painted. Buy Lizzie a birthday present because it's eating you up inside that you didn't bother yesterday. If and when you come back, I want your mind back on the job."

"Rick—"

"I've finished the floor in the main bedroom. Now fuck off, before I change my mind."

I can't help but smile. Seeing the look on my face, he takes a step back. "Don't even think about hugging me."

As pissed as I am with him, he's right. I make my way downstairs and storm to the lounge.

Lizzie's lying on the settee reading a book. I stand in the door frame; my heart is racing. I take a moment to compose myself. Ellie's toy box remains next to the settee. The dolls she played with yesterday are hanging out, which prevent the lid from closing. I kind of like that it's here, like part of Ellie is still here, even when she's not.

The card Ellie made for Lizzie's birthday is sitting proudly in a small silver frame. Lizzie's gained some extra brownie points for that.

I cross the threshold and step into the lounge. Lizzie must see me, but doesn't acknowledge my presence. She licks the tip of her finger and turns a page in her book.

I clear my throat. "Put your shoes on, we're going out."

She flips the book over in her lap, her mouth set in a hard line as she glances up. "Excuse me?"

"Fold the page over in your little book, get the fuck up, and put some shoes on."

"I didn't get so much as a good morning. You were extremely rude to me on my birthday—"

I've not got time for this. I pull her up from the settee and like a caveman I throw her over my shoulder.

"Put me down," she yells, pounding my back with her fists. "Seth, what the hell are you doing?"

"What I should have done yesterday. I'm going to buy you some damn flowers."

I don't put her down, I don't give her time to put her shoes on. I open the driver's side door of my van and throw her in. I sit down next to her, scooting over. She has no choice other than to move over. I sit for a beat, holding the steering wheel. I stare forwards. My heartbeat is finally slowing down and my breathing returns to normal.

"Seth—"

"I'm sorry, Lizzie. I've been completely out of order. I just feel so awkward around you. We crossed a line yesterday; I don't know how to get back to how we were."

She reaches for my hand. "Maybe we can't."

I take her hand in mine and squeeze.

She lets out a deep sigh. "Where do we go from here?"

I shrug. "The florist, definitely the florist."

I've never bought a woman flowers until today. Today I spend two hundred pounds on some roses and a bouquet full of God knows what, loads of different-coloured flowers all bundled together with a bunch of green shit poking out. The bouquet is so big that it takes up the middle seat in my van.

I pull onto her drive. We don't speak. I guess neither of us want to break the silence.

The cellophane crackles and she leans forward, sniffing the roses. "Thank you, they're beautiful."

I shake my head dismissively. "They're from Ellie."

"Well, tell Ellie thank you."

She sits, looking from me to the flowers as if waiting for me to speak. When I don't utter a word, she pivots around in the seat and opens the van door. I can see her slipping away, out of the van and out of my life. Without thinking, I lunge across the seats, flattening the ginormous bouquet with my stomach. I grab the door handle and pull it shut.

Lifting her hands, almost apologetically, she sits bolt upright.

"Dinner," I blurt out.

"What?"

"Have dinner with me, tomorrow night."

She picks at the flowers, trying to straighten the petals I flattened. "I... I can't, Seth."

"Why not?"

She turns her head, looking out of the window. "You know why." I don't know why women do this shit. Overcomplicate and overanalyse everything. "Why were you such a jerk yesterday?"

Raking my hand through my hair, I sigh. "I don't know. It was like I was a million miles away from you. All I wanted to do was stand at your side with my arm around your shoulders. Crazy, huh?"

I fail to mention that it pissed me off Cole bought her a house. I'll keep that to myself.

"Why did you kiss me?"

Why did I kiss her? I pinch the bridge of my nose, hoping to conjure up an answer, but the truth is I don't know what to say. I kissed her because I wanted to, and damn it, I couldn't sit back and watch Rick with his hands all over her. Something bubbled up in my stomach, something primal and possessive. Releasing my nose, I look over at her. She's so beautiful.

"We can't be more than friends, Lizzie, you know that?"

"So then why are you asking me out for dinner?"

Fantastic. I'm giving the poor girl more mixed messages. "Ellie wants us to go out for pizza, because it's your birthday and it's tradition."

Cellophane crackles in her hand. "Is that what you want?"

"Yes, Lizzie, it's what I want."

"Aren't you worried what Cole will think? The three of us going out for dinner?"

Cole's the least of my worries.

"Fuck Cole," I bark out. Fuck Cole with his money and his perfect uncomplicated life. "I'd like to think of it as a peace offering between two friends." I emphasise the word 'friends.'

I finish work at five pm. A lady called Monica swings by to pick Rick up. I stay at Lizzie's for a little while longer to inspect the work the subcontractors have done. The loft conversion looks great. The insulation has been fitted and all the boarding is complete.

"Lizzie, come up here," I call.

I hear footsteps. It isn't long before she joins me.

Her face transforms. "Wow. Looks good, doesn't it?"

She's looking at the room whilst I look at her.

"Yes, it sure does."

She's wearing a black t-shirt and knee-length denim skirt. Her hair is tied up in a ponytail, and her brown eyes are wide as she takes in the room. The urge to touch her is overwhelming. I fight the urge by pushing my hands in my trouser pockets. Smiling, she looks me up and down.

I'm not blind, I see how she looks at me. I imagine how Lizzie could fit into my life. Maybe I could see her when Ellie is at school, but by that time we'll both be working. Maybe weekends if Darcy minds Ellie, but then I'm sacrificing time with my little girl. I wonder how easy it would be to just let Lizzie fall into our normal, but that will never happen.

I envy anyone who has an uncomplicated life.

My eyes hover over Lizzie, her curvy body and her cute little ass. It would be so easy to take her to bed, and God, I want to, but she is not the girl you sleep with and forget about, she's the girl who once you have you never let go. She deserves simple and uncomplicated, which is something I can never give her.

A girl like her is too good for a guy like me.

`

Chapter Fourteen

Lizzie

The first thing I see when I wake is the flowers that Seth bought me. I mean I can't exactly miss them. The humongous bouquet fills four vases, which I've arranged on the hearth.

It's eleven-thirty am. Damn, I slept in. At five pm, Seth and Ellie are taking me out for dinner. We're not going to a playground or the beach, today we are going for a meal. Just the thought has transported me to cloud nine. I float out of bed as I think of the hours that lie ahead.

I fold the sofa bed away and replace the cushions. I stack the bedding neatly in the space behind the chair next to the window. I have to remind myself that sleeping in the lounge is temporary and soon I'll be waking up in my own bed in my new bedroom.

I make my way to the bathroom, where I take a quick shower. Once dry I wrap up in my baby-pink robe. After grabbing a light breakfast, I while away the hours watching daytime TV.

Lunchtime fast approaches. I make myself a mush-room omelette and think it's about time to get my outfit ready and possibly ironed. Seeing as I don't own a ward-robe as yet, I had to improvise. I grab my travel case from behind the bed, unzip it, then empty my clothes out on the cushions. I have no idea what to wear, how to style my hair, or what makeup to apply.

Chelsea's name flashes in my mind. I'm very fortu-nate to have a best friend who is a hairdresser and beauti-cian. She finished work at two pm, it's now two-fifteen. I grab my phone and shoot her a quick text.

Me: *You know you love me?*

Chelsea: *What do you want?*

I send a shocked emoji and beg her to come to my rescue.

Chelsea: *Let me get showered and I'll be right round.*

It's ideal that they live in the flat above the shop, es-pecially in emergencies like this. Twenty minutes pass before the bell rings. I rush to the front door. I can't wait to tell her about my meal with Seth and Ellie. The words are on the tip of my tongue when I open the door.

I step back. "Cole."

He holds out his hands. "The one and only. Shit, sis, don't look too disappointed to see me."

"I'm sorry, it's just I wasn't expecting you."

He raises a brow as he looks me up and down. "Clear-ly. I see you've not bothered to get dressed."

I gaze out at people walking across the street and pull my robe a little tighter.

"Well, I'm here, so are you going to ask your big brother in?"

I step aside. "Sorry."

He pulls a measuring tape from his trouser pocket. "It's only a quick visit. I need to measure the work the subcontractors did so I can pay them." He runs up the stairs, then stops on the middle step, peering down into the lounge. "Bloody hell, Lizzie, are you having a jumble sale?"

"Ha ha. If you must know I'm going out for a birth-day meal."

Backtracking, he makes his way down the stairs. "More celebrations? Who with?"

I glance down to the floor and contemplate if I should tell him, but I don't see the harm in him knowing. It's not like anything is going on between us. "Seth and Ellie. It was totally her idea, her favourite pizza restaurant."

"I see." A vein pops in his neck. "Have you forgotten what day it is?"

Two days after my birthday. Is that a trick question?

He passes me in the doorway to the lounge and makes his way to the settee. He notices the flowers, of course he notices them. He looks away as though they've personally offended him.

He sits down and places his hands over his face. "To-day would have been Granddad's birthday."

God, how have I not remembered? I was so wrapped up in myself. I've been a terrible person, a terrible sister.

"I was taking flowers to the cemetery after measuring up here. I was hoping you'd join me."

I look at the clock. Chelsea's due any second. I'll have to cancel our makeup session, she'll understand. "I made plans—" I begin.

"Your plans come before our granddad? You should be ashamed of yourself." He lifts his head. Imprints from his fingers redden his cheeks.

"No, it's not like that, but Chelsea is—"

"So now your friend comes before our granddad."

I place my hands on my hips. "Cole, that isn't fair."

He barges past me and storms upstairs, the tape measure held tightly in his hand.

I loved my grandparents, but he forgets, they passed away when I was young. They practically brought him up whilst our parents worked. He has lasting memories of them and a forever bond that even death can't sever, whereas they were strangers to me. Two totally different relationships, but that doesn't mean I wouldn't go and pay my respects.

I'll text Chelsea and tell her not to come. I feel in my pocket for my phone.

Crap. It's got to be here somewhere.

I pat my pocket again if somehow it'll be there. When I finally accept it won't magically appear, I start rummaging through clothes on the settee.

The ceiling lights tremble as heavy steps boom from above and doors slam. Cole and I have never argued. There's never been bad feeling between us. I can't leave things like this between us.

"Cole," I call, running out into the hallway. The doorbell rings just as my hand makes contact with the banister.

Oh, fudge.

I open the door.

"Hey," Chelsea singsongs as she bulldozes past me. She nearly runs over my feet with her carry case. Bypassing me, she hauls her pink sparkly makeup case into the lounge.

Why can't I look as good as her? She's wearing a black tunic and tight-fitting black trousers. Her blonde hair has been secured in a French braid. Not a solitary hair is out of place. She's wearing makeup, so natural that it enhances her already stunning features.

She drops the carry case onto the floor, flips the fastenings and begins sifting through bottles of foundation. "Spill, who's this big date with?"

I didn't mention a date. Great, I hope Cole isn't eavesdropping. "Chelsea, I'm really sorry, but I'm going to have to cancel."

She drops the cosmetics back into the case and stands. "Why? Don't tell me he's stood you up. What a jerk."

"No, nobody stood me up. There's somewhere I need to go."

Explaining as quickly as I can, I grab a floral summer dress from the pile of clothes. I step in it and pull it up under my robe. When my breasts are covered, I drop the towelling robe to the floor and push my arms into the straps.

We jump when Cole storms between us. His foot sends Chelsea's makeup case flying. The cosmetics scatter across the floor.

"Hey!" she hollers as she begins retrieving powders and eyeshadows.

He crouches momentarily to pass her a handful of products. "Shit, sorry, I didn't see it there. Let me help."

Chelsea's eyes go wide when she opens one of the eyeshadows and the broken powder falls to the floor. "No, I think you've done enough."

"I'll replace whatever I've damaged."

Chelsea turns her back on Cole and continues to gather the products.

Cussing under his breath, he bends down in front of the hearth and swipes a handful of flowers from the nearest vase. "For Granddad." He makes a beeline for the door.

I trip over my feet, makeup, and Chelsea in an attempt to match his steps. "Cole, wait."

He stops dead and turns to face me. His eyes are bloodshot and the flowers shake in his hand. "I don't get you, Lizzie. Playing happy families with Seth and his daughter." He pounds his fist against his chest. "What about me?" His voice breaks. "What about our family?"

My mouth falls open, and I grab his arm to stop him from leaving. "Cole, I'm coming with you."

"I wanted you to come because you wanted to, not because you feel guilty or obligated." He glowers at me, shaking his arm free. He's out of the door and in his car before I've had a chance to pull my shoes on. He reverses off the drive and speeds away.

I yank my cardigan off the coat hook. My keys jangle in the pocket. "Chelsea, I've got to go. Let yourself out."

She emerges from the lounge. "Go, I'll be here when you get back."

"Are you sure?" I ask, already halfway out of the door.

She nods. "Yes, go."

The cemetery is a ten-minute drive. I park besides Cole's Land Rover and make my way to Granddad's plot.

Cole crouches as he arranges flowers in front of the head-stone.

I stop at his side and place my hand on his shoulder. "They look beautiful."

He jumps to his feet. Without uttering a word, he opens his arms and wraps me up in his embrace. I close my eyes, letting out a long sigh.

We sit down and I listen as he reminisces. Granddad was an avid fisherman—Cole tells me about the hours they spent at the lake and the time Granddad pushed him in. Cole paints such a perfect picture; I can't help but feel that life cheated me out of time with Granddad.

"He told me I was the son he never had." Cole's voice breaks. He shakes his head as if trying to rein in his anguish, but try as he might, he can't hide his bloodshot eyes and sombre expression. He leans forward and squeezes my hand. "Means a lot you're here."

We get to our feet and stand a while, looking down at Granddad's grave.

Cole wipes his nose with the back of his hand. "I can't believe this is all that's left of such a great guy, you know."

A solitary tear makes a path down my face before falling to the grass. It's in this moment I feel a great loss. What gets to me the most is I don't remember him, I don't remember sitting on his knee as a child, I don't remember the tenor of his voice, I never got to hear his tales from when he served in the war. My granddad will only be a picture, a moment captured in time, and this headstone. "I wish I could have got to know him."

Cole nods his head in the direction of the car park. "Go, you've got to get ready to go out."

I kiss my finger, lean forward and press it to the head-stone. "Goodbye, Granddad."

I walk away and jump back into my car. Wiping my face, I take a deep breath, then start the engine.

Chelsea certainly worked her magic with the limited time I had to get ready. I'm wearing a long, flowing, green maxi dress. My makeup is subtle yet fitting. Chelsea added a little green to my eyeshadow to compliment my outfit. My hair has been secured into a neat bun. I don't admit this very often, but today I feel sexy.

Seth arrives at five o'clock on the dot. His work van parks up outside. I can see him unbuckling his seatbelt to get out and ring the doorbell.

I take a long and calming breath. *You've got this.*

I stand, grab my bag from the coffee table and pull on a pair of black sandals. I open the door as Seth stands on the welcome mat with his finger poised over the doorbell.

He looks me up and down. "Ding-dong."

I playfully hit him with my bag, and we make our way to his van. The passenger side door is already open. Ellie bobs up and down in her seat.

"We're going for a pizza," she singsongs.

I smile at Seth before sliding in next to Ellie. I can't miss how cute she looks. She's wearing a navy-blue summer dress; her hair has been braided and secured with a matching blue ribbon.

Seth, now seated in the driver's side, motions his hand around the interior. "I would have brought my Mercedes, but I thought we'd travel in style."

"You're spoiling me." I laugh and close the door. I don't know the ins and outs of his financial situation. Frankly I don't care. It doesn't bother me one bit that he doesn't own a car.

His deep blue gaze wanders over me. "Hi."

I bite my lower lip. "Hi."

Smiling, he slides the gear stick into reverse. It's only now as we drive away from the house that my gaze starts wandering. His brown hair has been sleeked back and his trim beard is a little neater than usual. My guess is that he's been to the barber's. He's wearing a short-sleeved white shirt, which makes his tattoo appear more striking.

My drooling over Seth is cut short when Ellie waves a colouring book in the air. "It's *The Little Mermaid.*"

Seth reaches across, pushing her arms into her lap. "Don't do that when I'm driving, please."

Ellie's shoulders drop, like Seth extinguished her excitement. I place my hand over hers. "I hope Daddy remembered to bring the crayons. I love colouring, maybe we could colour a picture together."

Ellie sits taller and nods.

It'd probably make more sense to have Ellie's car seat beside the window. I mean, I have no issue squashing in the middle, next to Seth. I know his hand would brush against my knee as he changed gear.

Within twenty minutes we pull into the small car park at the back of the restaurant. It's right on the beachfront. We have an amazing view.

I open the door and slide out. I'm about to close it when Ellie stretches out her arms and waits for me to help her out. I comply and hold her for a second before placing her feet on the floor. She grins up. "Thanks, Lizzie."

I smile. *Well, that was unexpected.*

Seth walks around to meet us, holding out his hand for Ellie to hold, but she doesn't take it.

"I'm going to get you," Ellie calls, jumping on my shadow.

Seth grins. He leads, watching out for cars, as Ellie runs in front of me jumping on my shadow.

When we reach the path, Seth slows and walks at my side. For a split second our eyes meet. It's one of those seconds I never want to end. His eyes say so much more than his words ever could.

"Come on, Daddy, she's getting away."

Seth laughs. At this point, Ellie is jumping on and off my shadow. Seth isn't quite as enthusiastic as Ellie. Instead of jumping, he takes a giant step forward and treads on my shadow's left leg.

I shove him and he falls forward onto my shadow's chest. "Be careful, don't stomp on my heart."

I hadn't meant the ambiguity of my words, but I guess they're apt. He's the only man to make it beat uncontrollably. He's also the only man who has the power to shatter it into a million pieces.

He gets my meaning; he pauses for a second before Ellie pulls him back into the game. I'm desperate not to dwell, so I run ahead.

"You can't catch me," I holler. Ellie and Seth run after me. I didn't think it was possible to have so much fun chasing shadows. In fits of laughter the three of us step, or more like fall, into the restaurant, struggling to catch our breath.

Chapter Fifteen

Seth

The moment we enter the restaurant we're hit by the strong scent of cheese, garlic, and pepperoni. Lizzie and Ellie follow as I lead the way to the front of house. With my girls either side of me we join the small queue and wait to be seated.

I cross my arms over my chest and look around. The restaurant has a modern feel, polished wooden flooring and high white ceilings dotted with spotlights. Tables with checked tablecloths are set a nice distance apart from one another. I motion around the large space. "I did the interior fit-out here a few years back."

Lizzie's eyes go wide. "Wow, you did a great job."

I smile big, feeling proud showing Lizzie my workmanship. My gaze focuses on the bricked cooking station positioned at the back of the room. Staff dressed in white uniforms knead pizza dough and apply toppings. The owner, head chef Francesco, is standing beside the clay oven, balancing a pizza on a wooden paddle. The Italian flashes me a smile before depositing the pizza into the oven.

Lizzie nudges me. "Seth, we're next."

A woman positioned front of house greets us. "Welcome to Pepper-Oni's Pizza Express. Do you have a reservation, or would you like me to find you a table?"

"My sister made a reservation, Darcy Summers."

Her finger moves down the list of names in her reservations book and stops at Mrs Summers. She squints at the writing. "It says here reservation for six."

I shake my head. "There was a last-minute change of plan." The conversation went something like, 'Thanks for booking the table. By the way, you're not invited.' In my defence, my sister bulldozed over Ellie's idea of taking Lizzie and took it upon herself to book the table.

"No problem. Right this way, sir." The hostess swipes three menus from her workstation and leads us through the restaurant. We pass through the main room and enter a large conservatory. She points to a round table next to the window overlooking the sea. Our table couldn't be more perfect—too perfect. It screams romance. Tonight was meant as a peace offering between friends, not a date.

I'm about to ask the lady if there's another table when Lizzie squeezes my arm. "Oh, my God, Seth, this is amazing."

Ellie is already sitting down with her colouring book open, her hand moving back and forth as she colours in the picture.

The woman eyes me speculatively when I don't sit. "Is the table to your liking?"

No, it is not to my fucking liking.

"It's great," I say through gritted teeth, forcing a smile. *Great, great, great!*

I pull a chair out for Lizzie.

"Very chivalrous of you," she says, about to sit down.

"No, Daddy, I want Lizzie to sit by me," Ellie says.

Moving around the circular table, I pull the seat out next to Ellie. I wonder if it'd be rude to sit at the opposite end. I stand surveying each chair. I don't want to be too close to Lizzie, but I can't be so far away that we can't have a conversation.

Lizzie pulls on my arm. "Seth, will you sit down already?"

Without thinking, I sit in the chair that may as well have a big warning light on it—the chair beside Lizzie. As the table is circular, we are in each other's personal space. My elbow touches hers and our knees meet under the table. She may as well be sitting on my lap. I jerk my knee away from hers and pivot my body around slightly.

Confusion skates over her features. "Is everything okay?"

I lean back in my chair. "Fine, why do you ask?"

"I don't know, you just seem a little tense."

I blow out. "I'm fine."

Lizzie turns her back to me. She's so close that I get a whiff of her strawberry-scented hair. She reaches across the table for a menu and reads Ellie the different types of pizzas and the list of toppings. It dawns on me how much Ellie is starting to relax around Lizzie, possibly even like her.

After a debate whether pineapple does in fact belong on pizza, we order a Pepper-Oni Family Feast, which includes two large Hawaiian-style pizzas, one garlic pizza bread, potato wedges, chicken bites, and three glasses of cola.

I tap my fingers on the table, thinking of what to say. "So, how was your day?"

Great, I've resorted to small talk. Next, I'll be asking her about the weather.

Lizzie shrugs. "I've had better."

I lean towards her on my elbows. "Why? What happened?"

Slumping in her chair, she looks heavenward. "It would have been my granddad's birthday today, I'd completely forgotten."

"I'm really sorry."

"It's fine. It's harder for Cole than it is for me."

This I know to be true. With career-driven parents, Cole lived with his grandparents well into his teenage years. "Your grandparents were good people."

She smiles, but it's forced. "When they died and Cole moved home he became a father figure to me. He's been the best big brother I could have ever asked for, and today I let him down."

Shit, that's heavy. What do I say after that?

I pinch the bridge of my nose. Cole doesn't deal with this time of year well. He's usually MIA in some swanky hotel room getting drunk and smoking pot. I make a mental note to call him later and check he's okay.

She fidgets with a napkin. "The house is coming along well."

"Sure is. The subcontractors Cole hired have finished boarding the loft. I think Cole said he's going to get an electrician to sign off the wiring upstairs so Rick can carry on with the plastering. Then the painters and decorators will be called, and finally Rick will lay the carpet. Job done."

Her eyes go wide. "Does that mean I won't see—" There's a crack in her voice as she looks from me to Ellie. She looks at us as though we're a package deal, which we are.

I run my fingers over my beard. "I'll be around. I'll have snagging to do."

Lizzie frowns. "What's that?"

"I'm sorry, snagging—going over anything we've missed or things that may need correcting. I have at least another three days of work."

She sits taller. She likes my company, and I'd be lying if I said the feeling wasn't mutual.

I give Lizzie a sideward glance. "I won't be around on Monday; I've got to go to an auction." In all honesty, I would rather spend my day with Lizzie than be stuck at an auction all day. "Cole has given me the go-ahead to buy a property for the three of us to invest in. We're going to try our hands at the domestic side of building, as opposed to commercial."

Apart from Lizzie's house, we usually work on big building sites—airports, shopping centres, schools. It'll be nice to take on smaller projects with fewer men to babysit.

"Come with me," I blurt out, before my brain has time to process what I've said.

Her large brown eyes flicker and I can see I've caught her off guard. "What, to the auction?"

It's too late to go back on it now. "Yes. You've been to one with Cole before, haven't you? You can be my wingman."

Did I just refer to Lizzie as a man? I immediately glance down at her breasts. They look amazing in her dress. I'm suddenly envious of the fabric hugging her cleavage.

"Wingwoman," I correct, glancing up.

Ellie pulls at Lizzie's arm. "We're going to the aquarium tomorrow; do you want to come?"

"I'm sure Lizzie has plans." As much as I want Lizzie to come, I can't let myself get too used to her. I'm scared that if I do that, I'll never want to let her go.

Lizzie smiles, though it doesn't reach her eyes. "Your dad's right, I have a busy day tomorrow."

We're all silent for a beat, and I picture Lizzie spending the day with us tomorrow. I'm not overly fond of fish. Eating them yes, looking at them no. Looking at Lizzie would be a damn sight better.

I clear my throat. "What about a walk along the seafront after dinner? We can take a look in the rock pools, see if we can find us some crabs."

Ellie squeals.

"Sure," Lizzie concurs.

I look from Lizzie to Ellie. "Looks like it's unanimous."

Before long, the waitress brings our food to the table. I love how Lizzie dives in. Cheesy strings hang from the corners of her mouth. She doesn't know they're there. I point and, laughing, she attempts to remove them—unsuccessfully, leaving me no option other than to lean forward and pick them off.

For a moment I don't care that our legs are entwined under the table, that her breast brushes against my bicep. I don't care about all the reasons why I shouldn't be enjoying this woman's company. I just live in the moment.

More than anything I love that she is the complete opposite to Anna. Anna and the fake world she liked to live in, the boring conversations we'd have about her—everything was about her. She couldn't even come here and eat a fucking pizza, it had to be a salad. That's a fantastic analogy for me and Anna. We were as compatible as salad in a pizza place. We just didn't go together. *Why didn't I see it sooner?*

By the end of our meal, Ellie tells me she needs to go to the little girls' room.

"It'll have to be little boys' room, I'm afraid."

She takes my hand and leads me to the toilets. I cover her eyes when we walk into the gents in case anyone is using the urinal. Empty, thank God. This is another thing that bothers me, bringing my little girl into the men's toilets. I've already had that awkward conversation with my daughter as to why she can't stand up to wee.

I uncover her eyes. "All clear."

She runs into the open cubicle and shuts the door.

I lean against the cubicle she's occupying. "Having a nice night?"

"Yes."

"What do you think of Lizzie?"

"She's nice."

What would you think about seeing Lizzie more often? How would you like it if Daddy cooked for Lizzie one night? Fuck's sake, what's wrong with me? This woman is dominating my bloody thoughts.

I jump back as the toilet door swings open and Ellie runs to the sink. I walk up behind her and press the soap dispenser; she lathers her hands up under the water.

After Ellie's hands are dry, we make our way back into the bar. I take a second to admire Lizzie sitting alone at our table. Shit, she's so beautiful. Tonight has been perfect. *She's* perfect—irresistibly so. It didn't feel as though I was having lunch with a friend. She feels like so much more, and I feel utterly powerless to hit the brakes.

I've tried hard to deny my feelings for her, but I'd be lying if I said I didn't feel something. I know she feels the same. Every time our gazes meet, her eyes sparkle. They say women are impossible to read, but not Lizzie. Her complete transparency beguiles me. I can't help wondering what she sees in a deadbeat like me. I have absolutely nothing to offer her. She has so much life to experience and all I'll do is drag her down.

Lizzie looks towards us and waves.

I point to the bar. "I'm going to pay."

I know she can't hear me, but she must be able to lipread. She grabs her handbag and rummages through. I sort the bill before she has time to get to her feet. Smiling, she shakes her head when the waitress rips off the receipt.

"I owe you," Lizzie says, waving a twenty-pound note in the air.

"Put your money away. It's on me."

"Thanks." Her eyes go wide when she glances at Ellie. She quickly bends down. "Oh, sweetie, we can't have you go out like that." She untucks the back of Ellie's dress from her underwear and pulls a long tail of toilet paper off her sandal.

Ellie glowers at me, giving me a thumbs down. "Daddy, that was so not cool."

I snort-laugh, ruffling her hair. "You've been watching way too much YouTube Kids."

Lizzie stands and playfully shoves me. "How would you like your panties and bum out?"

I raise a brow. "Panties? I'm not a chick."

"Daddy." Ellie's yanking on my t-shirt.

Ignoring her for a moment, I step closer to Lizzie, so that my mouth is inches away from her ear. I talk quietly enough so only she can hear. "People would have a great view of my bare ass. The word 'commando' would be a little more apt."

I'm joking. Lizzie's face turns crimson. So cute. I can't leave it there.

"What's wrong? I got a nice little glimpse of your ass on the beach when the wind blew your dress up, don't you think it's time you saw mine?" There I go, flirting. I can't help myself.

Lizzie turns. Our faces are inches apart. God, I want to kiss her.

In another life, Seth, in another life.

Ellie pulls on my t-shirt with more demand. "Daddy!"

I bend down. "Yes?"

She smiles impishly. "Lizzie said 'bum'."

I hit my hand on my head. "Oh, God, encouragement is the last thing this child needs."

I don't know what it is about certain words. 'Bum', 'fart', 'crap', words Ellie feels compelled to repeat.

"Bum bum bumtee-de-bum bum," Ellie singsongs.

I wag my finger at Lizzie. "You're in trouble."

Lizzie shrugs. "She's merely expressing her freedom of speech."

Why does this feel so natural, me, Lizzie and Ellie? I often wondered how a woman would fit into our hectic life. With Lizzie it's not as though she's trying to fit in, it's as though she belongs. Our friendship is walking across a tightrope and could easily fall into the unknown. I don't like not knowing, I don't like not being in control. I lost control when Anna left and I never want to be in that position again, and yet…

Lizzie and Ellie are walking towards the door to leave. I jog over, standing flush with Lizzie. Damn, I'm itching to drape my arm around her shoulders, but I don't. I've got to get my shit together before I decide how and when to tackle this head on.

Lizzie is talking away about who knows what as we walk along the pavement. I'm not paying attention; all I can think about is how hard I was at the party when we kissed. That kiss was something else. I was so tempted to throw her over my shoulder, take her in the house and fuck her.

"Would Ellie like that?" Lizzie asks.

I glance down. "I'm sorry, what?"

We separate briefly, allowing people walking in the opposite direction to pass.

Lizzie rolls her eyes. "I was just saying about a photoshoot."

I wave my hand in the air. "Stop, go back to the beginning."

Lizzie flashes Ellie a glance and circles her finger around her ear, insinuating I'm crazy.

Crazy about you, sweetheart.

"As I was saying. Chelsea is a qualified hairdresser and beautician. She and Amber own a photography shop. Amber is the photographer, Chelsea offers the clients a hair and makeup package, they're—"

"I know that, what about it?"

Lizzie's brows knit together. "They gave me a voucher for my birthday, they do special packages for children and I wondered if Ellie…"

144

I step aside to let a couple pass between us. My eyes go wide when I acknowledge the woman.

Hold the fucking phone!

I stand, dead still, as if I've been turned into a statue. Blonde hair, big tits, a short black dress and a baby bump—there's no mistaking it's her, a shadow from my past. I feel sick.

Lizzie turns, her hand on her hip. "Seth, are you okay?"

"Take Ellie." I point to a bench a few feet away. "Sit there, I'll be right back."

Ellie reaches for Lizzie's hand and without question walks to the bench with her. I should be jumping for joy. Ellie has gone with Lizzie, on her own. But I'm not, instead I've turned around and am weaving through the sea of people until I catch up with the blonde.

I wrap my fingers around her shoulder. "Anna."

The bitch. I look at the douche standing next to her, and know who he is before he turns.

My heart's racing, my palms are clammy. This woman has turned my world, my life upside down. Months of not seeing her and poof, here she is.

She and the guy turn.

I grit my teeth. "Barry."

Barry was the plumber I hired to fix our boiler three years ago. Now the dots are joining together.

"Seth." He nods, placing a possessive arm around her shoulders.

There's so much I want to say to her, so many questions I want to ask. But I say the first thing that comes to mind. "Aren't you going to fucking ask how your daughter is? You know, the one you gave birth to five years ago." I narrow my eyes at her baby bump. "Or was she so easy to forget about and replace?"

She says absolutely nothing, just stands staring at me.

"Don't be shy now. You certainly weren't the first night we met. Talk, damn you!"

I hadn't realised that I was drawing closer until Barry shoves me back. "Mate, she's pregnant."

I laugh sardonically. "Are you going to abandon this one too?"

Anna's face is stoic. She offers me no explanation, nothing. We stand for a few minutes just looking at each other. Our stare is finally broken when she fishes out a card from her bag and hands it to me. It's her business card, the holistic massage bullshit she did.

"Here's my new number. When you've calmed down, we need to talk."

Is she real? We needed to talk fifteen damn months ago.

"I would like to see Ellie," she continues.

"And cause more damage? Over my dead body."

Barry steps towards me. Anna takes his hand and guides him back to her side.

"Seth, this anger isn't good for any of us, and it's not good for the baby." She rubs her stomach, her very pregnant stomach. "I'd like the chance to speak to Ellie."

"About what? Oh, I know, how about, 'Hi, Ellie, I still exist. I've never stopped loving you'? That would be a great start."

She shakes her head. "This is too much negativity right now. I'm sorry. We can do this the easy way, or you'll hear from my lawyer."

I'm speechless, and just like that, they turn and continue on their way.

Damn it, why did I have to approach them? Why couldn't I have walked past? She wants to speak to Ellie, cause her more upset and confusion. My chest tightens.

Well done, Seth, you've opened Pandora's box.

Chapter Sixteen

Lizzie

It's not like me to run out of bread, but I guess there's a first time for everything. I grab two loaves from the shelf in the newsagent's and join the queue.

My phone vibrates. I reach down and pull it out of my pocket. Seth's calling. I swipe my fingers across the screen. Holding my mobile to my ear, I hand the cashier a five-pound note.

"What are you doing?" Seth asks.

I nibble on my bottom lip. "Shopping?"

"Where?"

"The newsagent's in Acorn Close, why?"

He clears his throat. "Ellie and I wondered if you wanted to come to the aquarium with us?"

"I'd love to. When?" That sounded way too desperate, but I can't take it back, so await his reply.

"Now," he says.

Instinctively I turn and look around the shop as if he's going to magically appear. "Like right now? Where are you?"

He doesn't answer. I can hear Ellie chatting in the background and the ticking sound of a car indicator.

"Hang on," he says.

A day with Seth and Ellie. I look down. I'm wearing a pair of jeans ripped at the knee and a baggy grey t-shirt. I'll have to change clothes first. I'm vacantly staring at a carrier bag the cashier holds out. I make no attempt to take it from her.

"Hello?" The cashier clicks her tongue and drops my change onto the counter.

I force a smile. "Thank you."

I can hear Seth's heavy breathing from the other end of the phone. "Sorry about that, I was parking up."

Parking up? Where is he?

The bell above the door chimes as I leave the shop. Seth's van is parked on the opposite side of the road. I hang up the phone. He wasn't joking when he said now.

I jog across the road and pop my head through the open passenger side window. Ellie bobs up and down in her seat with the most contagious smile I think I've ever seen. Her hair has been tied up into pigtails and she's wearing a bright yellow summer dress. She looks adorable.

I look at the shop and back to the van. "How did you get here so quickly? Were you following me?"

Seth laughs. "You said you were in the newsagent's in Acorn Close, and I happened to be in the neighbourhood." He taps his hand on the steering wheel. "Are you just going to stand there, or are you going to get in?"

I open the door and slide in beside Ellie. Seth looks at the carrier bag in my lap. "Do you need me to take you home to drop your shopping off?"

I lower the bag to the footwell below. "It's only bread, it'll keep. But I would like to go home and change my clothes."

"You look fine. I'm not taking you home to change."

Clearly he isn't big on paying compliments. I fold my arms across my chest. "I look fine? Now you've got to take me home to change."

"No can do, I'm afraid, Ellie simply won't allow it."

I look to the little girl, who's tapping the invisible watch on her wrist.

Cute.

Seth gives me the cheesiest smile ever. I know it's laced with sarcasm, but still, he manages to take my breath away.

He revs the engine. "You look fine, I look fine. Time's a-moving."

He certainly does look fine. He's wearing a pair of black shorts and a salmon t-shirt. It's a colour I am not fond of on men, but he owns it.

"We're going to see the fishes," Ellie squeals.

Seth pulls the van into first gear. "Come on, ladies, let's have some fun."

We drive along the coastal road for about half an hour. We park in a large roped-off section of the beach. Ellie reaches between us and unbuckles her seat belt. "We're here," she singsongs, pointing to the aquarium, a large domed building. We get out of the van and have to jog to keep up with Ellie. In her excitement she pulls us by our hands up a wooden ramp which leads to the entrance. Once inside we join the queue at the cash desk. Ellie's gaze darts everywhere. Her blue eyes sparkle under the long fluorescent lighting.

Seth inches closer. He gently strokes my arm. "Look at her, Lizzie, just look. I haven't seen her laugh or smile like this since…"

His words trail off. I figure he doesn't want to mention Ellie's mum in front of her.

"Working as many hours as I do, I feel like I'm missing out on so much." He's still stroking my skin. I know we're only friends, and that's how he wants it to remain, but I want more. Knowing the invisible boundary he's put between us, I should pull away, but I don't want to. The slightest touch from him makes me feel alive like never before.

Seth pays for our tickets and we're given the go-ahead to enter. Ellie doesn't wait—she bounds off towards one of the gift shops. They must sell every type of fish memorabilia known to man.

Smiling, Ellie throws her arms around a dolphin statue. Seth whips out his phone and snaps pictures. I think he took one of me, but I can't be sure. I'd like to think he did.

We exit the gift shop and head out towards the displays. Every exhibition tells a story. We see rock pools, grand Victorian tanks. Ellie loves pulling herself up on the large steps, bringing her eye level with larger tanks.

We burst into laughter as Ellie begins opening and closing her mouth, flapping her arms. I've gone from being an outsider to being part of a special unit.

I can't believe she's the same little girl from a few days ago. She's not scowling at me, she's looking for me, smiling.

I lag behind for a second, watching father and daughter. Ellie grabs Seth's hand. I'm dying for him to reach his free hand out for me, but he doesn't. Is it wrong that I want him to? I'd love to be the woman he seeks out in a crowded room. To be the woman he kisses at the beginning and end of every day. I wonder if the two of them could be a three. Would they let an outsider in? Would they let me in? I've never thought about children or a family—they were never part of my plan, only my career. The more time I spend with Ellie, the more I could picture her in my life. The question is, would she be willing to share her dad?

"Daddy, Lizzie, look! I've found Nemo." Her eyes are wide, her body is shaking with excitement. Seth crouches, sitting Ellie on his knee, and they watch a clown fish weave its way between a school of colourful fish.

I lean against a nearby wall. My hands fall to my side. It dawns on me how much I'll miss them both when the works have finished at my house. Will that be it? Will they disappear from my life as quickly as they appeared?

Ellie wraps her arms round Seth's neck. He sways a little as it seems she's knocked him off his balance. She turns, beaming at me. "Daddy said Nemo is a clown fish, that's funny."

I smile. "Sure is, sweetie."

"Daddy, I'm hungry."

He glances down at his watch and nods at me. I guess it's time for lunch. We make our way through the aquarium to the Blue Waves Café. Seth pushes the door open and we enter. The walls have been decorated with sketched images of pirate flags, compasses, and treasure chests. The tables have been designed to look like boats.

Ellie's already found us a table and is looking at an illustrated menu. Seth and I slide along the bench-style chair to join her.

Seth nods towards a soft play area in the corner of the

room. "Want to go play?"

Ellie frowns at the children jumping in the ball pit. Shaking her head, she shuffles closer to me. I'd completely forgotten about her separation anxiety; she's made such progress over the last few days.

Seth smiles my way. It's not a genuine smile. The way he looks from Ellie to the soft play area makes me think he's frustrated.

One step forward with Ellie, two back. We can't push her before she's ready.

I squeeze Ellie's hand. "We can have just as much fun at our table."

"Thank you," Seth mouths.

I feel lucky to be sat beside such a fine specimen of a man. He's gorgeous, his body perfectly toned. I can make out every rippling muscle beneath his salmon t-shirt. I'm not the only one who thinks so. I notice mums eyeing him up, so I sit a little closer, placing my hand over his. I don't care if we're a couple or not, that's merely semantics. While we're sitting together, he's mine.

He reaches under the table and rests his hand on my knee. I don't move, I don't breathe. My heart is beating so fast.

Ellie points to the desserts. "I want a muffin."

Tugging the menu from her, Seth gazes at me. "Are you hungry?"

I look down to his hand that still rests on my knee. My stomach is in knots, my face feels like it's on fire.

"A little." I feign interest, pulling the menu from his grasp, using it to hide my face. It's getting impossible to hide how I feel about him.

Seth chooses the chicken wrap; I tell him I'll have the

same. Ellie decides she'll have a chocolate muffin for her lunch. After a debate that lasts no more than a few minutes she finally settles on a ham sandwich as long as she can have her muffin for dessert.

Seth wipes his face, which glistens under the fluorescent lighting. "What's say we eat outside?"

Ellie pouts. "But I like my boat."

Seth begins fanning his face with a menu. "It's twenty-six degrees outside, and about fifty degrees in here." He motions his hands to the surrounding tables. "There's a reason people are going outdoors."

I'm glad my surge in body heat is due to the temperature, not purely down to me swooning over Seth.

Seth removes a napkin from the centre of the table and dabs his forehead. "Daddy's melting."

I snort-laugh as it appears the little girl has absolutely no sympathy.

He glances over at the open doors leading to the alfresco eating area. He squeezes my knee, then shuffles across the bench, ready to stand. "There's a sandpit outside. You could imagine you're at the beach."

Ellie's face lights up. "A sandpit!"

Seth leads the way and we follow him out. He wasn't kidding about the sandpit, it's massive. Kids are playing and laughing, buckets and spades lying around. We find a table on a large decked area and the waitress brings our food. Ellie tucks in. Her eyes are fixed on the sandpit. I know she'll need us to go sit with her so she'll play. Seth could do with the break; I'll go with her.

She's finished her sandwich and muffin by the time I take the first bite into my wrap.

Ellie points. "Lizzie, look, Freja's sitting in the sand."

Swallowing, I glance around. If Freja is here, then so is Amber. "Are you sure? Where?"

She doesn't answer, she jumps off the bench and skips to join Freja in the sandpit. I rub my eyes, at a loss for words.

"Oh, my God, Lizzie." Seth throws his arms around me, pulling me into him. "Tell me you're seeing what I am."

I glance down at his arms, which are wrapped around me, then back to Ellie. "I see."

"That's the first time Ellie has ever done that, ever. You don't realise what an achievement this is for her." Seth waves his arm in the air. Rick waves back in acknowledgment. He and Amber are sat together on a bench not far from where the girls are playing. "I wonder what's going on with those two. Like, are they sleeping together?"

I shake my head. "Honestly, I've got no idea."

Freja's hopping in circles round Ellie. Ellie is screeching and jumping. I'm watching her play like any other kid here. Sure, she still looks for Seth and occasionally she looks for me—that fear is still there and that won't disappear overnight—but I'd be lying if I said I didn't want to jump up and fist-pump.

Seth releases his hold on me, sits back and takes a bite of his wrap. "I blame myself, you know. That if I'd have been a better husband, a better dad, that—"

I swat his arm. "Stop it, Seth. Do you hear me? You're an amazing dad. You're an amazing guy."

Fudge, I didn't mean to say that. Our gazes lock. I have the strangest feeling, like it's just the two of us sitting in a bubble, a red-hot bubble that could burst at any moment. This isn't lust, this isn't a crush, I love the guy. I

155

love him, damn it, and there's not a single thing I can do about it.

Chapter Seventeen

Seth

She said, and I quote, *You're amazing*.

"You're damn right I am," I finally say after a long pause.

Her cheeks redden and she's quick to look away. I'm dying to tell her how wonderful she is, and that I'm falling for her, despite all the reasons I shouldn't. I feel as though I could tell her everything, every broken facet of my life. I want her to know everything there is to know about me, and I want to know all there is to know about her. Her strengths, her weaknesses, her annoying habits, all the idiosyncrasies that make her who she is.

Time to lay my cards on the table and start opening up to someone. I rub my hand over my beard, the coarse hairs rubbing against my palm. "Anna wants to see Ellie."

Lizzie's gaze shoots to mine. "Oh."

Oh? Her one-syllable answer prompts me to continue. "The night we went out for pizza, when I told you to wait on the bench with Ellie…"

She rubs her shoulder; her eyes go wide. "That was Anna? Oh, my God, Seth, she's beautiful."

Sure, physically Anna is pretty, but she's rotten to the core. "What kind of person, what kind of mum leaves her child without so much as a goodbye?" My tone is harsher than I had intended. "Shit, sorry, Lizzie."

"I don't know, Seth. Maybe she had her reasons."

Typical Lizzie, trying to see the good in people. I don't see good in anyone. I'm a cynic about everyone until proven otherwise. "Her reason, Lizzie, was that she wanted to jump on another man's cock and get knocked up by someone who wasn't her husband." I point to my left hand. To this day the outline of that damn ring is still slightly visible on my finger. "Technically we were still married when she got pregnant."

Lizzie shakes her head. "I'm sorry."

"Meh, I'm over it. I'm over her. But she wants to see Ellie."

My eyes move to my baby playing in the sand. Amber has joined them, and the three of them sit making sandcastles.

"Over my dead body. She's caused enough damage."

Lizzie's quiet. She avoids my gaze.

"Well?" I need to know what she's thinking. She's either with me on this one or she's against me, and I need to know where her loyalties lie.

Lizzie sucks her lips in and shakes her head. "It's not my place to say."

"No, go on," I prompt.

She takes a deep breath in before blowing out. "Anna's her mum, Seth, she has rights."

My jaw ticks. "She lost those rights when she—"

"You asked my opinion; I'm giving it to you."

I raise my brows. *I'm listening.*

"If Anna takes you down the legal route, they'll grant her access. Do you really want to put Ellie through that?"

"But—"

"Ellie's going to be a big sister, are you going to deny her the chance to get to know her brother or sister?"

Everything Lizzie said is right, but that doesn't make it any easier. My body is tense, my jaw is set.

Lizzie lays her hand over mine. "I know it's hard, and if you're asking me if Anna deserves to see Ellie, I'd say hell no. But like it or not, she's Ellie's mother."

We sit in silence. Lizzie shreds a napkin; the tiny pieces fall to the ground like confetti. Confetti thrown over a bride at her goddamn wedding. All I can see is Anna's face on the one day I regret more than any other.

Lizzie must be able to sense my mood. Without a word she jumps up and joins Amber and the girls in the sand. Ellie's whole face lights up when Lizzie sits at her side. Then Ellie does something completely unexpected— she shuffles closer to Lizzie, the same way she'd move closer to me. Is it possible that my daughter already has a bond with her?

"Yo, man, move your ass up." Rick swats my arm with a rolled-up newspaper. As requested, I move along the bench.

"You and Amber, eh?"

He unrolls the newspaper and glances down at the print. "Mind your damn business."

Rick is a closed book. I should have known better than to pry into his love life. Still, I'd like to at least get some information from him.

159

I tsk. "Monica the other day, Amber again today."

Rick closes the newspaper. "That's just nasty. Monica is my foster sister." His eyes narrow. "Are you done quizzing me?"

I yawn, feigning boredom. "For now."

"Are you still going to the auction tomorrow?" he asks, gliding to the sports section of the paper.

"I am. Lizzie is coming with me."

Rick whistles to himself. "Uh-huh."

I don't bother denying there's more going on between us. There isn't yet, but it's only a matter of time.

Rick flips to the pages at the back, displaying the properties for sale. "Cole had his eye on the house in Hedging Lodge Road. He went to see it a few weeks ago."

I know that street. It's a gated community in Devon. The houses there are nice. "Wait, have you spoken to Cole?"

Rick shakes his head. "Not since last week."

"What's our budget?"

Rick shrugs. "No budget. Cole's footing the entire bill."

"Excuse me?"

Rick leans closer to me. "Cole's loaded, like ridiculously rich."

"I don't believe you. We've been best friends since we were kids."

Rick mock-laughs. "He bought his sister a three-hundred-thousand-pound house, that was pocket change to him. I don't know how much is in his bank account, but I know there's a shit ton of zeroes on the end."

I'm quiet during the journey home. I keep replaying this afternoon over and over in my head. Ellie has formed connections to Lizzie and Freja in the space of one week. I know it's early days, but I feel more confident about her going to school in September. More so now as Amber said Freja will be attending the same school and they will start together. I always worried that I'd held Ellie back by not sending her when she was four, but I knew she wasn't ready. I'm happy she'll have a friend when she starts.

Stopped at a traffic light, I pass Lizzie a sideward glance. She and Ellie are playing rock, paper, scissors. Ellie doesn't seem to understand the rules of the game as she selects rock every time and bashes poor Lizzie's hand.

I'm not a romantic nor am I a fantasist, but Lizzie really does make me feel whole, and my heart feels empty in her absence. She started off as a bit of eye candy and has developed into an obsession.

"Any news from Cole?" Lizzie asks.

I shrug. "Nope, he's officially MIA." He does the same thing every year. He ends up staying in a hotel getting shitfaced.

"Seth, I'm worried about him. I saw Gail at the supermarket last night and she said they'd broken up. I hope he's not doing anything stupid."

Add getting laid to the list.

"He's a big boy, stop worrying." I try to sound confident for her sake, but the truth is, I'm worried about him. I have no idea where he is, and his phone goes straight to voicemail. Cole disappearing from radar isn't unusual, but the guy would answer a work call at the same time as taking a shit, that's how dedicated he is.

I park outside Lizzie's house. I turn the engine off, leave Ellie in the van and run around to the passenger's side to let Lizzie out.

She takes my hand and I help her out. "Thanks for a lovely day."

I squeeze her fingers. "The pleasure was mine."

The wind blows short strands of hair into her eyes and she brushes it away. God, what I'd give to pull her into me, place my hands on her ass and hold her.

She glances at her house and back to me. "So, what time do we need to leave for the auction tomorrow?"

"The auction starts at ten-thirty am. We'll need to make sure we're there for ten am. I'll need to register to receive my bidding paddle."

She pulls on my t-shirt, pulling me closer to her. With the sun in her eyes, she squints up at me. "I thought you were a newbie to auctions."

Instinctively, I grab her t-shirt and I too pull her closer. "That's what Google is for, baby."

Our bodies are flush. We're playing with fire, using our growing friendship to innocently tease one another, though it's not innocent when feelings are involved. I should stop touching her. I can't. I wrap my arms around her so that my hands are resting on the small of her back. I place my chin on her head. I can't look into her eyes. If I do, I'll kiss her. God, I want to kiss her.

I lean back, brushing hair out of her eyes. I'm past the point of giving a shit. I know she's Cole's little sister and therefore should be off limits, but the heart wants what it wants. I will speak to Cole, not to seek his approval, but to tell him of my intentions. I respect him and owe him that much at least.

I will be professional whilst she's a client, but when the works are completed on her house, I am going to take her out. I'm going to kiss her and probably do a hell of a lot more. The question is, can I keep her?

"See you tomorrow," I whisper. I release her and make my way back to the driver's side of the van. I start up the engine, then slide her into reverse. Ellie looks at me with a stupid expression on her face.

"What are you grinning at?" I ask.

"Nothing." She covers her face with her hands. It dawns on me that she must have got a pretty good view from the side mirrors. *Shit.* She's embarrassed seeing her dad hugging someone. I will always be honest with Ellie, but I will carefully select the information I feed her.

"You like Lizzie, don't you?"

She nods. "Is that why you were hugging her?"

I bite back my smile. "She's a friend, and people hug friends. Daddy would like to keep seeing Lizzie as a friend. Are you okay with that?"

I flash her a glance, and she's smiling. "Lizzie is my friend too, does that mean I get to see her as well?"

I can't let Ellie get too attached to Lizzie, though I fear she already has. "From time to time. But Daddy may see her on her own, when you're in bed. Aunty Darcy will babysit. Would that be okay?"

Ellie crosses her arms over her chest. "That's not fair."

As much as I want to pull Lizzie into our way of life, into our little family, I can't. There are conditions to dating this single dad. Though there's no reason that I can't be a great dad and have the woman I want. I just have to figure out how the two fit together.

Ellie doesn't speak for the remainder of the journey.

We pull up at home. Darcy's car is on the drive. Ellie sighs. "What's she doing here?"

Leaning over her, I unfasten her seat belt. "Ellie, that's unkind. Aunt Darcy does a lot for us."

"But Sunday is our day."

Sunday is Daddy and daughter day in our house, which was why she caught me off guard earlier when she begged me to invite Lizzie to the aquarium with us. What my baby wants my baby gets. I can't deny it's what I wanted as well.

I lock the van and we walk up the driveway. We live in a three-bedroom end-terrace house. Red brick walls wear ivy like an armoured suit. It's my home, my reprieve from the outside world. The interior is small, yet plenty big enough for what Ellie and I need. The house smells divine as we enter—freshly baked bread, cakes, and chicken. We find Darcy in the kitchen.

"Great news," she says, laying a pair of blue oven gloves on the side. "I've managed to swap my shifts around so that I'm starting work at seven pm. I can have Ellie every day until you finish work, then when you're back I'll leave. I thought it'd help you if you didn't have to cook when you got home." She motions over the worktop: spaghetti bolognese, fish pie, pizza, curry, all laid out in plastic containers, ready for freezing.

"So, where have you been today?" Darcy asks, removing a loaf of bread from the oven.

"We went to the aquarium with Lizzie. I played in the sandpit all on my own with Freja."

Darcy spins around, the bread nearly falling off the tray. "You need to be careful, Ellie, you shouldn't be by yourself, your dad or me need to be with you—"

Darcy carries on about stranger danger. Ellie's face becomes more drawn and her shoulders drop.

I'm about to say something when Darcy claps her hands together. "Guess what?"

"What?" Ellie asks, her gaze on me.

"I've handed my notice in at the hospital."

I blink rapidly. "What? Why?"

She lays the bread on the worktop and closes the oven door. "I weighed up what was important to me and where I was needed the most. Seth, we can't let Ellie go to mainstream school with her condition, it'll be far too upsetting. I'm going to homeschool her."

Ellie shakes her head. "But I want to go to school with Freja."

Darcy shoots me a glance as though I should be agreeing with her. "Freja, isn't she the child who was at Lizzie's birthday afternoon?"

I nod.

Darcy crouches so that she's eye level with Ellie. "Oh, no, honey, we don't want you mixing with children like that." She shakes her head, muttering under her breath. "Her mother was an utter disgrace—"

Darcy is just being a bitch; she knows as well as I do there is nothing wrong with Amber. I've heard enough, so raise my hand. "Ellie, go watch cartoons."

Ellie does as I requested. When she's out of the room I direct my attention to my sister. "Darcy—"

"You're spending way too much time with that girl, Libby."

I know her getting her name incorrect was intentional. Darcy remembered her name just fine a few seconds ago. I let out a harsh breath. "Lizzie."

"You're confusing Ellie. Having strange women in and out of her life isn't good for her."

One woman, the first damn woman I've felt anything for in a long time, and Darcy is trying to deny me that. I don't mention that Anna has moved on and is pregnant with another man's baby. Anna can do what she wants, screw who she wants. My teeth are clenched so tightly together than my jaw begins to hurt.

"Darcy," I seethe, "I'd like you to leave."

"Don't be daft, I love cooking, it's really no bother."

I walk across to the kitchen worktop, grab her bag and push it into her arms. "Not the kitchen. I'd like you to leave my house."

Her eyes go wide and she blinks several times. "Excuse me?"

"Take your bag, take your food, and leave."

Her mouth sets into a hard line. "I've been here for four hours preparing meals so that you didn't have to cook when you finished work. I'm trying to help."

"Help?" I laugh. "How are you trying to help? Ellie had a fantastic day, she left my side to go play with another kid. Something *you* said she was incapable of doing. Then you tell her she shouldn't leave my side. What the hell's wrong with you? Don't you want her to get better?"

Darcy holds her hands up. "I'm sorry. It goes without saying that I want her to get better. I just don't want anything to happen to her. She's safe with us."

"She needs to get used to other people, other kids. You need to un-hand your notice in at the hospital. Ellie's going to school in September."

Darcy's eyes tear up and she throws her arms around me. Her short hair is soft against my chin.

"You've got to back off, Darcy, you know."

I can feel her body quiver. "I'm sorry, Seth. I just love you both so much."

Her words tug at my heartstrings. I know she loves us, and I know she means well. Darcy and Dwight weren't able to have children of their own so I guess Ellie is the next best thing, but I am the parent. "I need you to babysit Ellie tomorrow when I go to the auction, but as for the other days, I promised Ellie we'd spend them with Lizzie as a family."

Darcy pulls away. "Excuse me?"

"I didn't mean to say that."

Her eyes narrow. "But you're thinking it?"

I try to look convincing. "Slip of the tongue."

Darcy's lips pull into a thin line. She doesn't believe me—hell, I don't believe me. For the first time, my sister doesn't call me out on my bullshit. She can't bear to hear the truth.

Is it wrong to admit, if only to myself, that being with Lizzie completes us, and together we feel like a family?

Chapter Eighteen

Lizzie

I line up three wine glasses on the kitchen worktop, one each for me, Chelsea and Amber. I have four bottles cooling in the fridge with our names written all over them. Now there's just one question left to ask.

"Red or white?" I call.

"Red," Amber yells.

"White," Chelsea contradicts.

Of course they would say the opposite. They leave me no option but to place the deciding vote. After opening a bottle of white, I place it and the glasses on a tray and carry them through to the lounge.

I slowly jiggle the tray up and down. "Wine o'clock, ladies."

A few glasses of wine is all it takes for our conversation to steer to Seth. Chelsea leans forward, her elbows resting on her knees. "How was your day?"

I bite my lower lip, remembering the way Seth held me, how his body felt next to mine. I suppress a smile. "It was okay."

Chelsea looks me up and down. "Just okay?"

Amber flutters her eyes. "They looked pretty cosy at the aquarium this afternoon. Quite the little family."

Is it wrong to admit that was exactly how it felt?

Chelsea wags her eyebrows at me. "Aren't you and lover boy going to an auction tomorrow?"

Amber and her big mouth. I shoot Amber a look, but her gaze is fixed on the ceiling. Of course it is, Rick's upstairs. He's putting extra hours in to give the plastering a push. He said he wants to finish the loft room ready for the painters on Tuesday. I personally don't think Rick has come to work on a Sunday evening to get a head start on anything other than Amber. Good thing Freja has a sleepover at her gran's on a Sunday. I'd say Amber will be having her own sleepover.

"He sounds busy up there," Amber muses.

"He is," I agree as floorboards creak from above. "He's like a machine, just keeps going."

Blushing, Amber sucks in her lips, her eyes not leaving the ceiling. Could she be any more obvious?

I clear my throat. "I have beer in the fridge."

She glances at me. "I'm sorry, what?"

"I was saying Rick might like a beer. Why don't you take him one up?"

She jumps to her feet and makes her way to the kitchen. Moments later we can hear her steps on the stairs.

I swipe the bottle of wine from the coffee table and refill our glasses. "More for us."

Chelsea gives me a knowing glance. "Told you you'd kiss your prince and live happily ever after."

I'd roll my eyes, but excitement bubbles in my stomach. "I think he could be the one."

Chelsea bounces up and down on the settee. "Oh, my God, no way. Does he know how you feel?"

I shrug. "I guess, but he's already said we can't be more than friends."

Chelsea rubs the back of her neck, her long hair cascading over her shoulders. "Sucks to be you."

I sink down into the chair. "You have no idea."

"Hey, Lizzie, could you come up here?" Rick's voice echoes down the stairs. We place our glasses on the coffee table and hurry upstairs to see what he wants.

He's standing on the landing, a plastering trowel in one hand, Amber's ass in the other.

I wag my finger. "Isn't there a saying about mixing business with pleasure?"

Amber squeals as he squeezes her ass.

"Have you decided on the colour you want the loft room to be painted?"

I shake my head. "No, but I have a few testers."

"As I thought. You women are always so indecisive." Rick's gaze shoots to Amber, and she mocks offence. There's a hidden message there somewhere, I'm sure, but Amber refuses to talk to anyone about their relationship.

Growing up, Amber and I told each other everything. She changed when she started dating this guy, Victor. I only met him once. He was a creep. I told her to stop seeing him, but Amber, being Amber, was too headstrong to listen. I went to uni and when I returned they'd split up. She's yet to fill in the gaps, but I know he hurt her.

Rick releases Amber's ass and focuses on me. "Tomorrow morning could you paint a thin layer of each tester colour on the wall? When the paint has dried you can pick the colour you like the best."

"Sure." I pull my phone from my pocket to check the time. It's seven o'clock. "Why don't you finish off what you're doing and join us downstairs for a drink?"

Rick drops the trowel. "I thought you'd never ask."

Seth and I leave Cornwall at seven am. Seth thinks there'll be traffic on the way to Bristol. He thinks wrong and instead of being stuck in queues we sail through. For the first time in my life, I wish for roadworks, diversions and standstill traffic.

Without Ellie's booster seat between us, I sit next to Seth. Every time he changes gear his fingers brush over my knee or thigh. The journey is hot and I'm sure the contact between us is intentional.

Turning off his satnav, he squeezes my thigh.

There he goes again, touching me.

"Would you like to go for breakfast?" Seth asks.

I glance at the time on my phone. Eight fifty-five am. We have over an hour until we need to be in the auction room and in our seats. The sale starts at ten-thirty. I kind of know what to expect as Cole and I went to an auction six months ago and purchased what's now my house. I loved the buzz, the surge of adrenaline when bidding, but I'm more excited knowing Seth will be at my side the whole time.

He clears his throat. "Well?"

"I'm sorry. Breakfast, yes, that would be lovely."

We pull in at the café opposite where the auction is

being held. He parks in a small car park to the right of the building and we make our way inside.

Pulling out his wallet, Seth points to the specials board above the counter. "What would you like?"

I'm not fussy where food is concerned, though with my nerves bubbling in my stomach, I don't know if I could eat a thing. "Whatever you're having."

God, he looks gorgeous. His hair and beard look more wild today, but I like that. He's wearing black trousers and a crisp white shirt. Sexy and professional.

He winks, nudging my ass in the direction of a booth. "Go, sit down, I'll get this."

My feet take me to the booth in the corner of the room. I sit and watch him place our order. I can't believe the change in him. He looks directly into my eyes when we speak, he's attentive, flirty, unabashedly touchy-feely. He's different. Are we finally crossing that invisible boundary between us? Who knows, but this is certainly a step, quite possibly a leap, in the right direction. The problem is, I don't know how he's feeling. Sure, he talks to me, but he doesn't tell me where his mind is. Without the foresight of a mind-reader, I'm scared to let my guard down. I'm scared to allow myself to hope, to imagine that one day we can be more.

He walks back to the table carrying a silver tray with two steaming mugs of tea on. "Our breakfast will be out shortly."

Our knees touch under the table, and neither one of us attempts to pull away. Smiling at me, he brushes a dark strand of hair off his brow. He studies my face. "It's nice to finally get some time alone."

I swallow. "Is it?"

He smiles big. I feel like my insides are on fire. How can I not want his kisses, his arms wrapped around me? How can I not want him?

He sips from his mug, clearing his throat. "So."

I tip milk into my mug, stirring it around with a plastic spoon. "So."

"Are you looking forward to the auction? I'm counting on you to help me get a deal."

I stop stirring. "Me?"

"Yeah, you, this is my first auction."

We spend the next half an hour chatting about the kinds of houses they're looking to purchase. Seth tells me one of the properties suffered fire damage, and it'll cost them a lot to renovate. He will only purchase that one if the price is right. Our conversation takes a detour, and he tells me about the surprise holiday he booked for him and Ellie to Disney World.

Seth smiles big. "I can't wait until we're on that plane."

My heart beats a little faster at the mention of a trip abroad. I've only been overseas once. The flight was awful—we suffered terrible turbulence and even hit an air pocket. The plane dropped thousands of feet before the pilot was able to gain control. As a result I'm petrified of flying, petrified of heights. The very thought makes me feel as though I'll throw up.

A waitress brings our full English breakfast. My hunger from moments ago vanishes. Seth looks up and frowns when I push the plate away. "Something wrong?"

"No, I'm just not hungry."

He leans forward and nudges the plate toward me. "Please, eat something. It's going to be a long day, you need your strength."

I take the cutlery in my hands and smile. I swallow away the nausea creeping up my throat and stab my fork into a mushroom.

Time ticks away, and in no time we find ourselves running from the café and across the road to where the auction is taking place.

The chairs have been arranged in rows with a narrow walkway down the centre. After signing in, Seth and I sit in the middle row. I watch people from all walks of life enter and take their seats.

Seth flicks through a glossy brochure. "This shows all the properties we can bid on today."

His arm rubs against me as he leans closer. He's pointing out a semi-detached property on the coast. I feign interest as he reads out some of the room measurements. I couldn't care less about the house; in my periphery I'm checking him out.

I jump as he prods my side. "Well, what do you think?"

"Erm—"

Our gaze meets but not for long. I can't, I want the guy so badly. He continues to talk, flicking through, until he stops at another property, a cottage this time.

He shakes his head, running his hand over his beard. "This one is a listed building; getting planning permission will be a bitch."

I glance down. The exterior to the property is lovely, with the signature white walls and thatched roof, but the interior leaves a lot to be desired.

"That won't be cheap to renovate," I say, trying to sound like I know what I'm talking about.

"Not cheap at all," Seth agrees. "Cole said he visited that property a few weeks ago, he estimated it'd cost between seventy and one hundred thousand to fix up to a high spec."

He pulls out a pen from his pocket, drawing a circle around the cottage, then places the pen behind his ear. He licks his finger and turns a few more pages. "There are five properties of interest. But this is the one we're here for."

I glance down, my eyes widening. I read 'Hedging Lodge Road.' The property is breathtaking. It is a Tudor-style detached house with green honeysuckle crawling its way up the front. The property is gated, with two acres of land, and has an indoor swimming pool. I could only dream of living in a house like this. Figures are flying around in my head and that's when I glance at the small print. The property has a reserve price of four hundred thousand pounds.

"Seth, have you seen reserve price?"

He nods. "Sure have."

I cough, clearing my throat. "Where's the money coming from?"

"Cole," he answers matter-of-factly.

My brother doesn't have that kind of money just lying around. This is a guy I used to help cut coupons with. I swallow hard. "Cole can't afford that."

"Well, according to Rick, he can. Don't forget he gave you a house last week."

Seth's right. Cole originally bought the house for me to rent from him, and on my birthday gave it to me. I was too overwhelmed to question him about it at the time. I sit, unblinking. I know their company was doing well, but it's not the company that's funding it, it's Cole. How?

Seth's stroking my thigh. "Will you stop worrying? You've got no idea how much money Cole has."

No, but it's something I intend to speak to my brother about. I hope he's not doing anything illegal. No, he wouldn't, I know Cole better than that, but jeez, where is he getting that kind of cash from?

Leaning back in his seat, Seth takes a deep breath. He moves the brochure aside and picks his bidding paddle from his lap. Our number is six hundred and twenty-four.

"We've got this," I whisper.

His hand moves from his leg to my knee, which he squeezes. "Let's hope so."

We stand as a couple of middle-aged businessmen squeeze past us to take their seats. Voices around the room lower as the auctioneer walks behind his wooden stand. He smooths the front of his shirt and clears his throat.

"Right, ladies and gentlemen, if I can have your attention. The first lot for today is lot 137. A two-bedroom bungalow…" The auction proceeds in quick succession.

Ten properties are called, two don't make their reserve price so remain unsold.

"Lot 148, three-bedroom cottage, in need of some restoration. Need a bid. Eighty thousand."

I nudge Seth. "How about this one?" It's so sweet, a little chocolate-box cottage with a thatched roof. "Seth, it's perfect. It's a five-minute walk to the beach."

He shakes his head, leaning into me, his mouth nearly touching my ear. "Cute, but no way we'll make enough profit."

Giggling, I scrunch up my shoulder. "Seth, your beard's tickling me."

"Oh, right." He edges away. His fingers brush my hair back into place.

My pulse quickens as one of the houses Seth circled is called out. Seth's incredibly blasé when raising his paddle. He keeps flipping to the back of the brochure and to the Tudor-style house. When bids slow, he retreats, letting the competing bidder claim the property. The same happens with the next two properties.

"Lot 190. Five-bedroom Tudor-style house, built in the early 1600's. Who's going to start me off with three hundred and fifty thousand?"

Seth grabs my hand, holding it tightly. I squeeze his fingers; I feel as excited as he does. "Lizzie, this is us."

Seth's about to raise his paddle in the air when someone calls from behind. "Three hundred and eighty."

"I have three eighty, can I see three ninety?" the auctioneer calls.

Seth grabs my hand, our fingers laced around the paddle. He raises it into the air.

The auctioneer nods at Seth, and continues to raise the offer. The higher the price goes, the fewer people raise their paddles. Painfully long seconds separate each new bid.

"Can I see five hundred thousand?"

Seth looks at me—for luck? Reassurance? I have no idea, but I nod.

"Last one, Lizzie." Seth raises the paddle above his head. His pulse flickers in his neck, his Adam's apple bobs as he swallows, and there's a sprinkling of sweat across his brow. Well, I'll be damned, he's nervous. If he doesn't get this property, we'll leave empty-handed. I know he feels pressure from Cole to come home with something, and I know how much he has his heart set on this property. My hands are clammy. I rub them down the material of my jeans before crossing my fingers.

The room falls silent after Seth's bid. I'm holding my breath, too nervous to breathe. Seconds feel like minutes, and minutes feel like hours. *Come on.*

The auctioneer's glance sweeps the room one final time. "Okay. In that case, going once."

Seth's hand snakes around my shoulders.

"Going twice."

His arm tightens, pulling me into him.

"Sold to the gentleman in the sixth row."

Seth pulls me into him, my head against his chest. His heart is pounding, and it dawns on me that this is the first time I've heard his heartbeat. I can feel him start to pull away. God, no, not yet, I want to bask in our closeness a little longer.

He cups my face in his hands. "I needn't have worn my lucky shirt. You're my lucky mascot."

In that case, take the shirt off.

I've not got the confidence to say that aloud. I'm about to reply when he kisses me without warning. His lips crush mine. Our breaths dance as our lips become one. I'm unsure if I should pucker up, if I should part my lips to allow his tongue to seek out mine. His eyes are closed, which tells me there's more to this than a quick celebratory peck. Wishful thinking on my part, perhaps, but is it wrong to want him to want me?

In my head the kiss lasts a lot longer than it does in reality. He pulls away and punches the air. "We did it."

Chapter Nineteen

Seth

*F**uck, yeah!*

I fist-pump the air again. I want to kiss Lizzie again, but shit, if I go in for round two I won't stop kissing her.

I do all the official shit when the auction is over—hand over my ID, give our business account details. I hold Lizzie's hand as we leave. I've got my house and my girl.

Stop, rewind. Not my house, not my girl. Not yet. I wanted to speak to Cole before I told Lizzie how I feel, but I can't contact him. His phone doesn't even ring out when I call. It goes straight to voice mail, and he deserves better than a recorded message.

With each step we make towards the café, towards the car park and my van, I feel like I'm going to explode.

Once in the car park, I circle her wrists and pin her against the van.

Her doe eyes go wide as I unintentionally wind her. "Seth."

"It's no good." I take a deep breath. "When the job's been signed off, I'd like to still see you. I need to still see you."

Her mouth drops open. "But I thought—"

I place my index finger to her lips. "It's just a meal, don't make more of it."

I don't mention that our meal will be in the most expensive restaurant in town. I want to strut in with her on my arm. Not only is she beautiful, she's clever, intriguing, she's great with my daughter, she's perfect. She somehow completes the fucked-up mess that is my heart.

She shakes her head. "Do you mean as friends?"

I push my body into hers, my groin pressing into her. My cock is throbbing so damn much it's in need of release. "Does it feel like I want to be your friend?"

She looks down at the fabric that separates us.

"No, Lizzie, I'm done pretending. When the work is finished and you are no longer my client, I am going to take you out"—I push my cock closer, pressing it harder into her stomach. She groans—"we are going to have an amazing night"—I move her hair away with my nose and bite her earlobe. She trembles—"and then I'm going to fuck you so damn hard you won't be able to sit down for a week."

"Seth—"

I release her. "Do me a favour."

She nods.

"On the drive back can you sit by the window, please? I can't have you sitting right next to me, not now."

As requested, Lizzie occupies the adjacent window seat. It goes without saying that I make things incredibly awkward during the journey home, which of course is spent stuck in traffic.

The satnav shows a road closure ahead. I'm guessing it's roadworks or a collision. Either way, we will be delayed for a few hours.

Great.

I can feel her gaze on my profile, and as I turn to face her, she looks away.

The traffic isn't moving. The van's stationary. I pull up the handbrake, reach across, unfasten her seat belt, grab her jeans and pull her towards me.

"Much better." I say, switching on the radio. Whereas I relax, she sits bolt upright. Her chest rises and falls— good, she's still breathing—but I can't see her seat belt.

My bad.

Reaching over her, I yank the seat belt free, then work it down. With the metal fastening between my fingers I pull it slowly over her shoulder. She shivers when I move it down between her breasts and past her pelvis where I finally clip it in. "There. All safe."

She doesn't speak, she doesn't even look at me. I tap my fingers on the steering wheel. Maybe I've misread the signs and she doesn't like me, in which case I've made a complete twat out of myself.

I turn the volume down on the radio, shuffle around on the seat. "If I've misread the signals, please accept my sincere ap—"

"You haven't," she mutters, her gaze locked on her hands, which are fidgeting in her lap.

"Then why are you so damn quiet?"

She laughs and then shrugs. "I don't know."

I take her hand and place our entwined fingers in my lap. Her hand is inches away from my groin. God, I want her fingers wrapped around my cock. Her arm is so bloody tense, it feels like one wrong move and it'd snap right off.

"Relax, Lizzie."

She sucks in a deep breath. "I'm trying."

What we need is an icebreaker. The traffic is at a standstill. I stroke my fingers down her cheek.

She closes her eyes at my touch. "Is this real?" she whispers.

I loop my fingers around her hair and tug her closer to me. "We're about to find out."

I stop when our faces are inches apart. Her gaze is fixed on mine. She bites her lower lip. "Hi."

"Hi," I say back. Batting my eyes, I pucker up. I'm trying to inject a bit of humour into a moment I can clearly see she's overthinking.

It's not an equation, Lizzie. Get out of your thoughts and let's kiss already.

We sit for a beat, our breaths the only things that are intimate. She nods, as if winning the war raging in her mind. Shutting her eyes, she closes the distance between us. Her lips brush against mine. I push into her, cementing our union, our lips as one. She's shaking, she's nervous. I keep cool and go at her pace. The kiss is slow. Her hand finds its way to my cheek, my hand cups the back of her head. I'm dying to deepen the kiss. Damn, I want to take all she has to offer, to bite, to suck, to tease. Without meaning to I nip her lower lip. I'm about to pull away and apologise when her teeth press down on mine. I crack open an eye. She's looking at me, a mischievous glint in her eyes. She's following my lead, and if she wants to learn, I am happy to teach. I'm about to push my tongue into her mouth when our kiss is interrupted by the beeping of horns.

I break our kiss. The traffic is moving slowly. I push the van into first gear and crawl forward to join the traffic. Lizzie's hand rests on my thigh. I know she can't miss the bulge in my jeans, but she doesn't touch it. I want her to touch it. It dawns on me that her actions are tentative—she isn't comfortable making the first move. I wonder if she's had many, if any, sexual partners. It's not something I can just ask her, is it? I can't rush her, I won't rush her, but when we fuck, I know the earth will move.

We don't talk for the remainder of the journey; I look her way and she looks out of the window. When I do catch her gaze, the smile she gives me is amazing.

I watch Lizzie's ass as she exits my van and makes her way up her drive. I power-walk to her side and walk her to her front door.

She places the key in the lock. "I enjoyed today."

I step closer to her. "Me too." I wrap my arms around her waist and pull her into me and we share a cheeky kiss.

We break away and I brush my thumb over her lower lip. "See you tomorrow."

I don't rush home, nor do I drive slowly. I look at all the surroundings as I drive, thinking how much clearer I'm seeing, and for the first time in a long time I feel as though every aspect of my life is good.

I pull onto my street. A red car is parked next to Darcy's on my drive—Anna's red car. I yank the handbrake up and run into the house.

My heart's racing, and I grab the banister. "Ellie. Ellie!"

She isn't ready to see her mum. Anna's caused way too much damage to just walk into Ellie's life when she feels like it. No movement from upstairs. I run into the kitchen.

"Ellie," I call again. "Ellie!"

Darcy enters the kitchen with a cup of tea in her hands. If she weren't a woman, I'd wring her damn neck.

"Why have you let that fucking bitch into my house?" I say between clenched teeth.

Darcy's hazel eyes go wide. "Seth, I—"

"Because this fucking bitch is Ellie's mum, and I have a right to see my daughter." Anna stands in the open door, her hand over her stomach.

Ignoring her, I turn to my sister. "Where's Ellie?"

Darcy attempts to hold my arm, which I shake free from her embrace.

"Seth, it's okay," Darcy tries to reassure me, but fails. "Imogen took her out for ice cream."

I feel slightly more at ease that my younger sister has Ellie. I glare at Anna, then focus back on Darcy. "Did Ellie see her?"

Anna pouts. "Excuse me? She has a name."

I scrunch up my nose, looking over her body and her huge baby belly. "I can think of a few." I can feel the venom dripping off my tongue.

Darcy waves her hand in front of my face. "No, I told Anna to go for a drive and return when Ellie had gone."

My heartbeat begins to slow and return to normal. I grit my teeth. "And she's still here? What does she want?"

"Seth, I'm right here, you know." Anger laces Anna's voice.

I wave my hand in the air, dismissing her comment. "Tell me what you want, then get out of my house and out of our lives."

Anna's heels click against the tiles as she enters the kitchen, placing the mug she's been drinking out of on the worktop. The stained red lipstick around the mug's rim turns my stomach. *Note to self: toss said mug into the bin.*

"I'm moving to Australia," she says after a long silence.

I make a cross on my chest and hail Mary. "Praise the Lord, there is a God."

Anna places her hand on her hip. "I really think we should go and sit down in the lounge."

I have no idea what she was expecting. For me to jump for joy that she's here? For me to be sad she's leaving? I'm neither.

How does she think this is going to go? Amicability? Discussing the child we created? I raise my hand. "Whatever you want to say can be said here."

She does that thing with her nose, the little twitch she does when she's nervous. She takes a deep breath, and I know I'm not going to like what she has to say. "Okay. I want ten thousand pounds."

I fold my arms across my chest. She's got a damn nerve. "On top of the seventy thousand pounds' worth of gambling debt you left me with? We lost our home because of you."

Anna couldn't get a credit card due to her poor credit, so being the doting husband, I gave her mine. I was so busy looking after Ellie and working that I didn't notice the statements no longer arrived in the mail—or rather they did, and Anna hid them.

"Ten thousand pounds and Ellie is yours. If you don't cough up the cash, then I'm applying for full custody of Ellie and she'll be coming with us."

I take a step towards her, and she steps back. "You want to thank your lucky stars you're a woman and pregnant."

Her face is unchanged because she knows I wouldn't lay a hand on her. She stands tall. "Ten thousand pounds, and you'll never see me again."

I narrow my eyes. "A hitman would accept less."

Darcy steps between us. "Okay, I can see emotions are running high, let's just put our foot on the brake a little bit."

I glower at my sister. "I'd like to speak to Anna, alone."

Darcy looks between us, and Anna nods. "I'll be okay."

I snort. "Of course you will, you've always made sure you were."

Anna's eyebrows draw in, but still she tells Darcy to leave us. Tossing her long blonde hair over her shoulder, Anna struts into the lounge. She wiggles her hips from side to side as she walks, as if she knows I'll be looking at her ass. I'm not.

Taking a deep breath, I follow her into the lounge. She's sitting on the settee, her shoes are off and her feet are spread across the cushions.

I look at her with disgust. "Do you mind?"

Ignoring me, she points to the easy chair opposite. "Please, sit."

It hits me that the longer it takes me to hear her out, the longer she'll be here. Blowing out, I do as she requested. "I'm listening."

"Ten thousand pounds and I'll relinquish all my parental rights."

I snort-laugh. "Darlin', you did that the moment you walked out."

"In the eyes of the law I've done no such thing." Her eyes leave me, and she begins flicking varnish off her nails. "Darcy tells me you're taking my daughter to Disney World."

I nod.

"Not if I don't get my money."

Is she for real? "And how do you plan to do that?"

"You can't take my daughter out of the country without my consent."

"I don't need your consent for a week's holiday."

"You're kidnapping her. You'll hear from my lawyer."

Evil, spiteful bitch. I know I'm within my rights, but she can make things complicated and I've not got time before we leave to sort legal stuff. "You'd deny our little girl her first holiday for ten thousand pounds?"

Anna's stare meets mine.

"You're bluffing," I spit out.

"Are you sure about that?"

We stare at each other for a beat before she eventually gets to her feet. "It was nice seeing you, Seth. I trust you'll make the right decision."

She brushes past me, taking all the unanswered questions with her. I take her arm and she glances down at me. I stare up into a face I etched onto my heart—I memorised every scar, every freckle, the exact shade of her eyes. Looking at her now feels as though I'm looking at a stranger. "Why did you leave?"

Her hand makes its way to mine. "I told you when we got together that I wouldn't be second best to anyone."

Second best? What the hell is she talking about? She was my queen. "There was no one else, only you."

She looks away. "I'm not talking about another woman."

"But then who—" It becomes clear the moment the words leave my lips, and I don't believe the words that are about to leave my lips. "You were jealous of our daughter?"

A tear escapes her eye and trickles down her cheek. "The day she came along, it was as though I didn't exist."

"You had postnatal depression; Ellie needed me."

"*I* needed you, damn it." She sniffs, wiping her tears away.

"And I was there for you every minute, every second of the day. I took months off work so I could be there. But we had a baby who wasn't going to feed herself, and bills that needed paying."

She glowers at me. "You gave up on us."

I shake my head. "*You* gave up on us. You refused to get help; I did the best I could. I was exhausted. I went to work seven days a week to make up the money we had lost. Darcy would stay with you till I finished. When I got home I waited on you hand and foot, I got up in the night to feed Ellie then got up the next day at six am to start the whole thing all over."

Anna looks away, but she needs to hear this. I need to say it. "We worked through your depression, you got better. You told Darcy not to come over during the days, you insisted on doing the night feeds. Things were great with us, better than they ever had been. We were happy, weren't we?"

Anna shakes her head. "No, Seth, you saw what I

188

wanted you to see. I'd meet up with Barry, and he complimented me, made me feel beautiful."

"Are you kidding me right now? I told you every day you were beautiful."

"And then you'd focus all your attention on her. I was always going to be second best, and I could see that. I don't know, maybe I missed the romance, missed the excitement."

"Tell me, Anna, was it depression or boredom that split us up?"

She doesn't meet my eyes. She can't. With her eyes on the floor she continues. "Sometimes the things that are meant to bring you closer together end up tearing you apart. I loved you so much, Seth, I really did. But having her is the biggest regret of my life. I didn't love her then and I don't love her now. It's her fault our marriage broke down."

I'm floored by her words, the honesty, the pain. I still hate her, but I also pity her. I don't know what possesses me, but I stand and place a hand on her stomach, knowing new life is only inches away. "Get help, Anna, don't make the same mistake twice."

She narrows her eyes. "Barry loves me."

"I'm not doubting he does, but he's also going to love the baby. You're going to have to get used to being second best, because the moment your child is born into the world, he or she should be the most important person in your lives."

Anna's eyes go wide, and her lips begin to tremble. "I miss you, Seth, I wish things could have been different."

I wish I could say the same and mean it, but the truth is, I'm glad she's out of my life, out of Ellie's life.

"Me too," I lie, in the hope she'll fuck off to Australia and never look back.

"I meant what I said though, I need the money."

"Why do you need money? Barry is loaded."

Her eyes leave mine, and it's as though she looks through me.

"You're gambling again, aren't you?"

She runs her fingers through her hair. "I can't help it, I've been really low recently."

"Low? How can you be low? You're moving to Australia and you're pregnant."

She glances down at the baby bump. "Don't you think I know that?"

It's the first time in fifteen months I've felt an emotion that isn't hatred for this woman. I feel sorry for her and the child she's carrying. Anna may not know it, but she's traveling down a road of destruction and she'll only leave casualties in her wake. Another guy she'll run away from, another baby she'll leave motherless.

Chapter Twenty

Seth

I don't allow Anna the power to get into my headspace.
I do all I can to block her out.

When I get to work the following day, I find Lizzie alone in the loft room, staring at three lines of blue paint. God, she looks hot. She's wearing a baggy black t-shirt and a pair of tight-fitting black trousers. Her ass looks amazing.

I attempt to sneak up behind her, but the floor creaks and she turns. Her hair is wild, the kind of wild I'd imagine after a serious sex session.

I adjust my trousers. *Nonsexual thoughts, Seth.*

She sweeps her hair up in her hands, pulls it into a low ponytail and secures it with a hair tie from her wrist. "I can't decide which colour."

I nudge her aside and take a look at the colours. I raise a brow. "They're exactly the same."

She shakes her head and begins pointing to the lines of paint. "No, that's duck egg, that's turquoise, and that one is aqua."

I squint. "Really? They look virtually the same."

She playfully nudges me back. "You would say that." She looks past me and down. "No Ellie today?"

Shoving my hands in my pockets, I blow out. "No, Darcy has taken her shopping to pick out her school uniform."

"That's nice."

"It is," I agree, but I really wanted to take Ellie. The problem is, with how my hours fall I don't know when I'll get time. The uniform shop is attached to a small boutique in town and is by appointment only. Darcy was lucky to snag a last-minute cancellation. The next available appointment would have been the week before Ellie started back at school. That wouldn't leave me enough time to iron in her name tags and return items that didn't fit her right.

Lizzie looks back to the wall. "So, which colour?"

I press my index on the middle. "That one."

She frowns. I'm sure she knows I picked one at random. "Why that one?"

I shrug. "Because I think it's nicer than the other two colours. Happy?"

"No, which colour do you prefer? And why?"

I grab her waist and lift her from her feet. She laughs as I march her in the direction of the large window and kiss the end of her nose. With the reflection of the sun on her face, her eyes sparkle up at me.

"What time are the painters coming?" she asks.

I scuff my shoe on the floorboard. "That's what I came to tell you, they're not."

She scratches the top of her arm. "I don't understand."

"Cole was meant to be sorting it. I guess he didn't."

Her shoulders drop and she gazes at the brown plastered walls.

"I'm sure they'll be here tomorrow." I hope I sound confident. I sure as shit don't feel it. If the painting is delayed, then the floor will be. We need to be finished by the end of the week.

I haven't got much snagging to do. I guess I could work a paint brush. "What about if we painted the walls?"

She points between us. "As in me and you?"

I grab the waistband of her trousers and pull her into me. She doesn't resist, instead wraps her hands around my waist.

It feels nice, natural between us. I hold her. She feels so good in my arms.

"Okay. I can do that," she says. "I've got to drop by work first to check on my art supplies and rearrange some displays, but once I'm done, I don't see why not."

Hearing footsteps on the stairs, I release Lizzie and we stand apart. Rick's gaze bounces between us and he snickers. He holds his hands in the air. "I ain't saying nothing."

I flip him the finger. "Ha, ha."

"So I managed to get hold of Donald, the owner of the painting company. He said Cole didn't pay the invoice from the last job."

It's not like Cole not to pay an invoice. "Really?"

"Not Cole personally, there was a mixup between the accountants. Anyway, I've got to go to the bank and withdraw some cash from the business account."

I pinch the bridge of my nose. "Great, more hold-ups."

"I could go to the school another day," Lizzie suggests. "We can make a start on the painting right away if it'll help?"

Rick looks around the loft room. "I'm not going to lie, it will give the job a push forward. The plaster will soak up a few coats of paint before you're happy with the finish."

"I'll take Lizzie to the hardware store, we'll pick up a big tub of base coat and a few tubs of duck egg."

"Aquamarine," Lizzie corrects.

Rick waves his hands dismissively and heads back down the stairs.

My keys jangle as I yank them from my trousers pockets. "Aquamarine it is."

The drive to the hardware store is nice. We don't talk, but we hold hands at traffic lights. I love how her hands feels in mine. Her skin is soft and smooth. Makes me feel a little self-conscious knowing mine are rough and dry from the hands-on work I do. I hope she doesn't mind.

I reverse-park in one of the trade parking bays and shut off the engine. "Two days, Lizzie."

She looks up from our entwined fingers. "I'm sorry, what?"

I rub the inside of her palm with my thumb. "I have two days left on the job, then you're no longer a client."

Not sleeping with a client is a big deal. We took on a job at the Bull's Head pub in town a little over three years ago. Cole started seeing Gail, the landlady. Needless to say the invoice was halved, our profit was slashed, and we took on additional work at no extra cost. I truly believe that mixing business with pleasure is a recipe for disaster. Plus, I'd never live it down after all the shit I gave Cole for getting involved with Gail.

Lizzie giggles, squeezing my fingers. "I'm looking forward to our meal."

"Not as much as I'm looking forward to my dessert."

Blushing, she swats my arm. The hardware store is quiet. It's nice, as we have time to look around. We find an assistant on the painting desk. Lizzie is still indecisive as to which colour to choose, so decides to have her own colour made up. The assistant mixes a bit of this and a bit of that before Lizzie approves.

We leave the shop with two tubs of base coat, blue emulsion, paint tubs, rollers, paint brushes, and some edging tape. I can't say I'm a fan of painting, but I am looking forward to getting my hands dirty with Lizzie.

We arrive back to her house and hurry up the stairs. We pass Rick on the landing as he continues to plaster the walls. He nods his head in acknowledgment. "I've sorted it. The painters will be here tomorrow."

Fantastic news. I'll be finished with the job before I anticipated. I'll have the snagging done by the afternoon, then I'm free the rest of the week.

It doesn't take us long to set our workstations up. Lizzie suggests working opposite ends so we'll meet in the middle. I don't like the idea of working too far away from her, but the idea of us getting closer together the more we paint spurs me on to paint quicker.

I switch on the radio on my phone, place it in centre of the room and it blasts out some tunes. It has the desired effect on Lizzie's ass, which she sways in time to the music, but the opposite effect on her. She doesn't talk to me, doesn't even look at me.

I turn around a few times, hoping to make eye contact. She's completely oblivious, rolling the roller up and down. I'm surprised how much of the wall she's covered.

I dip my brush into the paint. When I lift it up, it drips onto the floor. I lift the brush behind my head and flick the brush in her direction. Blobs of white paint mottle her black t-shirt and hair. She stands still. The roller doesn't move an inch.

She turns slowly. "You did not just flick paint at me."

I take a step towards her. "What are you going to do if I did?"

She takes slow, calculated steps in my direction. She's like a tiger about to pounce.

That's right, baby, keep coming. She waves the roller in front of my face. I grab the fluffy head and, using the long pole, pull her closer. Our bodies are inches apart. Her breathing has increased.

"Look at the mess you're making," I say, placing my paint-covered hand on her t-shirt, right underneath her breast. I made sure not to touch her there. I want my first time touching her breasts to be memorable.

She drops the roller to the floor and looks at the handprint. "You're in so much trouble."

I walk forwards. She walks back until her ass is pressed firmly against the newly painted wall.

"See what I mean, Lizzie? Look at the mess you're making."

Chapter Twenty-One

Lizzie

I gulp. My heart is beating so fast in my chest. After a few long seconds of caging me between his arms, he smiles, retreating to the opposite side of the room.

I glance down, pulling my t-shirt up for a better look. Seth's handprint has stained the material directly over my stomach. I peel my jeans off the wet wall and peer over my shoulder at my butt, which is now smeared in white paint. Great, two items of clothing I won't be able to wear again after today.

Narrowing my eyes, I look over at Seth, whose back is toward me. *He can't even face me, the coward.*

"You've ruined my clothes," I call, biting back a smirk. "I'm sending you the dry-cleaning bill."

He waves his arm dismissively. "You should be thanking me."

I raise my brows. *This should be good.*

"Wearing all black made you look like Catwoman. The paint adds"—he pauses, as if thinking of the right word—"character."

"Character. Right."

His shoulders rise and fall. No doubt he's laughing. Still, he stands resolute, attempting to look as though he's taking his work seriously. I look at the small amount of base coat that he's applied and surmise there's more paint on me than the wall he's working on.

I crouch down, retake the roller, and continue to paint. The music blares and I force myself to relax, swaying slowly in time. I can see Seth in my periphery checking me out, yet I don't turn. I can't.

What's wrong with me? The guy I've wanted since forever wants me. I should be throwing myself at him, but I can't. Something is holding me back. It feels as though I've placed him on a pedestal, one too high for me to ever be able to reach. Damn it, I'm ruining this before it's even begun.

He's removed his t-shirt. Sweat shimmers on his broad back. My gaze moves down to his tapering waist and his ass. Even in his work trousers, it looks pretty fine. He turns his head. He must have noticed me checking out his ass, as he gives it a little wiggle. My gaze meets his. He doesn't speak. He doesn't need to—the intensity of his stare says it all. He winks and I look away.

I want nothing more than for Seth to remove my clothes, for his hands to explore every inch of my body. I imagine him lying next to me totally naked, but I'm scared, I'm terrified of messing up. I've only had one sexual partner. Seth's a man, he's eight years my senior. He has eight more full years of experience.

I turn when Seth turns off the radio on his phone.

"Sorry," he says, pushing it in his pocket. "The battery is dying."

I want to say something. I feel he does too, but we just stand in a strange silence. Time passes slowly as we apply two coats of the white base coat.

"Daddy, Daddy!"

We both turn, hearing Ellie's voice. I realise my t-shirt is showing a little too much cleavage so yank it up.

Footsteps draw nearer before Ellie and Darcy appear in the doorway. Darcy looks formal. Her short hair has been sleeked back and she's wearing a grey pinstripe skirt with a matching jacket and cream blouse underneath. I smile in her direction, but her gaze is fixed on the little girl as she readjusts one of her pigtails. Ellie looks adorable. She's wearing a green summer dress.

"Daddy, Lizzie, look at my new school uniform," Ellie squeals, shaking a plastic bag in her hands. Darcy clicks her tongue, moving the little girl's head back in place as she continues to adjust her wonky pigtails.

Seth drops his brush in the paint tub and runs his hands down the front of his trousers. "How about we grab a drink and we'll take a look at your uniform downstairs?"

Ellie frowns, hugging the bag into her chest. "But I want to show you now." She stamps her little foot on the floor.

I drop the roller and walk towards her. "Sweetie, you don't want paint on your new clothes, do you?"

Her frown dissolves. Pointing, she chuckles. "Look, Aunty, Lizzie's got paint on her."

Darcy's gaze leaves Ellie and she focuses on me. Her smile drops, her eyes narrow. The woman clearly has a problem with me. I look away, not challenging her stare.

What the hell have I done wrong? I scuff my shoe on the floor, glancing down when my foot hits a raised floorboard. That's when I see it. The handprint that Seth left on my t-shirt has moved from my stomach and is covering my breast. It must have moved when I pulled my t-shirt up. Great, now it looks as though he's had his hands all over me.

"I can see you've been busy 'painting.'" Darcy uses air quotes to emphasize the word 'painting', her stare bouncing between my t-shirt and her brother's bare chest.

"Er, er…" I stutter, pulling my t-shirt down. Sure, my cleavage is exposed, but Seth's handprint is back in its rightful place. "I think I should change."

Darcy smooths down her skirt. "I think that's a good idea."

Rubbing the top of my arm, I turn my attention to Seth. "You guys carry on without me. I'll have a tea and one sugar."

I run past Ellie and Darcy. I make my way down to the second floor and lock myself in the bathroom. I keep my clean washing in a cupboard under the sink. I undress, toss my paint-mottled clothes in the wash basket and grab a pair of skinny jeans and a blue floral t-shirt.

I sit on the edge of the bath for a few minutes, trying to compose myself. I pull my phone from my pocket and scroll to the one person who I know will be able to help me.

Me: *Help.*

Amber: *Go on.*

I send her a monster text. I begin with the handprint incident and Darcy. I end with how Seth told me he wanted me.

Amber: *OMG, that's hilarious.*

I glance to the wash basket, completely mortified. God knows what Darcy must think of me now.

Me: *Not funny.*

Amber: *It is a little funny.*

I stare at my phone, waiting for her to say something about Seth. She doesn't.

Me: *What do I do about Seth?*

Amber: *He wants you, you want him. I don't know what you're asking me.*

I tap my foot on the floor. What am I asking her? The man of my dreams wants me, he actually wants me, and I'm scared. Without thinking I text her back.

Me: *What if I'm no good?*

Amber: *I think it's time Sandy ripped off that cardigan and put on her catsuit.*

Sandy from *Grease* is a great comparison for me—safe, predictable, dare I say boring? I know Amber's right, and I don't want to risk losing him.

Me: *I'll try.*

Amber: *I accidentally left some condoms in your medicine cupboard.*

Oh, fudge. Seth and Darcy are downstairs. What if he happens to find them?

Me: *AMBER!*

Amber: *You're welcome.*

She also inserts an emoji of a bone. A bone? I have no idea why, it's obviously a sexual reference, but I don't get it.

I've been sat up here way too long. I can't hide up here forever. Holding my breath, I make my way downstairs.

Darcy's in the lounge sitting on the settee. Her legs are crossed and she swings her shoe forward and back. Damn, I feel like I'm standing up in court and she's my judge and jury.

I look from Darcy to Ellie. She's sitting in front of the TV watching *Finding Nemo*, a glass of milk in one hand, a cookie in the other.

Seth walks in from the kitchen, a mug of steaming coffee in each hand. He places them on coasters on the coffee table. Seth nods in my direction. "Yours is coming."

Darcy doesn't take her drink. She's too busy watching every single move I make. I sit on the easy chair, and after Seth brings my drink, he stands in the open doorway. At least he isn't planning on getting paint on my furniture as well as my clothes.

"I've eaten my cookie," Ellie pipes up, uncrossing her legs. "Now can I try my new school uniform on?"

Darcy jumps up, grabbing a tissue from her jacket pocket. "Let me wipe your face. Put your drink on the table. We don't want any spillages, now do we?"

I place my mug down and rub my hands together. "Come on, Ellie, let's see what goodies are hiding in your bag."

She smiles, tipping her uniform and a pair of black patent shoes onto the floor. Looking at me, she lifts her arms in the air. I pick up on her cue and help her off with her dress.

Darcy is still watching me. She runs her fingers through her short dark hair. Her jaw is set.

Seth kneels at my side and reaches for my hand, taking Ellie's dress from me. "Thanks, Lizzie." Seth helps Ellie button her shirt, then holds her hand and she steps into her pinafore. A blue cardigan with an embroidered logo on the left breast completes her uniform.

My heart melts. I blink rapidly, my eyes welling up. "You look so grown up."

Darcy hitches her skirt up and kneels. "Right, little lady, let's get your uniform back in the bag."

Ellie is out of the uniform and sitting back in front of the TV in no time. Darcy folds each item of clothing perfectly, placing them back in the bag with precision. "We're picking the rest up tomorrow."

"The rest?" Seth quizzes.

"Her PE kit, backpack, lunch box, pencil case, crayons."

I frown. I don't understand why Darcy is rushing to

get her stationery—oh, wait, I do. Darcy is trying to keep Ellie and me apart and playing the doting aunt certainly does that. But if she wants to take Ellie out tomorrow, who am I to stop her?

Tomorrow? No, I booked Ellie in at Amber and Chelsea's shop. I shoot a glance at Seth. "We have plans tomorrow, remember?"

He raises a brow. Clearly, he didn't remember. "Right."

Darcy sits forward. "Surely this is more important?"

"Really, sis? School doesn't open for a month."

Darcy's mouth drops open. She reaches forwards and swipes the remote control from the table and mutes the TV. "Ellie, honey. What do you want to do tomorrow? We can get that lovely unicorn backpack you pointed out earlier. Remember there was only one left in the shop. Or you could spend a day out with your dad and Lizzie."

That's a low blow, bribing a child with a backpack.

"Lizzie and Daddy," Ellie chants, clapping her hands.

Darcy lets out a long, low sigh. "I guess we could pop back to the shops in a few hours."

Ellie nods.

Seth clears his throat. "That settles it."

Chapter Twenty-Two

Seth

Lizzie prepares sandwiches and Darcy and Ellie stay for lunch. I may have been imagining it, but Darcy is warming to Lizzie. No, strike that. Darcy rolls her eyes when Lizzie speaks and turns her nose up at the sandwiches.

We're discussing Ellie's new school when the lounge door swings open and Rick appears. "Do you guys want to explain how the ass print got in the wet paint?"

Lizzie's face turns red and she looks away. Unsurprisingly, Darcy stands. She and Ellie say their goodbyes and leave.

By seven pm, Lizzie and I have finished painting the loft. The walls were like a goddamn sponge—they soaked up three coats of base coat. I wrap my arm around her and we step back and take time to appreciate the large room.

I nod. "Not bad."

"Not bad at all," Lizzie agrees.

I point to the wall opposite. "You know, a double bed

would go nicely there."

Lizzie shakes her head. She's told me a dozen times today that this is going to be her art room. Such a damn shame.

I raise my hand. "Just hear me out. Imagine waking up in the morning to that view."

"Yo, yo, are you two decent?" Rick's standing in the doorway, covering his eyes.

I shake my head. "Yes. Don't judge me by your standards."

Rick cracks his fingers open before removing his hands. "Plastering done, snagging done." He holds his hand high. "Give it to me, baby, don't leave me hanging."

I stroll over and we high-five.

Lizzie frowns. "What does that mean?"

Rick clears his throat. "It means we've pretty much finished the job. All that is left is the painting and laying the carpet."

Lizzie runs to Rick and wraps her arms around his waist. "Oh, my God, thank you. You don't know how much it means to me to finally sleep in an actual bed."

"Teamwork, that's what it's about." Rick beckons me over. "Team hug, bro, get your ass over here."

I don't pass on a chance to wrap my arm around my girl. *Not my girl,* I have to keep reminding myself.

I stand between Rick and Lizzie and do the whole group hug thing. Rick lowers his hand.

I shove him. "Get your paw off my ass."

Rick laughs. "I like it when you're all feisty." He pulls away, looking us up and down. "I'm going to head home. Have fun, lovebirds."

Rick slaps my and Lizzie's asses and runs down the

stairs. I'm sure he bangs the front door extra loud to make a point.

Alone at last.

I undress Lizzie with my stare. "And then there were two."

She looks down, wrapping her arms around her waist. "Can I wine—" She trips over her words. "Can I get you a drink?"

As much as I want to have a drink with her, I know it's getting close to Ellie's bedtime and I'll need to be heading off. One quick drink won't hurt though. "Tea, please. No sugar."

She nods, staring at me when I don't move. "Are you coming?"

I pull my phone from my pocket. "I'm just going to give Darcy a quick call, make sure Ellie is okay."

Lizzie smiles before heading downstairs. I glance at the screen and notice that I've had a text from Darcy. She sent it ten minutes ago.

Darcy: *We came back to mine after shopping. Ellie's fast asleep in my bed, she's welcome to stay the night.*

She's never spent an evening away from me. I start typing back, asking Darcy to bring her home, when I stop typing. She's staying the night at Darcy's; this is huge for Ellie.

Me: *Does Dwight mind?*

Darcy: *He's working a night shift.*

I flip the phone around repeatedly in my hand. This is big for Ellie, this is big for me. I've never spent a night without my baby under the same roof.

Let go, Seth.

Ellie is fine with Darcy. She's used to her. It's going to be a bigger deal to me than it is to Ellie. I take a deep breath.

Me: *Okay. But call me if she wakes up in the night, I'll be right over.*

Darcy: *She'll be fine. I put leftover chilli in the fridge. Put it in the microwave for five minutes, stir it, and then put it on for another minute.*

Me: *Yes, Mum.*

Darcy: *You deserve a night off from being a dad. Do you want me to drop her off in the morning?*

Me: *I'll pick her up.*

I don't expect that Ellie will stay at Darcy's house without me till morning. She always sneaks into my bed in the middle of the night. She'll know I'm not there.

Darcy is with her, she'll be fine.

I have an evening off. I'm here and Lizzie is downstairs. We're alone. The job's finished and she's no longer a client. All the boxes are ticked—nothing is holding me back, not any more.

I can hear Lizzie pottering around downstairs. I make a fist and pound my chest.

You've got this, I think, giving myself a quick pep talk.

I stroll downstairs, noticing that Lizzie has pulled out her sofa bed. *Perfect.* Walking with more of a spring in my step, I make my way into the kitchen. Lizzie's spooning sugar in a mug.

I sneak up behind her and wrap my arms around her waist. "I said no sugar."

She jumps in my embrace. "Fudge, Seth. You gave me a heart attack."

I spin her round. "Fudge? Who the fuck says fudge?"

Apparently, Lizzie does. Come to think about it, I don't recall ever hearing her swear.

"So." I slide my hands into her jeans pockets and pull her closer to me. "Ellie is staying the night at Darcy's."

"Your cup of tea." Her voice cracks.

I lean forward, sandwiching her against the worktop. "Fuck the tea."

I bend down and cover her with kisses. She trembles in my embrace, and I'm in two minds whether to deepen the kiss, but I do. I push my tongue into her mouth, and within seconds she goes from nervous to hungry, her kisses dripping with lust. I grab her ass and pick her up so she's sitting on the worktop.

She pulls away and shakes her head. "Not here." She's looking in the direction of the lounge, to where I know she has a sofa bed.

With our lips locked, I take us to the lounge. It's a bonus to see the bed is already up and made.

She pulls back slightly. "I, I need to change the bedding."

I half-shrug. "It's a bit counterproductive."

"What is?"

I lower her onto the bed. "Changing the sheets when

we're about to get them dirty." She laughs. My face is unchanged, stoic. I just watch her. "God, you're beautiful."

She stops laughing. "Do you think we could just lie together for a little bit?"

She lifts the covers and slips in. Her gaze hovers over the empty place to her right. It's not exactly what I had envisioned, but whatever. I don't need prompting; I manoeuvre myself round the bed, lift the covers and lie by her side.

We lie in complete silence. She reaches for my hand. Our little fingers link together, a small link binding us together. It doesn't take long before my hand seeks out her hand. Her foot brushes against my foot. She nudges my thigh with her knee.

She clears her throat. "You must be hot in those, why don't you take them off?"

I raise a brow. She's looking down. I assume she means my work trousers. *Take them off*, she said.

With pleasure.

I lower the blanket and unbutton my trousers. I lift my ass and pull them down, tossing them onto the floor.

I know she's looking at the bulge in my pants. I leave the covers pushed down and don't make any attempt to hide it from her. She needs to see the way she's affecting me.

My stare goads her. "Aren't you hot in yours?"

I watch as she unfastens the metal button and lowers the zip. She lifts her hips, pulling them down. Her legs are beautiful. Her thighs are significantly paler than her calves. I imagine her wearing her cute little shorts in the garden whilst the sun kisses the skin free from clothing.

I run my tongue over my teeth. "You really should

wear less when sunbathing. Or maybe, I don't know, wear less as a rule."

Her black lace panties peek out from under her T-shirt. They're almost see-through, but not quite. I need to see more. More skin, more of her. I lean across, brushing my finger along the hem of her t-shirt. "Surely you're hot in this?"

Biting on her lip, she sits up and pulls it up over her head. She has the daintiest pink bra on. The half cup of the material barely covers her nipples. Her breasts are sexy as hell, on the smaller side, her nipples small and cherry pink.

Her gaze rests on my torso, but she doesn't need to ask. I'm already removing my t-shirt. We lie side by side in our underwear. I reach across the bed. Our fingers inter-link and she inches her body closer to mine.

Her eyes are wide. "I don't want to be someone you sleep with and forget about. You mean more to me than that. I'm worth more than that."

How could she think that of me? I mean, yeah, I did proposition her on the night out. Things are different now, surely she knows that. "I've never been a one-night stand kind of guy. I want this, Lizzie, I want you. Not just tonight. I want you more than I've ever wanted anyone. To tell you the truth, I wanted you way back when you were eighteen, but you were still a kid."

Her forehead creases. "I was not."

"Eighteen and twenty-seven is a huge gap. You had your future ahead of you, university, your life. I couldn't get in the way of that."

"I wonder how things would have been if you had?"

Now that's a question that plagues me. Where would Lizzie and I be now? One thing for sure, I wouldn't have

211

Ellie. I can't picture a world she isn't in.

I turn side on to face her. Lizzie mirrors me and we lie gazing into each other's eyes. I hook my finger under the material of her bra, not to expose her breast, but just to caress her, to know how her skin feels under my touch. "I think things happen for a reason, at the right time."

She gulps. "Is now our right time?"

I flash my teeth. "I'd like to think so."

She wiggles forward.

Come on, baby, a little more.

"What about Ellie? How do I fit into your lives?"

I take a deep breath. "Ellie will always come first. Always. But I can't deny how much I want you, how much I want you in our lives. Things will have to move slowly, and maybe it'll take us a while to be a conventional couple, but what's conventional? The hell should I know? I believe if two people are happy, loving one another, nothing else matters."

As much as I want to grab her, I don't. Her gaze is fixed on my lips and she slowly shuffles closer. I can't take this any longer. I wait till her body is flush with mine before I close the small distance between us, crashing my lips onto hers. This time she kisses me hard.

I grab her ass and pull her closer so that I'm pulling her into my erection. My body reacts to that contact, that touch immediately. My hips start moving in a silent question. Her hips silently answer as she rocks into me. Our bodies dance on instinct—it's a slow, tentative dance whilst we familiarise ourselves with one another, but at any moment we could lose control and become completely feral.

"Tell me to stop, and I'll stop," I say into our kiss.

"Don't stop." Her words send me right over the edge. That want, that desire, that carnal need erupts in my gut and I ram my hips ferociously into her, showing her what's to come.

I guide her hand over my cock, asking, begging for her to touch me. God, when she finally makes contact and her fingers glide over my length for the first time, I lose it. My heart is beating at record pace and I don't want it to stop.

I waste no time in rolling her over so that I'm on top. I drop down, placing my lips over her lips, taking away her will to breathe. I want her to want me as much as I want her. Her legs wrap around my waist, and she shudders, my cock grinding against her sex.

I know she's nervous, I was trying to go slow, but the moment my cock presses against the heat of her underwear, it's all over. Her arms lasso around my neck, her legs hook around my thighs. I grind harder into her. She pushes herself into me.

The only thing separating us is the thin material of our underwear, but that's easily sorted. The predictability I thought was Lizzie has been washed away, and lust stares back. She bites her lip. I fist her hair. She lets out a whimper, and I retreat. God, I've been fighting this desire for so long, I'm like a damn volcano about to erupt.

I tighten my grip on her thighs, wanting more of her, wanting to take everything she'll give me. Our kiss is so hard that our teeth clang off one another as our tongues plunge into each other's mouths. Our tongues are ravenous as they battle. Hungry, greedy, indulgent kisses that I never want to end.

"You're mine, baby," I breathe into our kiss.

I reach into her panties and she opens her legs, opening herself up to me. I dip my finger into her delicious wetness and then glide it up and down her clit. Our kiss grows more demanding with every glide of my finger.

I drop my head to the crook of her neck, biting, sucking on her skin. "You're so wet."

Her nails match my torturing strokes. She digs deep and hard down my back.

I wriggle out of her hold, making my way down her body. She closes her eyes when I reach her panties. I don't remove them with my teeth as I'd planned. I prise her legs open and pull the material to the side, fucking her with my tongue, pleasuring her with my fingers. She fists my hair, her hips rising for more, more of this, this explosion between us. I lick, flick, suck, and nibble on her clit until her legs begin shaking. She pushes me away whilst her body reacts violently to her orgasm.

"Oh, sweet Jesus," she cries out, but I'm not letting her get away, I move her hands aside and I ride the wave she's on, tasting all her pleasure. God, she's deliciously wet. My cock is aching to get inside her.

I've got to get inside her before I come in my pants. I stand, leaving her on the bed, looking down at her beautiful body as she quivers. I bend down, remove my wallet from my trousers and fish out a condom. She leans up on her elbows and watches me sheathe up.

Lizzie doesn't flinch when I step towards her. Instead, she opens her legs wider, inviting me in. I place my left hand on the bed, and then the right, walking my hands towards her. She lies back, looking down at my cock as it gets dangerously close to the point of no return.

I groan as she takes me in her hand.

She gasps. I'm going to plough my hard cock right into her. She isn't ready, not yet. My finger strokes her sex. I circle her clit, pressing firmer until she starts to quiver under me. I slowly sink one finger into her and then another. She feels so tight against my fingers. As much as I'm dying to dive into her, ripping through barriers that I put into place, I know I can't. I can't ruin this for her. "Are you ready?"

Gulping, she nods.

I take my cock in my hand and hover it over her wetness. I can feel her warmth through the condom. Damn, it feels good. I'm fighting the urge to thrust into her. Slowly, I push myself in, inserting one inch at a time. I give her time to adjust to my size, slowly moving in and out, pushing a little deeper each time.

I lean down, my nose in her hair. I inhale her beautiful scent; she smells so good. She's so perfect. Our bodies are hot and sweaty as I inch further into her. "Is this okay?"

Her hands lock around my neck and she pulls me down, my body falling onto her, my cock closing the final distance between us. I'm fully inside her. She moans. Her inner walls are so tight around me. Rising up on my arms, I look down at our bodies, joined as one.

I lift her leg, placing her foot on my shoulder. I look down, getting the perfect view. I can't hold back any longer. I thrust deeper, harder, I groan as my balls tighten and my cock throbs violently inside her. I drop her leg and allow my body to drop. I don't want to crush her, but I want her in my arms.

With me still inside her, I wrap her up in my arms and roll us onto the side. I kiss the tip of her nose. She blushes.

She can't pretend to be shy after that.

She bites down on her lip. "Hi."

There's so much I want to say, but only one thing that comes out. "Hi."

Chapter Twenty-Three

Lizzie

We lie staring at each other. I prop my elbows on the pillow, gazing down at Seth. His toned chest is glistening with sweat.

"That was…" Seth runs his hand through his hair. "Shit, that was intense."

He's sure right about that. Is that how sex is meant to be? I'm not a virgin but have only been with one other guy. I do not remember sex feeling so damn good. With Gary it was awkward, the lights were always turned off, and we dressed the moment it was over. Seth didn't turn the lights out, he didn't shy away when putting on the condom, he stood there, tall and confident. He made sure I saw every inch, and in return he explored every inch of me. It's hot, verging on awkward, but in the same way it's helping with my insecurities.

He runs his fingers gently down my arm. "You have no idea how much I've wanted you."

If only you knew how long I've wanted you.

LAURA RILEY

I turn my back and shuffle into him. His legs wrap around my legs and my ass presses into his groin. He wraps me up into his chest, pulling me close. He breathes against my neck. Each exhale causes goose pimples to ripple down my skin. God, I love how his body fits perfectly against mine. I love how we fit, in every sense of the word.

Squeezing my hand, he lets out a long breath. "As much as I don't want to move, I think I'm going to have to."

He kisses my cheek. Butt-naked, he gets up and walks into the hall. I'm almost too scared to look, but steal a peek at his ass before he makes his way up the stairs. I can hear him moving around upstairs, the water running, and the floorboards creaking.

Oh, my God, did we really just have sex? It feels so surreal. Closing my eyes, I smile, thinking back to the years I fantasised about him. Back then I never thought in my wildest dreams that I'd be anything more to Seth than Cole's little sister.

Clutching the covers to my chest, I fall back onto the bed. My heart is still racing, my lips still swollen from our kisses, my body still tingling from his touch.

I can hear the bathroom door open and close. Our gazes meet as he makes his way down the stairs. He winks, standing in the open doorway. He makes no attempt to dress. Instead he places his hands above his head, holding the frame. His chest rises and his tapered waist narrows as he reaches up.

Don't look down, don't look down.

But I do.

"Just can't get enough of my cock, can you?"

I grab a pillow and toss it in his direction. He catches

218

it. The covers I was gripping moments ago fall from under my arms, exposing my breasts, and he stares. His eyes are hot and hooded, and he sucks in his lips. "God, how did I get so damn lucky?"

I sit up, suddenly feeling more exposed than I did minutes ago. I hold the covers over my chest.

"Get used to me looking at you, Lizzie, because I'm going to. A lot."

I look away for a beat. The intensity in his voice and stare are causing a reaction between my legs that I can't explain.

Seth rocks back and forth on his heels. "I don't know about you, but I've worked up quite the appetite. Do you want to go into town and pick something up?"

I nod, pressing my hands over my stomach to stop it rumbling. "Sure."

He steps aside, leaving the doorway clear. "The bathroom's all yours."

I gather my clothes together and hug them to my chest as I make my way out of the room.

Seth raises a brow.

"What? I'm shy."

"Because that's the impression I got when my tongue was between your legs."

I playfully shove him as I pass, and he slaps my bare ass.

After cleaning up, I dress and stand looking at myself in the bathroom mirror. I'm sure some women can carry off the just-had-sex look. Unfortunately, I'm not one of those women. Washing my face, I wipe away the smudged mascara. I grab my vanity case from the windowsill and run a brush through my hair and apply some foundation and eye makeup.

By the time I get downstairs Seth's already dressed. He stands in the hallway holding one of my jackets in his hands. He helps me into it and takes my hand as we head outside to his van. When he unlocks the passenger side door, he holds it open for me.

I know we're not officially a couple, but it feels as though we are. I sit beside him in the front seat. When his hand isn't holding mine it's stroking my thigh as he changes gear.

We park not far from the beach and amble along the sea front holding hands. Giving me a little tug, Seth guides me towards a narrow alleyway which leads into the town. Town isn't overly busy, but people stagger out of bars, whilst others head into takeout restaurants.

The shops don't look anything special, especially of an evening. An array of different-coloured awnings frame the red-brick buildings. Shutters have been pulled down and 'closed' signs hang in the doors. The few shops that remain open have fluorescent signs hanging above the door. That's when I notice 'Cornwall Art and Prints' lit up with bold red font. I remember seeing an event here being advertised. It looks as though there's an exhibition inside.

Seth juts his chin in the direction of the shop and looks at me as he awaits an answer.

I love anything arty. "Sure, why not."

As we walk in Rick and Amber walk out. Smiling, we exchange glances, but don't stop to talk. Everywhere we go, they seem to be. I wish she'd open up to me about her relationship with Rick. All I can get out of her is, "It's complicated."

The interior of the shop is large and open-plan.

Frames hang off the walls showcasing photography and paintings. Numerous sculptures in a variety of media line the back wall.

We're greeted by a middle-aged man dressed in a dark suit.

"Not bad." Seth admires the art.

"Thank you." The man hands us a flyer. "Please take a complimentary glass of champagne whilst you look around." The man points us in the direction of a table where long-stemmed glasses have been laid out.

Seth takes two glasses and hands one to me. "To us." Licking his lips, he takes a sip. I'm not sure if it's Seth's toast or the alcohol warming my insides but whatever it is, it sure feels nice.

I glance down and read the front page of the flyer. It seems the exhibition is solely Cornish landmarks and wildlife.

Seth places the glass down and holds out his hand, which I take. Hand in hand, we take a slow walk around the room. The photography is beautiful—landscapes, seagulls in flight, guillemots with their striking brown and white plumage.

One picture grabs my attention and I stop walking. Seth stands by my side. His eyes are wide as his gaze flits between black and white infrared and aerial photos. "I never realised photography could be quite so diverse."

I point to the photographer's name directly below.

"Amber took that?"

"She sure did. I knew I'd seen that particular photo before."

We move on to the paintings. My favourite is Cornwall's Lanhydrock House and gardens. It's a nineteenth-century country house that has been recreated in soft pastels.

Seth nudges me. "Lizzie. There's a couple over there who have been trying to get your attention."

I turn and wave in their direction. "It's Mr and Mrs Jones. Their daughter Daisy is one of my art students."

Mrs. Jones bustles towards us. "I had to come say hello and thank you. Daisy's art has come on so much, and it's all down to you."

I drop my gaze. "It's nice of you to say, but it's not all down to me. She's very talented. I'm simply pointing her in the right direction."

"Well, that's not what our Daisy says. I also hear you're quite the artist."

"I guess I'm okay."

Seth wraps his arm around me. "Will you learn to take a compliment, woman?"

Mrs Jones beams. "Well, I best get back. It was lovely to see you."

Seth studies me for a beat. "Why don't you paint a Cornish landmark and have it displayed here?"

I shake my head. "I'm not that good."

"I'd like to be the judge of that."

I smile, though I know it doesn't reach my eyes. My artwork is good, but it's not something I've shared with anyone outside of the classroom. It is something I'd like to share with Seth when I'm good and ready.

We spend about half an hour in Cornwall Arts and Prints looking around. Seth donates twenty pounds on the way out, and I purchase a small replica of Amber's photograph and a copy of the nineteenth-century house printed on a postcard.

Linking fingers, we walk outside and head for the Dolphin chip shop. We're served straight away and, holding a cone of chips each, we sit down on a bench overlooking the beach.

I stare out at the sandy beach. With dusk fast approaching, the sea resembles a large navy-blue cloak. People interrupt our view as they sporadically walk past.

Seth shuffles closer. Our arms brush one another's as we eat our chips with small wooden forks. He hasn't spoken for a while; it looks as though he's in a trance.

God, I hope he's not having second thoughts.

His fingers stiffen as I reach for his hand. I glance back up and to his face. "Are you okay?"

He looks down at our fingers. "Yes, fine, just a few things on my mind."

"You can tell me—that is, if you want to."

"It's Anna."

I frown. "Anna?"

"She turned up at my house last night."

I don't feel hungry anymore. There's a horrible feeling creeping its way into my stomach. Anna's gorgeous, she and Seth have history together, and it bothers me. "What did she want?"

He closes his eyes and shakes his head, like the thought alone is too awful to recite. "She's emigrating to Australia."

I smile to myself. *The further away she is, the better.*

He lets out a sharp breath. "She wants to take Ellie with her."

I gasp. "She can't! Surely she can't do that!"

He shakes his head. "I'm not worried, she's bluffing, I know she is. If Ellie meant that much to her there's no

223

way she would have walked out on her fifteen months ago."

"If you're not worried, I wish you'd tell your hand that."

He loosens his grip. "Sorry, Lizzie. Shit, I don't know. Darcy keeps pecking my damn head over it and I guess her worry is starting to project itself on to me." He tosses our empty containers into a bin. "I could always come back for a nightcap." A wicked smile twists his features. "Round two?"

"You're incorrigible."

He lifts a brow. "You're only just coming to realise that?"

Streetlights flicker as we make our way to Seth's van. Once inside, he pulls his phone from his pocket and sighs. "Round two is going to have to wait."

"What? Why?" That sounded more desperate than I had intended it to.

"Ellie's awake and is asking for me. I'm going to drop you back and go pick her up." He places his hand on my knee, working it all the way up. "I'm finding it hard to resist you."

So don't.

Chapter Twenty-Four

Seth

"Home, sweet home," Lizzie says.

I pull the handbrake up and turn in my seat so that I'm facing her. I capture a lock of her hair between my fingers and tug her closer. "I'll see you in the morning." I kiss the tip of her nose. God, what I'd give to spend the night with her. To hold her in my arms, have her head rest against my chest, and have her wake up beside me. I'd love to think it could be a possibility, but realistically it'll never happen.

I rest my forehead against hers. "I wish I could give you all of me."

"I'm happy to have whatever is available."

I take her hand and hold it against my chest. "I hope you know what you're saying, because I don't think my heart could survive another break."

For the first time she initiates the kiss. Her kiss is soft and sweet, just like her. I don't deepen the kiss. I just enjoy the feeling of having her in my arms, knowing she

225

wants me as much as I want her.

There's an innocence, a vulnerability about Lizzie that intrigues me. Is it wrong for me to want to preserve that vulnerability?

"I'll ruin you," I say into our kiss.

"So ruin me."

I push my hand down her jeans, and my finger is pressing against her clit. She squirms in my embrace.

I break our kiss. "Does that feel nice?"

She doesn't answer, but by the way her hips chase my finger I'm guessing the answer is yes. With my free hand I undo my trousers.

Her body tenses. "Seth, not here."

"What? You're not into public displays of affection?"

She pushes my forehead away with her palm. "Not when my neighbours have front-row seats."

I press her clit one final time before pulling my hand free. "Then we'll take the party inside," I say, licking my finger. "God, you taste so good."

Her face turns a nice shade of red. I'm dying to pull her onto my lap and fuck her right here, right now.

"Do you want to?" Her voice is low.

My finger slowly teases the material of her t-shirt. "Do I want to what?"

"Come inside?" she whispers.

"First you initiate the kiss, and now you're propositioning me for sex. I like this side of you."

I love how hard she's trying, and the fact she's pushing herself out of her comfort zone.

I'm so tempted to take her up on her offer when the feel of my phone vibrating in my pocket brings me back to reality. I ball my hand into a fist and bite my knuckles.

"As much as I want to, I've got to head back."

Disappointment twists her features, and she starts to shuffle towards the van door. I take her hand in mine and place it on my groin. My cock is rock hard and I want her to feel what she's doing to me. "I just want you to know that today was the first time of many, Lizzie. I have no regrets."

"Neither do I."

"Good. Now get that sexy ass in the house before I give your neighbours an X-rated show they won't forget."

I walk her to her door. Back in my van I turn on the engine. I shoot Darcy a quick text to let her know I'm on my way. I push the gear stick into reverse, pull off the drive and head straight to my sister's.

Darcy greets me at her front door. She's wearing a pink fluffy robe. Ellie is asleep in her arms.

"I'm sorry, Seth, she went straight back to sleep. I shouldn't have disturbed you."

My baby's face is squished against Darcy's chest. Her mouth is open and a small line of drool seeps from the corner.

"There's no way I'm taking her home in that state. By the time I've got back and fucked around getting her into bed she'll be wide awake."

Darcy nods. "Why don't you take the spare room tonight?"

By the spare room, she's referring to her twenty-year-old stepson's old room. He's currently at Edinburgh Uni studying economics. I know it's not ideal as it only has a single bed, but I'm sure Ellie and I could squish together for the night. "Has she been to the toilet?"

Darcy winces. "Yeah, in my bed."

I bite the insides of my cheeks. "Sorry." I try not to laugh, but it's kind of hard not to. Darcy's husband is a pretentious prick and it amuses me to know that Ellie's pissed on his Egyptian cotton sheets.

"If I wasn't holding Ellie, I'd slap you." She knows I hate Dwight, she knew from the moment I first met him.

"Am I really that transparent?"

She rolls her eyes. "As glass." Stepping aside, she welcomes me in. "Here, take Ellie. I'll put some fresh sheets on the bed for you."

Ellie and I meet Lizzie at the photography shop the following afternoon. The 'closed' sign hangs in the door. Chelsea and Amber have kindly blocked out a two-hour slot for us. I'm not keen on getting my picture taken, but I'm excited to see what they're going to do with Ellie.

Damn, Lizzie looks beautiful. She's wearing a white summer dress. Her hair is loose with a daisy in the front. A daisy my daughter picked for her.

Lizzie smiles. "Hey."

I look her up and down one more time, making sure she knows that I like what I see. "Hey, yourself."

We stare at each other for longer than would be deemed acceptable for friends. Ellie's gaze bounces between us and, looking down, I can see the grin she's wearing.

"What's put that grin on your face?" I quiz, running my knuckles back and forth over her head.

She grabs my forearm and like a little monkey she

clings on. I raise my arm, lifting her feet off the ground. Playfully, I shake my arm till her vice grip loosens and her feet return to the floor.

"Tell her she looks pretty, Daddy."

Lizzie runs her fingers through her hair, dislodging the daisy. It falls to the ground. I don't know what possesses me, but I bend down and retrieve it and secure it back in her hair.

I step closer. "So my annoying daughter wants me to tell you that you look pretty."

The sun reflects in Lizzie's brown eyes as she gazes up at me. "And do you think I look pretty?"

Ellie giggles. Lizzie looks down, scuffing her shoe against the concrete step of Amber and Chelsea's shop.

I clear my throat. "Yes, I think you look pretty."

She looks up into my eyes, sucking in her lips. Pretty does not do her justice, she's stunning. It's so hard not to kiss her, not to hug her, but I have to put Ellie first. I know the day will come when I'll need to sit her down and tell her that Lizzie and I are an item, but today is not that day.

We jump as the shop door swings open and Chelsea appears.

"Oh, my God," Chelsea says. "I've been watching you for the last ten minutes. Are you going to get your butts in here?"

Ellie tenses and she steps behind me. I turn and my heart tightens in my chest. Ellie is pulling on the skirt of Lizzie's dress to be picked up. Lizzie's face lights up as she scoops her up in her arms. With her fingers she brushes Ellie's hair behind her ears. "Sweetie, this is Chelsea, Amber's sister. Do you remember her from my birthday?"

Ellie saw Chelsea at Lizzie's birthday afternoon, I'm

sure, but I don't recall seeing them speak. Ellie pushes her face into Lizzie's neck. I guess the logic is, if she can't see Chelsea, then Chelsea can't see her. It's my daughter's ingenious way of making herself invisible.

I stroke Lizzie's arm. It feels as though my heart could jump out of my chest and reside between my two girls. This, this is the moment I fall head over heels in love with this woman. If I could pause time and save it in a bottle, I'd bottle this moment.

"Ellie!" a little voice squeals from inside the shop. Ellie's head shoots up as Freja joins Chelsea in the doorway. Ellie begins bouncing up and down in Lizzie's arms until Lizzie's forced to put her down.

Ellie runs over to Freja. Holding hands, they disappear into the shop. When my daughter's out of sight I grab Lizzie's ass and pull her into me. "I can think of a few other places that daisy would look good."

Lizzie draws her lower lip between her teeth. She removes the flower from her hair, stands on her tiptoes and places it behind my ear.

I lean down and brush my lips against hers. There is so much I want to tell her, so much she needs to hear, but not now. I pocket the daisy as a keepsake. Damn, I'm sentimental.

When my gaze returns to Chelsea, she's glancing at her watch and tapping her foot. "When you've finished, we need you inside. We aren't insured to have under-twelves on the premise without a parent present."

"Yes, ma'am," I say, saluting her.

Laughing, Lizzie slaps my arm. "Will you get in the shop already?"

The shop is a modest size. A hair and makeup station

is positioned at the front of the shop next to a small reception area. A section at the back is lined with shelves containing different-sized frames and mugs to be personalized. In the opposite corner is a pull-down projector green screen.

Amber appears out of a back room with a tripod and a camera in her hands. She rests the tripod against the back wall and crouches down so that she's eye level with Ellie. "I hear you're a big fan of *Finding Nemo*?"

Ellie clasps her little hands together under her chin and nods.

Amber motions around the room. "Chelsea will do your hair and makeup. From there, you and Dad will join me at the green screen and we're going to take some pictures. How does that sound?"

My nostrils flare. I don't know how I feel about my five-year-old having makeup on. Amber's face straightens when she looks at me. "Relax, Seth, the makeup is only very light, it's just to even out her skin tone for the pictures. Today is about Ellie, and making her feel like a princess. Or rather a mermaid."

Even out her skin tone? What does that mean? I'm sure it's just something she's made up to shut me up.

Chelsea takes Ellie's hand, which Ellie snatches away.

Chelsea's eyes are wide as she glances at me. "I'm sorry. I didn't hurt her. I mean, maybe my nails caught her. My God, I'm so sorry." She tries to close the gap between herself and Ellie, who at the same time is walking back trying to widen it.

I lift my hand. "It's okay, she has—" I take a long breath in. I've always felt too ashamed to tell people about

Ellie's issues, that somehow it makes me a bad dad. I feel as though admitting she has a problem is making it real and therefore that's all she'll be known for, the kid with separation anxiety, the girl who's broken. But by not telling people about her issues I'm making life harder for her. People don't know how to act around her. I'm causing her unnecessary stress.

Let it go, Seth. Time to man up.

"She has separation anxiety," I spit out with relief.

Chelsea stops walking forward, and Ellie stops walking back. It's as though they've established a mutual ground. They stand looking at each other.

This is the first time I've told someone who's practically a stranger about her condition. It feels like a heavy burden has been lifted from my shoulders. For the first time in fifteen months I've accepted Ellie's issues and confronted my demons. I've never been ashamed of her, but ashamed of me that I couldn't fix her. Sometimes people just can't be fixed, you simply deal with the cards you've been dealt.

Chelsea rubs her hands together. "How about you take a seat with Freja on my special mermaid stools, and I'll do your makeup? Would you like that?"

Mermaid stools? I glance to the makeup station. What is she talking about? They're just white stools. Ellie will never buy into that for a second.

Ellie takes a small step forward. "Can I sit on Lizzie's lap?"

As lovely as that is, I can't expect Lizzie to sit still for God knows how long with Ellie on her lap. No doubt Lizzie will want to have a drink in the back and chat with Amber.

I kneel beside Ellie. "Don't you want to sit on Daddy's lap?"

She shakes her head. "The mermaid stools are for girls; you're not allowed there."

Wow. Well, that's me told. Looks as though the mermaid stools have worked.

Chelsea giggles. "Oh, Daddy will need his makeup doing. He needs to look pretty for the pictures as well."

I make an X with my arms. "I'm sorry, no. There is no way you are putting makeup on me."

Amber reels off the 'even skin tone' bullshit again, and Ellie does a sad puppy-dog face.

"Okay, okay. But we are falling out if you breathe a word of this to Rick or Cole."

Amber, Chelsea, and Lizzie all mimic zipping their mouths.

I flip them the finger discreetly, and by discreetly, I mean using my middle finger to scratch my cheek.

The ladies high-five and Ellie and Freja high-five.

"You're all conspiring against me," I say, throwing my arms up in the air dramatically, causing Ellie and Freja to giggle.

Chelsea applies Ellie's makeup, curls her hair, and pins it up. When she's finished with Ellie, she turns to me.

I close my eyes, leaning my head back. "Just get it over with."

I'm sure I hear a phone capturing a picture, but I've committed now. Chelsea applies a thin layer of foundation to my face using a sponge, and then bloody eyeliner to my eyes. She pulls out a palette of eyeshadow and that's when I draw the line. "No. I'm done."

Ellie and I sit in different positions on the green

screen and wait for Amber to give us the go-ahead that the session has started.

Ellie points. "Daddy, look, an umbrella. Is it going to rain inside?"

Amber laughs. "This is my special umbrella. It will flash when I take a picture." Amber presses the button on the camera and as she said, the umbrella flashes.

She smiles, her face disappearing behind the camera. "You just need to pretend you're underwater. Do you think you can do that?"

If there's one thing Ellie can pull off, it's how to be a fish. I nod. "I think we can be inventive."

"Are you ready?" she asks, her finger poised over the button.

"We are," I say, holding Ellie up in the air. She puffs out her cheeks as if she's holding her breath. I've got to admit, she's quite the natural in front of a camera. It doesn't take long before Freja joins us, their summer dresses opening like parasols as they twirl one another around.

I glance at Lizzie, who's standing at the reception desk next to Chelsea. I know they're talking about me from the way Lizzie blushes and looks away.

"Hey, Lizzie, want in on one of the photos?"

She walks over and joins us for several pictures. Her hand finds its way into mine, and when the girls are lying flat on their stomachs kicking their legs that's when I kiss her. The kiss lasts seconds. I hear the camera click, see the flash under my eyelids and pull away. Lizzie looks around the room as though feeling all eyes are on her.

"Group picture?" Lizzie calls, beckoning Chelsea over.

Running like a duck in her high heels, Chelsea hurries over. Amber secures her camera on the tripod and sets the timer. I wrap my arms around Ellie's and Freja's waists and lift them up. Lizzie stands directly in front of me, Chelsea and Amber either side.

"Say cheese," Amber says, turning her face to the side and puckering out her lips.

Lizzie relaxes back into me, her head pressed against my chest. I don't see the camera, I don't see the shop, I don't see anything. Just her. My baby balanced on my hip, my woman in front of me. Surely this is too good to be true.

After the session finishes, Amber, Ellie and Freja sit together looking over some of the digital images on the camera. With a pen and paper in her lap, Amber makes a note of Ellie's favourites.

Ellie presses her finger on the small screen. "Can I have that one?"

Amber smiles. "I've got to load it on Photoshop first and tweak the background."

Ellie shakes her head. "I want it like that."

"Sure." Amber disappears into the back room and appears moments later with the photograph, which Ellie grabs, hugging it to her chest. "I'll upload the edited images onto the iPad and drop it off at Lizzie's when I've finished work."

"You're all welcome to stop by for drinks after," Lizzie says.

Amber smiles big. "I'd like that."

Chapter Twenty-Five

Lizzie

After the photoshoot we decide to grab lunch at a small pub. From there we head to the park, where the three of us sit side by side on the swings. We have a contest who can swing the highest. Ellie wins.

At four pm, we make it back to mine. Perfect timing, as the painters will be finishing work soon and we will have the house to ourselves.

I stand on the doorstep, gazing at the lock.

Seth stands behind me, resting his chin on my head. "Forget something?"

"You could say that."

My house keys are in the pocket of my jacket, which, of course, is hanging up in the hallway. Technically I've locked myself out, but lucky for me, the workers and Rick are inside. I raise my hand, about to press the doorbell when Ellie tugs on my dress. "Can I?"

I glance at the white button and down to Ellie. "Sure, sweetie." The moment I lift her off the ground she lunges forwards and presses the doorbell. With Ellie in my arms, Seth wraps his around me.

We wait for a beat. I can hear voices and footsteps from inside. The front door finally swings open, and Rick stands looking out. His gaze roves over the three of us.

"Quite the little family," he says with a smug smile.

My grin widens. It'd be a dream to call these two incredible humans my family. Seth must feel the same. He stands tall, his arm tightening around me as though he's claiming me. Ellie pushes her face into my neck, and I feel the need to squeeze her into me. I want her to know I'm here for her and always will be.

Seth rolls his shoulders, puffing out like a bull. "So what?"

"So nothing," Rick shoots back, crossing his arms over his chest. I know their exchange is light-hearted from the mischievous glint in Rick's eyes. It's a battle of who has the best poker face. Rick leans forwards, squinting at Seth. "Bro, are you wearing guyliner?"

Seth's gaze shoots to me.

I bat my eyelids. "I'm sorry, I didn't notice."

He gives me that 'you're talking total bullshit' look.

I smile sweetly. "It kind of suits you."

I've never seen Seth move so fast. He pushes past Rick and bolts up the stairs. The bathroom door slams shut.

Sure, I could have mentioned it to Seth at the pub when he went to order our meals, I could have mentioned it at the park when he bought our ice creams, but it amused me to say nothing.

I step onto the hessian mat. Ellie shuffles behind me, clutching my dress, as workmen pass us in the hall. When they eventually make their way upstairs, I reach my hand out. "Come on, sweetie, you can come out, they've gone."

Her face inches out from behind my legs. She stands straight. She takes a small step towards Rick, placing her hands on her hips. "I've got makeup because I'm a mermaid."

Rick crouches down, gazing into her eyes. "Well, I think you make a damn good mermaid. Though I can't say the same about your old man."

His face straightens when I shake my head.

"Sorry, Lizzie, back to business. Your bedroom is nearly finished, and I even made your bed."

"What, seriously?" I have to literally pinch myself. For the first time in weeks I've got my own bed to sleep in, not that uncomfortable sofa bed.

"I only speak truth," Rick says, dusting down his shoulders. "I just have to finish assembling your bedroom furniture and we're good to go."

Ellie seems to have grown bored with our conversation. Yawning loudly, she kicks her shoes off and runs into the lounge. She huddles up on the easy chair and pulls the folded photograph from the breast pocket in her blue dress. Ellie said it was a secret and refused to show either me or Seth the image she asked Amber to print.

"I best get back to it." Rick pulls a screwdriver from his work pouch and rushes up the stairs. I remove my shoes and join Ellie in the lounge.

I sit on the edge of the settee, wishing Rick would hurry up. I bounce up and down on the cushion. I am not going to miss sleeping on this old thing. I can only imagine snuggling on a new mattress, not having springs poking into me every time I turn over.

Seth, now makeup-free, peers around the door. He gives me the thumbs up. "The painters are done; they're loading their van as we speak."

I clap my hands together. "Ellie, do you want to be the first person to jump on my bed? Mess it up a little?"

Seth raises a brow. "I could mess it up a little."

I smile but say nothing.

"Yes, I do," Ellie squeals, bouncing up and down on the chair. I smile. She really is so sweet.

The cushion dips as Seth sits by my side. His eyes are a little bloodshot and blotchy from where I gather he's been scrubbing off the eyeliner. I can't let him see me laugh, so glance out of the window, focusing on a long-haired man who balances stepladders over his shoulder. He's followed closely by another man who's holding paint tins. Ellie runs over and props her elbows on the window-sill.

I'm excited to see my bedroom but hope the loft room has been fitted with laminate flooring. Finally, I will have my very own art studio, a perfect room to paint in. I can create all sorts—with brushstrokes of oil, watercolours or pastels I can bring the world to life.

I envision my wooden easel besides the window with its beautiful sea view. I feel inspired to paint.

I think back to last week when Ellie and I created the Nemo mosaic. I think about how much fun we had together. There's an artist inside her, I just know it.

"Hey, how do you fancy painting together one of these days? I'm sure you'll love my art studio."

She jumps up and down. "Can I, Daddy, can I?"

"Of course you can," Seth says.

Doors slam. The painters are getting into their van.

Ellie turns her attention back to the window, watching them drive away. This gives Seth just long enough to reach over the cushions and squeeze my fingers, followed by his warm lips stealing the briefest of kisses.

"Are you ready to see your bedroom?" Rick calls down.

I smile at Ellie. "Hey, are you ready to mess up my bed? I think a good old-fashioned pillow fight is in order."

I lead the way, and like a miniature convoy we walk up to the second floor.

"Stay close, Ellie, some of the paint is still wet," I say, about to walk across the landing into the master room.

"Up here," Rick calls.

I look to Seth, who shrugs. We carry on up to the loft. I figure they're using the free space to store stuff. I freeze on reaching the threshold. My bed has been assembled and positioned in the middle of the room, the boxes containing my bedroom furniture have been opened, and pieces of wood and fixing have been laid in neat piles. One of my bedside tables has been partially assembled, and instruction manuals litter the floor. With my mouth open, I step onto the laminate flooring.

Ellie wastes no time running and jumping on the bed.

I try to blink away the tear that's threatening to fall. "Rick, this is—"

"Amazing. I know, right?"

I rub my temples. "Rick, this is supposed to be my art studio." My excitement swims in a pool of disappointment, and I could burst into tears.

Rick clicks his fingers, pointing his index finger in my direction. "Very funny."

"Rick, I'm serious."

"But I heard Seth saying—" He stops talking and studies me for a beat. He blows out, scratching his head. "Oh, shoot, sorry, Lizzie. I promise I'll sort it tomorrow."

I sigh but can't help but smile seeing Ellie jumping up and down on the mattress. She's holding a pillow and swings it towards Seth's head. He dodges, grabs a pillow from the bed and uses it as a shield.

"Lizzie, help," she squeals.

I blink, looking away as my eyes fill with tears. It's not only Seth who wants me, Ellie does too. I'm becoming part of something very special. I feel as though two have just become three and I'm no longer an outsider.

Rick gathers the unassembled furniture and stacks it up against the wall.

Panting, Seth looks at Rick, who's methodically placing fixings in the correct bags. "Looks like you've built up a sweat. Do you fancy a beer to cool down?"

Rick flips Seth the finger but doesn't need asking twice. The men head downstairs.

Ellie sits on the bed; I walk over and join her. "Do you like the colour I chose for the walls?"

She glances around the room, scrunching her nose. "It's okay."

"Just okay?"

"Something's missing."

I laugh. Something is missing—my easel for one, my paints for another. "Go on," I prompt.

Her blue eyes widen. "It's the fishes, fishes live in the sea."

I look around. "And I suppose the blue walls are the sea."

She claps her hands. "I want fishes."

How can I magic fish?

I smile and jump from the bed. I turn over a blue instruction manual. There's writing on one side, but the back is blank. A blunt pencil lies nearby. Ellie slides off the bed and is kneeling by my side.

Her eyes are filled with interest as I begin to sketch. Nemo comes to life before her eyes.

She snatches the manual from me and hugs it to her chest. "I love it. Can we colour him in?"

I stand, dusting down my dress. "Sure, just not right now. I need to find my crayons. When I do you can help me."

Ellie wraps her arms around my thighs.

We turn, hearing footsteps on the stairs. Amber and Freja appear in the doorway. Amber opens her handbag and pulls out an iPad.

I look past them. "Is Chelsea with you?"

She shakes her head. "She had plans." Tucking her long blonde hair behind her ears, Amber sits on the edge of the bed. "Do you want to take a look?"

The girls sit either side of her. I sit beside Ellie; she crawls onto my lap. I wrap my arms around her, holding her small body against me. I'm enjoying the closeness. It feels so natural. Maybe one day we can be a family.

Ellie pulls my arm. "Look at that one, Lizzie."

I glance down at the screen. Ellie and Seth are standing in a three-dimensional image. The green screen they were photographed in has been replaced by a crystal-blue ocean. Nemo is kissing Ellie's nose, Dory is in Seth's open hand, and a school of fish are in the distance.

"Wow, Amber, that looks amazing."

She nods. "Thank Photoshop."

Ellie leans forward, flicking though the images. "I want that one," she says with complete certainty.

Before I get a chance to look at the photo she selected, Amber hugs the device to her chest. I'm about to demand she show me when Rick calls up. "The pizza is here."

Ellie and Freja race ahead. When the girls have finished eating, Seth grabs Ellie's toy box from the lounge and hauls it upstairs to the loft room.

Rick eats the last slice of pizza. The four of us sit in the lounge chatting and drinking. We don't feel like friends, we feel like two couples, meeting for the evening whilst our daughters play together upstairs. I know Ellie isn't biologically mine, but that doesn't stop the strong maternal feelings I'm experiencing when I'm around her.

We take it in turns checking on the girls. By nine pm we can no longer hear their echoed voices and the floorboards above stop creaking. Rick goes up to check on Freja and returns moments later with her asleep in his arms.

"Ellie?" Seth questions.

Rick tilts his head to the side, closing his eyes.

Amber stands, finishing her glass of tonic water. "Guess it's time we call it a night."

Rick and Amber bundle Freja into her booster and we stand in the doorway and wave them off. I can feel Seth's body pressing against me. When the car pulls off the driveway he reaches over my shoulder and slowly closes the door. His arms snake around my waist and he turns me round to face him.

He tugs at the hem of my dress. "This has been driving me crazy all night."

He places a hand either side of me, trapping me against the door. His lips press against my neck, his tongue making small circles before he licks and sucks the bare skin. He pushes his groin against me, his cock deliciously hard. My sex is throbbing, and instinctively we begin grinding against each other.

Who knew dry-humping could feel so good?

I cry out. Seth places a hand over my mouth.

"Do you think you can be quiet?" he breathes into my ear.

No.

"Mmm-hmm." I nod, but I know I'm a terrible liar.

He backs away, readjusting the waistband of his jeans. "Fuck. We can't, not with Ellie upstairs. I should call for a taxi."

"Why don't you stay? I'll go check on her if you pull out the sofa-bed. We can snuggle up in bed and watch a film."

He rubs his hand over his beard, then stands on the bottom stair, his head tilted slightly as if trying to listen. "Okay. But I'll go and join her in bed when the film finishes. She's co-slept with me since her mum left, she can't wake up in a strange place alone."

Chapter Twenty-Six

Seth

I wake up next to Ellie. She's asleep, asleep between me and Lizzie. I sit bolt upright. Rubbing my eyes, I glance around. The three of us are in the lounge lying on the sofa-bed. Last night's wine glasses remain on the mantel next to the clock, which tells me it's six-thirty am.

Fuck. I clasp the blanket in my fist, squeezing it tightly. How could I have been so damn irresponsible? I didn't join Ellie in the loft room in the double bed as planned. I specifically said I was going to be there when she woke up.

This is the last thing I need. It will only confuse Ellie. I've never had another woman in bed with me, that is except for Ellie's mother. Will she think Lizzie is her new mum?

I look at my little girl, who is fast asleep. I play out all the scenarios in my head. I loose the blanket and take a deep breath. I just need to get out of bed and carefully pick her up. I've lifted her many times when she's been asleep and she's not woken up.

Okay, I can do this.

I'll carry her up to the loft room where she'll wake up next to me. Problem solved.

Holding my breath, I push the blanket aside, pivot my body so that my legs are on the floor. Good, she's still asleep. I slide one arm under her legs and the other under her neck. I pull her against my chest and slowly begin to lift.

"Hi, Daddy."

Jesus fuck almighty. I never understood the saying 'to jump out of one's skin' until now. My sudden movement causes a half-asleep Ellie to become fully awake.

I glance at Lizzie, who is sitting up watching our exchange. Her eyes are wide. Shaking her head, she places her palm over her face.

Ellie looks from me to Lizzie. "Is it time to get up? I want pancakes." Ellie wriggles out of my arms and saunters her way to the kitchen.

"Seth," Lizzie says, reaching for my arm, which I pull away. She looks hurt.

"Shit, Lizzie, I'm sorry." Standing in my boxers, I scramble to put on yesterday's clothes that are lying on the floor.

Lizzie jumps out of bed—thank God she put her pyjamas on last night. She uses her fingers to brush her hair into place, which doesn't work. It seems her bobbed hair is a classic bedhead. Every time I've seen her first thing in the morning it has been totally wild.

She drops her hand and uses it to rub the top of her arm. "I'm, erm, I'm going to have a shower."

"You have to make pancakes first; Daddy always

burns them."

I turn in the exact moment I'm pulling my trousers up over my thighs. "Lizzie, you don't have to—"

"It's okay, I'd like to. I might not have pancake mix, but I can make you an omelette, if you'd like?"

Ellie nods and holds her hand out for Lizzie. I catch her glance as she walks past me and joins Ellie.

The morning is surprisingly normal. I was so worried that it would be awkward, but it's anything but. Ellie helps Lizzie crack the eggs and cut the mushrooms. I even get involved tossing the omelette, pancake-style. Every so often my arms find their way around Lizzie's waist, and she mirrors my gesture.

Lizzie, Ellie and I just work. I never envisioned letting another woman in our VIP club for two, but the more time I spend with Lizzie, the more I see her being part of my life, our lives.

I plate up the omelettes and carry them over to the red breakfast bar where we sit. I drum my fingers on the top and sigh.

Lizzie gazes up from her plate. "Is everything okay?"

"Not really, no."

"What's wrong?"

I glance around at the high-gloss red units, shaking my head. "I hate the colour of your kitchen."

Her knife and fork clang as she drops them on her plate. "That wasn't funny."

I bring my index finger and thumb together, leaving a small gap between. "It was a little funny."

She folds her arms. "I like the colour red."

"Yeah, I got that impression when I stepped into your lounge and took a look at the colour of your furniture. All you're missing is a damn disco ball."

Lizzie snort-laughs into her glass of orange juice. El-lie laughs, though I'm sure she doesn't know why. Fuck it, I start to laugh.

We eat our omelettes in total silence, though when we lock eyes with one another we laugh. Knowing Ellie can't see, I reach under the table and place my hand over Liz-zie's leg. Her hand rests over mine, and we lace our fin-gers together. I want to bring up this morning to Ellie, but if I do, I'd be making a big deal out of something Ellie hasn't even mentioned. I decide to say nothing, well, at least until she asks.

"I best head off," I say, pushing the chair out from under the breakfast bar. The time is approaching seven-thirty am. Rick will be here any moment to begin the car-peting. Not just that, Darcy will be waiting at home to look after Ellie.

Lizzie stands and helps Ellie off the ladder-backed chair. "Will I see you later?"

I shrug. "Maybe."

I send Ellie upstairs to retrieve her shoes. She returns minutes later clasping the photo Amber printed off for her yesterday.

"Are you going to show Daddy the picture?"

Ellie doesn't answer, but her hold tightens.

Lizzie stands in the open doorway watching as I strap Ellie into the van. Shutting the passenger's side door, I blow Lizzie a kiss, which she catches. I get into my van feeling like the richest guy in the world. I honk my horn and reverse off the driveway and watch her get smaller and smaller in the side mirrors.

Ellie's quiet on the drive home. In my periphery I can

see the green background of the photo she's looking at. Every time I turn my head to steal a glance, she angles the photo away from me.

I wasn't going to mention this morning to her, but I can't say nothing. My daughter's mental health is paramount to me. I want to know how she's feeling, I need to know.

Flicking the indicator, I clear my throat. "Ellie."

She folds the photograph unevenly, makes a sort of square and places it in the breast pocket of the dress. "Yes, Daddy."

"So, last night you fell asleep with Freja, because she's your special friend. Well, Daddy fell asleep with Lizzie."

"Because she's your special friend."

"Right." This is easier than I thought.

"Lizzie is my special friend too, so does that mean I get to fall asleep with her when we have our next sleepover?"

"Yes." *Wait, what?*

I pull into a side road when it registers what she asked. I can't afford the lines to get blurred, it's all about managing expectations. "No, no more sleepovers at Lizzie's. Last night was a one-off."

She scrunches up her face. "Why not?"

"Because—" I falter on my words.

Why the hell not?

How do I explain in a way a five-year-old would understand? I ponder for a few minutes. She sits in silence awaiting my answer.

"Because I said so." Oh, my God, I've turned into my mother.

"That's not fair." Crossing her arms, she turns in her chair so that her back is toward me.

Well, that didn't go exactly as I'd hoped. Maybe it would have been better if I had said nothing.

I turn into my street. Darcy's car is parked on the driveway, of course it is.

Ellie unfastens her seatbelt, and I wrap my fingers around her wrist. "Hey, baby, do you think the sleepover at Lizzie's could be our little secret?"

She bites her bottom lip and she looks up as if giving my request some thought. "On one condition."

On one condition? What the hell's my sister letting her watch on her iPad?

I eye her speculatively. "Go on."

"I want a Dory teddy to go with Nemo."

"Done."

The last thing I need is a lecture off my sister. I'll tell her about me and Lizzie in my own time, on my terms.

I jump out of the van and I unlock the front door. Darcy is waiting in the hallway, sitting on the bottom step.

Here goes.

She's sitting with one leg crossed over the other, rocking her foot from side to side. "Your beds haven't been slept in. Where have you been?"

I think of a few believable scenarios, like we got up early and went for a drive, or Ellie felt unwell and I took her to the pharmacy to grab some medication. I open my mouth to reply—

"We had a sleepover at Lizzie's," Ellie announces, clearly forgetting our little deal.

Darcy's hazel eyes narrow. The pace she's rocking her foot increases. She leans forward, resting her chin in her hands. "And where did you sleep?" She raises an accusing brow.

Ellie glances at me and back to Darcy.

Don't do it, kid.

"I slept with Daddy and Lizzie."

Ellie is completely oblivious to the shit show she's created for me. Humming, she skips past us and into the lounge. I can't be angry with her. I instilled into her how important it is to tell the truth.

I toss my keys onto the floor and make my way into the kitchen. I can hear Darcy's steps as she follows closely behind. I'm waiting for it, the moment she starts pecking my head.

Let's get it over with. I turn and, were Darcy taller, we would be standing nose to nose.

"What the hell do you think you're playing at? Don't you think Ellie is damaged enough?"

I walk around her, grab the OJ from the fridge and drink from the carton. I do this purposely knowing Darcy drinks orange juice when she's minding Ellie. I swish it around my mouth a few times before placing it back in the fridge and close the door. I casually lean against the worktop and fold my arms.

Darcy places her hand on her hip and takes a long breath in.

The doorbell chimes.

I quirk my lip. "Saved by the bell."

My joke isn't well received. She flares her nostrils. As I jog out of the kitchen, I turn around to see her tipping the orange juice down the sink and tossing the empty carton into the bin.

I don't bother looking through the peep hole when I

get to the front door. Shit, if it's a sales guy I'll invite him in for a coffee. I unlock the latch and open the door.

My eyes go wide, and for once I'm rendered speechless.

Cole's standing on my doorstep. His face is flushed and his jaw is set.

"Cole—"

He lunges forward, grabs my t-shirt and yanks me into him so that we're nose to nose. I can't miss the strong scent of alcohol on his breath. "I should rearrange your fucking face," he seethes.

I shove my head forward so our foreheads crash together. "I'd like to see you try."

Our gazes are locked on one another and the intensity in his stare is bordering on erratic.

"Can you take this outside, boys? There's a child inside." My sister's voice slices through the tension, and the grip Cole has on the collar of my t-shirt loosens. Darcy is standing in the doorway; her expression is hard as she watches our exchange.

Plastering on a smile, he wraps his arm around my neck, squeezing. "Nothing's going on, Darce, just a heart-to-heart amongst friends."

I return his gesture, wrapping my arm around his shoulder. I squeeze his neck, making sure to match his force.

"Seth was just going to invite me in for a drink, weren't you?"

I want to tell him to go home and sober up, but he's got something to say, and I should hear him out.

Darcy shifts so that she's occupying the centre of the doorway, making it harder for Cole to enter.

I wag my finger in the air. "It's okay, sis."

Reluctantly, she steps aside. Cole removes his arm from around my neck, and I lead the way into the house. Darcy closes the door behind us. "In the kitchen. I'll keep Ellie in the lounge," she tells us.

Cole barges past me, making his way into the kitchen. I follow close behind, shutting the door.

Cole leans against the worktop, crossing his arms over his chest. I'm not going to patronise him and ask what this is about. I rub my hand over the back of my neck and let out a deep sigh. "Look, man—"

"I don't want to fucking hear it. My little sister, how could you?"

With clenched fists, he spins around and thumps the kitchen cabinet directly behind him. His fist makes a dent. He cries out, immediately shakes his hand, cradling it in the other.

"I bet my face wouldn't have hurt that much," I say, grabbing an ice pack from the freezer, tossing it in his direction. He makes no attempt to catch it, and it falls to the floor. "Mate—"

"I'm not your fucking mate," he spits out. "I'm here to give you this."

He paces forwards, and I clench my fists in readiness. His hand disappears in his pocket and he pulls out a chequebook.

Well, that was unexpected.

He opens it and tears out a cheque which has been pre-signed and dated. He shoves it against my chest. "A blank cheque. There's fifteen thousand in that account. I trust we have an understanding."

When I don't take it from him, he tucks it into the

253

collar of my t-shirt.

Is he paying me to break up with Lizzie? "Do you pay all her boyfriends off?"

He shakes his head as if brushing off my comment. "The moment you pay the cash into your account you are under contract. Breaching the contract will mean the money will need to be paid straight back to me, with interest."

I mock-laugh. "What makes you think your money interests me?"

Cole leans into me. His cheek briefly glides across mine. "I could make things very difficult for you, Seth. The mates' rate rent I charge, doubled. The new business venture, gone. Your share in the company, dissolved. I'd be very, very careful if I were you. You do not want to make an enemy out of me."

He taps my cheek several times. I lean back to look directly into his eyes. Eye contact sometimes is more powerful than a brawl. It portrays complete and utter honesty and I'd rather him see my soul bleed than my nose. I hope my eyes speak a thousand truths that I'm too chickenshit to say aloud.

I love her. I'm in love with her. I can't, I won't lose her. "Mate, we've been friends for over thirty years—"

"I've told you already, I'm not your fucking mate." His stare is dark, demonic. He's so angry. There is more behind his anger than me sleeping with Lizzie. He takes a step back. "Don't even think about repeating our little conversation to Lizzie. Remember we have no formal tenancy agreement; you are living in my house as a friend and paying me peanuts for the privilege. If you refuse to leave it will be considered breaking and entering and will be a police matter."

I flip Cole the finger. "Squatters' rights, motherfuck-er."

"Good luck with that one," Cole says, donning his imaginary cap and dipping his chin.

Sarcastic piece of shit.

Cole is fully aware of the law of the land. He can't kick us out of our home, he knows it and I know it. But he's drunk and he's saying anything to gain control of the situation.

"Give Ellie and Darcy my regards." With that, he walks from the kitchen.

The second the front door closes Darcy re-enters the kitchen.

I'm ready for round two.

I take a deep breath. "So, how much did you hear?"

"Enough." She opens a folded piece of card, the fold-ed photograph, the one that Ellie has been guarding for the past twenty-four hours. Darcy glances at it before holding it up for me to see. The background is completely green, unedited. It's a picture of Lizzie and I kissing. Ellie and Freja are lying on their stomachs on the floor, oblivious to what was happening behind them. Of course this was the picture Ellie selected. It's what Ellie wants, Lizzie in our lives. Shit, it's what I want.

Darcy places the photo on the worktop behind me. "Anna only wants ten thousand pounds from you, and we get to keep Ellie. Think about what you could do with the rest of that money." She reaches up, takes my jaw between her hands. "Tell me, Seth, is Lizzie worth more to you than fifteen thousand pounds?"

This is a no-brainer for me. I know I've not been see-ing Lizzie for long, and we aren't even official, but no one can put a price on love, and I love the girl.

Darcy's eyes narrow when I don't answer. "Is Lizzie worth losing your little girl forever? Anna could get full custody, take her to Australia and you'd never see her again."

I shake my head out of Darcy's hold. "Anna's bluffing, Darce. She's been absent for all this time, courts won't take her seriously."

"Are you prepared to take the risk?"

Chapter Twenty-Seven

Lizzie

I've spent the day watching Netflix and making drinks for Rick and Dave whilst they fit the carpet upstairs. I recognised Dave the moment he arrived, the bald guy from the night out at the Golden Kite. He told me how he and the redhead hooked up that evening and are still together. I wanted to tell him about me and Seth, but news travels fast and I figure Cole should hear it from me.

After binge-watching eight episodes of *Mystery of Tess*, it's time to stretch my legs. I contemplate going for a jog, but not before checking my phone. I scoop it up from the coffee table and press the button, expecting to see a notification. Nothing. Just the time and my screensaver, a selfie of me, Amber and Chelsea.

I texted Seth to see if he and Ellie got home okay after our morning together. He hasn't replied. In fact, Seth hasn't called or texted all day. I stare at the screen, willing a text, a call, something. I sign onto my social media account and find a message from my brother.

Cole: *Hi, sis, lost my phone. I'm home nursing the hangover from hell. I'll come and see you tomorrow.*

Me: *Are you okay? Where have you been?*

Cole: *See you tomorrow.*

The green circle that tells me he's online disappears. Strange, Cole is never short with me. I hope he's okay. I make my way out of the lounge and head upstairs. Rick is sitting on the landing fitting the carpet, and Dave is assembling the wardrobe in my bedroom.

Standing on the top step, I glance down at Rick. "I'm going to head out. Would you like a tea or coffee before I leave?"

The floorboards creak as Dave appears in the doorway of the master bedroom. Dave nods but Rick shakes his head. His eyes are wide and it's as though he's trying to tell Dave something.

Rick clears his throat. "No, thank you, we're nearly finished. We will have a drink at the pub on the way home."

"Oh, that's right," Dave agrees, and winks at Rick. Clearly Dave has not yet mastered the art of being subtle.

I fold my arms. "Okay, what's going on?"

Rick shrugs. "I have no idea what you're talking about."

"Rick." My tone is sharp.

Rick forces a smile. "All I know is that Seth wants to talk to you. He said it was important and he wants us to hurry up."

I purse my lips. "He said that?"

He drops the carpet he's working on and blows out as though I'm inconveniencing him. "His exact words were 'hurry up and fuck off.'"

"What could be so important he'd need to tell me in person?"

"Shit, I don't know, Lizzie. Give us an hour and we'll be out of your hair."

I spend the next hour trying to watch another episode on Netflix, but instead watch the clock.

Does he want to stop seeing me? What have I done wrong? He's going to break up with me, I just know it.

Memories of our time together flash in my mind, from the night out, the park and beach with Ellie, the auction, when we slept together. The past few weeks have been amazing. Now all of a sudden cold reality hits me that it could be all over. I look down at my phone and as I do a solitary tear escapes from the corner of my eye, the tiny droplet splashing on the screen.

I have such a bad feeling bubbling up in the pit of my stomach. I can feel bile creeping its way to my throat, which I swallow down.

After the longest sixty-eight minutes of my life, I hear movement. I spring up from the settee and meet Rick and Dave as they hurry down the stairs. I make my way into the hall and catch up with Rick just before he slips out.

Rick doesn't stop. He's still pulling his shoes on when he pulls the front door open. He and Dave hurry out.

I grab his sleeve. "Rick."

Halfway out of the door, he turns. "Seth is on his way. Now. I really must go."

My eyes go wide. I'm silently begging for an explanation. "Should I be worried?"

He exhales. "Honestly, I have no idea, but he didn't sound in a good place."

Rick looks at me, and I stand staring back. It feels as though he's driven a knife straight through my chest and into my heart. He wiggles his arm free, and I release him.

"I'm sorry, Lizzie, I've got to go. I have a pint with my name written all over it." He smiles as though trying to lessen the growing tension between us.

I close the door behind him and stand with my back pressed against it. Banging my head against the solid wood, I slowly slide my way down so that I'm sitting on the floor. I bend my legs up to my chest, wrapping my arms around my knees.

I've been so excited about my bedroom and now it's finally done, I couldn't care less. All I can think about is how I've been floating on cloud nine and that cloud is slowly disappearing from under my feet and I'm about to fall.

My ass stays firmly rooted to the spot. I never realised how thin the door was until now. Sitting in total silence, I can hear traffic, the sound of children laughing, dogs barking. I hear the slam of a door, shingle crunching underfoot until finally the doorbell rings.

I don't know if I want to move, I don't know if I can move. I question if it's better to live in my ignorance, in the reality where everything is fine between me and Seth. To live happily in the moment right before he's about to break my heart.

The doorbell rings for a second time. I wait, holding my breath, feeling like I'm in limbo. The waiting and not knowing is torture. I stand, spin around and open the door.

Tears forge tiny streams down my cheeks, and I'm

scared to look at him. But the moment I do, the moment we make eye contact, he lunges forward, crashing his lips into mine.

He walks forward, forcing me to walk back. I continue walking back until my back crashes against the kitchen worktop. His tongue is in my mouth, his hands are gripping my ass and he sits me on the cold surface.

"Seth," I moan into his mouth and pull away.

His eyes are bloodshot, his lips are swollen. "Yes?" He pushes the material of my dress up, giving himself easy access.

I tense as his hand nears my sex, and I push him back. "What the actual fuck? You've not contacted me all day. Rick says you have something you want to talk to me about. I spent over an hour thinking all sorts, thinking you were going to end it with me."

Seth's eyes go wide, and he places his hand over his mouth. "Did you just say the F-word?"

I frown. "No. Yes? Did I?" I shake my head. "Stop changing the subject. If this is break-up sex you can forget it."

He takes small, calculated steps towards me. Placing his hands on my thighs, he reaches right up to my underwear. He doesn't attempt to reach in, nor does he withdraw.

"No, Lizzie, I have no intention of breaking up with you. It's not going to be easy, and we have a shit-ton of hurdles to get over, but in the end I see us, us and Ellie. I love you, Lizzie."

Tears fall again, though this time they're tears of happiness. "I love you."

I take his hands in mine, pulling them so that they're

wrapped around my waist. His erection presses into my sex, and with my legs wrapped around his ass I pull him closer, needing him closer.

I feel like I've been hit with a rush of adrenaline. I've never been so hungry for sex before. I push him back and slide down. I'm not gentle, I'm not shy. I grab the buckle of his belt, undo his jeans and yank them down. The head of his cock pokes out of his black boxers, which I also yank down.

I've never performed oral on a man, it was always a no-go with Gary, but with Seth, I don't even ask him. I work my hand up and down the length of him, feeling his velvety skin under my fingers. With my gaze focused on him, I drop to my knees.

"Lizzie, you don't have to—"

I angle his cock so that it's inches from my mouth. "Shut the fuck up." I say, slowly licking the tip. It's saltier than I imagined, and tastes a little of soap, making me think he showered before coming here.

"I love it when you talk dirty." He groans. Closing his eyes, he tilts his head back.

His cock is thick, it's long, it's intimidating. For a beat the old Lizzie tells me not to do this, but I'm done being her. In the bedroom, I like this Lizzie better. And with that, I open my mouth and move slowly down, all the way down until I'm close to gagging.

Okay, that's my limit.

I begin moving my head up and down, occasionally releasing his cock so that I can run my lips around the head. I don't know what I'm doing, but I don't care. I jerk him off at the same time he's in my mouth, I massage his balls, I do everything our bodies are silently telling me to do. I can feel him harden even more, his hips begin undulating, and in no time at all his fingers are fisted in my hair and he begins moving my head quicker.

"Fuck, Lizzie, I'm going to—" He pauses for a beat, his grip loosening in my hair. "Shit, I mean, you can stop now if you don't want to."

I know what he's asking, and I don't want to stop. I grab his ass and I push myself to the limit, pushing past that gag reflex, taking all I can.

This is the green light he's been waiting for. His fingers tighten in my hair and he picks up the pace, forward and back. His cock is rock hard in my mouth. I can taste the saltiness of pre-come. He lets out one final groan before he explodes into my mouth, strong, confident squirts that I swallow.

I glance up and he glances down. Slowly I rub the back of my hand over my mouth and get to my feet.

I'm waiting for him to pull his trousers up. I figure now he's come, it's all over.

I thought wrong.

He turns me around, pushes my dress up so that it's over my head. He pushes my knickers aside and begins rubbing his cock around my opening.

He retreats. "Fuck."

I lift my head and peer round. "What's wrong?"

He points down. "I forgot the condoms."

"Oh." Is one syllable really all I can say? I've never had sex without protection before. Sure, I'm on birth control, but I don't want to take any chances.

I smile, pointing above my head. "In the medicine cupboard, I have condoms in there."

Thank you, Amber.

He slaps my ass. "Upstairs," he demands.

Laughing, I make my way to the stairs. I can hear his feet as he runs behind me. I make it to around the middle step when he grabs my waist. I turn, my ass landing with a thud.

Seth is directly below. Taking my foot in his hand, he slowly kisses his way up my inner leg.

"You don't need these," he says, reaching for my underwear, pulling them down. He throws them over his shoulder into the hallway. He buries his nose into my sex, then fucks me mercilessly with his tongue.

Damn, this has never felt so good. My legs are shaking around his head. He stops and begins kissing his way up my stomach.

"You don't need this," he says, pulling my dress up over my head. He kisses a path between the valley of my breasts, all the way to my ear. "You definitely don't need this." He lifts me up, releasing the fastenings of my bra, watching as my breasts fall free. With his finger rubbing my clit, he licks and sucks my nipple. "I want you to come for me, Lizzie."

He lowers his head back between my legs, his fingers dipping into me and his tongue licking and sucking my clit.

"Seth," I cry out. My body is on the cliff edge about to fall off when he suddenly retreats.

He takes his sheathed cock in his hand. "I've got to be inside you. Now." It isn't the comfiest position, but he angles my legs up and pushes into me.

"Oh, my God, Seth."

His thrusts are demanding, full of emotion. My desire matches his emotion and with my feet I pull him in, more and more. I want to take every inch of him.

He grabs my ass. I wrap my legs around him. Still inside me, he carries me to my bed.

He lowers me onto the mattress. "Time to christen this, baby."

I reach up, lasso my arms around his neck and pull him down, my nails ripping their way down his back. I want him, long and hard, I want him. The thought of losing him pushes me to the edge of insanity, stripping me of my inhibitions.

We're messy, we're feral, we're frantic and we're perfect.

Our lips lock. I can taste myself in his kiss like I'm sure he can in mine. He thrusts deeper, causing my body to shake uncontrollably. There's a glint in his eyes, satisfaction, and we both ride the wave of my orgasm. When my body has no more to give, he tenses in my embrace and his cock pulsates inside me.

We stay as one for long minutes. He pulls out of me, pulls me to my feet and holds me. Our bodies are sticking together with the sweat we've accumulated with our sexathon, but I don't care.

"I meant it when I said I love you," I mumble.

"Me too."

I glance down, admiring his cock. The condom is hanging off, but I can see it's done its job.

"Just can't get enough of my cock, can you?"

I shake my head. "Nope, I love your cock."

He laughs. "I told you I'd ruin you, and I was right." He kisses my forehead and leaves me to clean up. I jump on the bed, I don't hide under the covers but lie on top of them. I want him to see me, every inch.

The toilet flushes and I can hear him walk along the landing. His smile widens when he sees me. He doesn't reach for his clothes. I lie on my side and he lies directly behind me. I can feel every inch of him and if I'm not mistaken, he has a semi.

He's stroking his fingers up and down my arm as we lie on my bed together and watch the shadows slowly move across the room. With my head now on his chest we just hold one another, love one another. We are one.

I open my eyes; we must have fallen asleep. Dressed, Seth is sitting on the end of the bed. "I've got to go."

I sit up. "Ellie?"

He nods. "Darcy sent me out to take care of something. I didn't expect it'd take me this long."

I laugh. "And did you take care of it?"

An expression skates across his features, and it's one I'm unable to decipher. "I did, just not in the way that she'd hoped." I don't question him further. He stands and blows me a kiss. "See you tomorrow, beautiful."

Chapter Twenty-Eight

Lizzie

With a cup of hot chocolate in my hand I make my way upstairs. Finally, my first night in my own bed, in my room. I've placed the mug on my bedside table and I'm about to get in bed when the doorbell rings. I'm hoping it'll be Seth for round two, but it's nearly ten pm, he'll be in bed with Ellie tucked up next to him.

Dragging my feet, I make my way downstairs and to the door. "Darcy?"

She's wearing a pair of dark blue dungarees, her short hair spiked up. I'm sure it's the first time I've seen her in casual dress. With her thumbs wrapped around the denim straps, she rocks back and forth on her heels. "I knew I couldn't send a boy to do a man's job."

"Excuse me?" I say.

She takes a step forward and instinctively I step back. "I think you and I need to have a little chat." She barges past me and makes her way into the lounge.

Sure, Darcy, come right in, after you.

I close the door and make my way to the lounge, where she's sitting on the settee inspecting her nails.

I stand in the doorway. "To what do I owe the pleasure?"

She glances up from her nails. "I think you know by now that I don't like you."

I hold my hand over my heart and pull the most pathetic puppy-dog face I can. "But we were getting along so well, where did it go so wrong?"

"I'm going to drop the pleasantries."

I snort. "I think you dropped those a long time ago."

I don't know how she does it. She's mastered resting bitch face, or maybe it's just her face, who knows.

"You have to end things with Seth."

"Let me tell you right now that isn't going to happen." I don't sit down, I don't offer her a drink. Instead I turn my back on her and walk towards the front door. Her cue to leave.

"He'll lose Ellie if you don't."

I freeze. My feet feel as though they're rooted to the spot.

"What?" I say, in no more than a whisper.

"Come, sit down, I'll put the kettle on."

I don't feel as though I'm walking, but rather floating. I take a seat in the easy chair opposite and sit in silence as Darcy goes into the kitchen to make us drinks.

Seconds feel like minutes and minutes feel like hours as I wait for her to join me. She re-enters the lounge and puts a steaming cup of tea on the table.

I look up and she winks. "I added a little something stronger to give it a kick."

Robotically, I take the mug and take a sip. I cough as soon as I swallow. Jeez, I'd guess at least half of the contents is whiskey.

I place the mug back on the table and Darcy sits on the settee. Narrowing my eyes, I lean forward. "I'm listening."

"Anna came to see Seth—"

"I know, he told me."

Darcy raises a brow. "Did he tell you she wants to take Ellie to Australia?"

I relax back into the chair and nod. "Yes, he's already told me this." Seth told me about Anna the day after she went to see him. He wasn't concerned. Darcy's overreacting. I smile. "We have no secrets."

Her brows knit together. "Did he tell you she's blackmailing him?"

I feel as though she's stuck a pin in me, and like a balloon, everything I am is seeping out and I'm deflating.

"She wants ten thousand pounds. If she doesn't get the money she is going to apply for full custody of Ellie."

My mouth falls open. "Okay." I run my hands down the length of my pyjama bottoms. "I could speak to the bank, see if I could take money out of the house."

She holds her hand in the air. "My brother wouldn't even consider taking money off you."

I want to argue with her, tell her she's wrong, but she isn't. There is no way Seth would take a penny off me, but surely, I can try. I'll speak to Seth tomorrow; we can get through this, I know we can.

I stand. "Okay, thank you for your concern."

"Sit."

Like a dog I obey. I sink down with my elbows on my

knees, resting my chin in my hands. "What has any of this got to do with my relationship with Seth?"

She steeples her fingers in her lap. "It has everything to do with your relationship with him."

"Why's that?" I challenge with a raised voice.

"Because your brother has offered him fifteen thousand pounds to finish with you, and if Seth doesn't agree Cole is threatening to make them both homeless. Seth will lose everything, the roof over their heads, his business, Ellie, and it'll be all your fault. Now I'm not telling you what to do, but if he loses Ellie because of you, he will never forgive you."

I laugh. "Cole wouldn't do that, I know my brother."

She shakes her head. "Not as well as you think you do."

I pull my phone from my pocket and she grabs my wrist. "If you breathe a word of this to Cole, he'll make them homeless." Releasing me, she stands, dusting her skirt down. "Seth was too much of a coward to tell you. I'm not. Sometimes in life you have to hurt the people you love because you put their needs before your own. I trust you'll make the right decision for Ellie, for Seth."

Chapter Twenty-Nine

Seth

All good things have to come to an end, and a heat wave in England is sadly one of those things. I'm sitting in my lounge. Large raindrops have been hammering against the window for the past hour.

It's unusually quiet in my house today, and, feeling completely relaxed, I leave the TV switched off and enjoy listening to the melodic ticking of the clock.

Darcy offered to take Ellie shopping to get ballet shoes. It seems Freja convinced her to try a dance class. At first Ellie was a bit unsure, but when they told me I could stay and wait in a side room with the other parents, she decided that she wanted to give it a try.

With the house to myself for the first time in a long time, I sit and ponder what to do. I know I can't go see Lizzie. Rick told me Cole has been hanging around and as Cole has been MIA for the past few days, I know she'll want to spend time with her brother. I might be a loved-up motherfucker, but I'm not a selfish one.

I've dropped Lizzie several texts throughout the morning, and it bothers me that I can see she's read them and not replied. I scroll to Rick's name.

Me: *Is Cole still hanging around?*

I drum my fingers on the arm of the settee, go to the kitchen to make a coffee, and watch a forty-five-minute documentary before I get a reply.

Rick: *He's just left.*

I don't know what possesses me, but I call her instead of texting. She answers after the fourth ring.

"Hello." Her voice is muffled.

"You've not been answering your phone."

She blows out. "I'm sorry."

"Are you on your own?" I can hear running water in the background.

"I'm about to jump in the shower, so yes."

Fuck, yeah. Lizzie naked, getting into the shower. The line goes quiet. I can't hear the running water in the background, so assume she's turned the shower off. It's not like Lizzie to be this quiet. "Is everything okay?"

Silence for a beat. I can hear her faint breath from the other end. "I'm sorry, Seth, I can't do this."

"Do what?"

"I can't do any of this. I think we should stop seeing each other."

I don't know what possesses me, but I laugh. Her words only register in my mind when I realise that she isn't laughing with me. She's serious. I spring off the settee and begin pacing up and down. "Yesterday you told me you love me and today we're over? This is Cole, isn't it, is he bribing you?"

"What? No. This has nothing to do with my brother." I can hear her sobs at the end of the phone. "I'm sorry, Seth, but the work on my house has finished and, well, there's no point us dragging this out. It's been fun but I've got to focus on my job. You've got to focus on Ellie. Maybe in another life we could have been happy."

Is she actually serious right now? "Is Ellie too much for you, is that it?" It feels as though my heart is shattering, like it's tearing from each vein and artery and is bleeding out in my chest. I push my feelings aside. "How is this going to affect Ellie?"

"I'm not her mum, Seth, she'll get over me."

Wow, just fucking wow.

I storm upstairs. The doors almost fly off their hinges as I make my way into Ellie's room. "You know the photo Amber printed off of us all is stuck to her bedroom wall. The photo is right beside the taped-up mosaic of Nemo you two did together. This will crush her."

"Seth, I'm sorry, but I think it's easier to do this now than months down the line. Trust me, I'm doing this for you. I'm doing this for Ellie."

"Like hell you are." I can't believe she's splitting up with me, just like that, no explanation, no nothing. I take a deep breath and try to claw back some of my dignity. "Have a good life."

I cut off the call and stare at the phone. How the fuck do I tell Ellie that another woman has abandoned her?

I sit on Ellie's bed and glance up at the pictures taped to her wall. Pictures she wanted to look up at every night before going to bed. The family Ellie clearly wanted, the family I wanted is gone.

I sit tall and think about how I handled the breakup with Anna. Truth is, I didn't. I crumbled. Anna was everything to me. I spent months trying to track her down, months emailing and texting her. Finally it dawned on me one day that she was gone and she wasn't coming back.

Okay, I have to take stock of the positive in my life— my little girl. It's us against the world and I don't need anyone, which reminds me.

I leave my heart in Ellie's bedroom. Looks like I won't be needing it any more. I pull the blank cheque from Cole out of my wallet and consider my options. I unlock my phone and scroll down to my building society app. I know if I do this, there is no going back, but I don't feel as though I have an option. My finger hovers over the call button. I press the screen.

After I've spoken to my bank, I call Anna. The call's diverted to voicemail, and I take a breath, knowing I'm signing my soul over to the devil. "Anna, it's me. It's about the money. We need to talk."

Chapter Thirty

Lizzie

The mug I'm holding slips from my fingers and smashes in the sink. I jump, grabbing my chest.

I facepalm. "Absolutely amazing." I run the tap, ridding the basin of any shards before tossing the broken pieces into the bin. That was my fourth cup of herbal tea in the last couple of hours. The camomile was meant to calm my nerves. The camomile failed.

I drag my feet into the lounge. Sighing, I sit on the chair nearest the window. I purposely face away from the sofa-bed. I can't bear to look at it—it just reminds me of all the special moments Seth and I shared. I can imagine the two of us on the bed together, laughing, sipping wine, lying beneath the covers wrapped up in one another.

My eyes are glazed with tears. The view out of the window is a blur, much like the last seven days have been. A week since I've seen Seth, and incidentally a week that I've isolated myself in these four walls drinking camomile tea and binge-watching Netflix.

After living as a recluse, I conclude it's time to re-enter the rat race called life. Problem is, I've got too used to my own company. I know that I can't do this alone. I stand and take my phone off the mantel. The screen's blank, and it doesn't turn on when I press the button. I turned it off as soon as Seth cut the call ending our conversation, and it's been off ever since. I plug it into the charger and wait for it to load.

I ignore the ream of messages that flash on my screen. Not one is from Seth. When I click onto my contacts, Amber is the first name I see. I press her name, my ear pressed against the screen as I listen to dial tone.

She answers on the sixth ring. "Decided to rejoin the land of the living?"

I coil the charger lead around my finger. "Sorry, I've been preoccupied."

"Preoccupied? Is that all you've got to say for yourself? I haven't heard from you in a week, you've not answered the door when I came round, you've not returned my calls, what the hell?"

"I can't go into that now, but I'd really like someone to talk to. Are you free today?"

"Depends."

"On what?"

"If you're going to tell me why you split up with Seth." Her tone isn't exactly sharp, but there's a hint of agitation in her voice.

I scratch my head. "Wow, news travels fast."

Of course it does, she's seeing Rick. Rick is one of Seth's best friends. I feel awful for how things ended with Seth, but I know I did the right thing. "How is he?"

She sighs down the phone. "How do you think? You

broke up with the guy over the phone. That's cold."

I couldn't say it to his face. I know if I did, I'd never have ended it. I'm starting to think calling Amber was a bad idea. I'm about to say bye when she speaks.

"I stop for lunch in half an hour. We have no appointments this afternoon so I can always shut the shop early."

"Meet you at the park?" I suggest.

The park of all places, the same park I went to with Seth and Ellie. I'm a glutton for punishment but I deserve it—the torment, the pain. I said the most horrible things imaginable to him, I said what I needed to so that he'd hate me. *Congrats, Lizzie, you succeeded.* Seth hates me, no doubt Ellie hates me. *I* hate me.

"Park it is, see you there," she says.

I cut the call. I haven't changed out of my pyjamas for a week. I seriously need to freshen up. I have a quick shower, towel-dry my hair and slip into a knee-length black dress. I grab my keys from my jacket pocket and shut the door on my home, on my gilded cage.

Finally outside, I take a deep breath, breathing in the sweet scent of summer. I set off down my driveway and head in the direction of the park.

The sun's particularly bright today and is reflecting off the metal slide. Using my hand as a visor, I glance around. There is no sign of Amber. Instinctively I look toward the bench I sat on with Seth. A poignant smile tugs at my lips when I see it's occupied. A young couple are sitting side by side, the man blowing bubbles for a little boy. The child looks around the same age as Ellie. What I'd give to turn back the clock to when it was the three of us sitting together.

Spotting an empty bench opposite, I pass the family blowing bubbles and sit down. Instead of watching them, I glance down at my phone. I scroll down my list of text messages, briefly listen to my eighteen voice mails and hop on my social media account. I should be glad Seth hasn't tried to contact me, glad he's moving on, but I'm not. It leaves a hole in the bottom of my heart that I can't fix. The more it beats the bigger the hole gets until my heart disappears altogether.

I turn my phone off. It's only a matter of minutes before I spot Amber heading towards me, Freja walking to her right. Freja is smiling at me, but I can see her looking towards the slide and climbing frame.

"Where's Ellie?" she blurts out.

What the hell do I say? I look to Amber for help. "She... she's—"

Amber picks up on her cue and tugs the little girl's jacket off. "Freja, there are plenty of children playing, go and join in. You'll soon make friends."

"Okay, Mummy," Freja says before running towards the playground.

Amber sits down beside me, folding the jacket in her lap. "Talk," she says, offering me her profile as she watches Freja.

"What do you want me to say?"

She looks at me for a beat. Her eyes are narrow. "You've obsessed over the guy for years, you finally get him and let him go? Just like that?"

She's right, but what choice did I have? I couldn't stay with Seth and watch him lose everything because of me.

Amber nudges my arm. "So, are you going to fill in

the blanks?"

I sit forward, crossing my arms, thinking what to say. "It's complicated."

The young family are sitting blowing bubbles. I'm mesmerised. There's something hauntingly beautiful about bubbles. How something so ordinary can be transformed into something so elegant. A kaleidoscope of colours merge together, flying to the heavens. Except they don't reach their destination. All good things have an expiration—youth, beauty, happiness, it's only a matter of time before the bubble bursts.

Amber rubs her temples. "Complicated? What's complicated?"

I sigh and can't stop a tear escaping. "Life, that's what." I can feel a lecture brewing. Turning to face her, I squeeze her hand. "Please, Amber, stop with the questions. I just need a friend."

Her face softens and she throws her arms around my shoulders, hugging me. Her long blonde hair sticks to my face, I push the strands aside. Squinting, I glance towards the play area. Freja is playing with another little girl, a little girl who should have been Ellie. A lump makes its way into my throat. I wilt in Amber's arms, but as I fall apart she squeezes me that bit tighter, holding my broken pieces together.

"Thank you," I whisper.

"We're best friends, I'm here any time you need me."

We sit and make small talk. I enquire about her and Rick's relationship, to which Amber tells me it's just a bit of fun. "Victor broke me, I'll never trust again."

This is the first time Amber's opened up to me about her ex. Sure, I have the fun-loving Amber sat beside me, but she doesn't let me in, she doesn't let anyone in. As insignificant as her statement is, it feels as though the spell he had over her is losing its power.

There are so many questions I want to ask her. "What hap—"

Panting, Freja runs towards us. I stop speaking as she wiggles her bum between me and Amber and sits between us on the bench. I will speak to Amber, when the times right. I'll be there for her when she's ready to open up.

Freja huffs. "I'm bored. Can we go to the beach?"

It feels as though an arrows been shot right into my heart at the mention of the beach. Today feels like a trip down memory lane. Next we'll be going to the Sea Life Centre and finish off eating at Pepper-Oni's.

We cram into Amber's tiny car and head for the coast. It's mid-afternoon by the time we park up. Amber pops into a shop and comes out with three bottles of chilled water and a bucket and spade for Freja.

Once on the beach, Freja runs off in front. "I'm going to make a magic castle," she sings, carrying on to the water's edge.

I gaze along the beach. It's lovely being here on such a beautiful afternoon with my best friend and her daughter, but I can't help feeling detached somehow. I had my own little family in the making, two people who I love with all my heart, and I let them go.

Amber and I sit on the warm sand and watch Freja jumping between the shallow waves.

"I'm going to get you," Freja chants, kicking water up at me. Though for a second it's Ellie's little face I see and her high-pitched squeals I hear.

"Not if I get you first," I chant back. I make my way

over to Freja. Amber reclines back on the sand, closing her eyes. Being a single parent is hard work, I imagine it's nice for her to have a break, if only for a few minutes.

I charge after Freja, joining her in the shallow water. I pick her up by her waist and spin her around. Laughing, she begs me to put her down, which I do. Holding hands, we jump over the waves together. I even show her how to be a horse.

Freja doesn't have the same concentration level as Ellie, I guess being slightly younger. It doesn't take her long to get bored and want to do something else.

With our hands filled with small shells, we walk back up the beach. Amber's standing up, dusting sand off her dress. "Sorry, Lizzie, we've got to go. I said I'd pick Rick up from work."

My heart starts beating quicker. I can't go home, not yet. "I'm going to stay a little while longer."

Amber gives me the once-over. "Are you sure?"

"Yeah, I'll get a taxi home."

Freja holds her arms up. Amber smiles, sweeping her hair to the side, and picks her up. Freja's chin rests on Amber's shoulder and I wave at her as they disappear further up the beach.

I sit back down, burying my feet in the sand. It's nice to feel warmth, if only for a few minutes before the cold beneath penetrates my skin.

I sit in silence, listening to the cry of gulls, the splash of the waves. As I look towards the horizon Seth's face seems to come to life in the clouds below. Like the clouds, he's too far away for me to reach. Dusk comes and goes; people start leaving and the surrounding town begins to light up.

I could sit here forever and while away the hours. The truth is I'm dreading going home, pushing my key in the front door and walking back between those four empty walls. I made a huge mistake splitting up with Seth, but I did it for him, for Ellie. Whatever the reason, I can't go on like this—it's not living, it's existing. I'll wait till they're back from America and I'll get him back.

Chapter Thirty-One

Seth

The door to the dance studio swings open. Boys in leotards and girls in fluffy tutus run in. Gathering inside, they begin stretching.

When the door closes, I lean forward and peer in through a small viewing window. I make eye contact with one of the dance teachers and she waves. After weaving between children in the class, she opens the door and joins us in the narrow corridor. She holds out her hand, which I take.

"You must be Seth. I'm Miss Kavanagh." Her handshake is soft, yet confident, and she smiles up into my eyes. Miss Kavanagh is a petite middle-aged woman; her dreadlocked hair has been scraped back into a bun. She's wearing skin-tight grey leggings and a baggy t-shirt that has the dance school's logo, a pink flamingo, embroidered on the left breast.

She places her hands on her knees and bends down. "And you must be Ellie."

Ellie squeezes my hand a little tighter and hides behind my back.

"Sweetheart," I say, her ballet shoes dragging on the floor as I give her a little tug forward.

Miss Kavanagh smiles sweetly. She doesn't attempt to reach for Ellie, she just stands and waits patiently. I filled her in over the phone about Ellie's separation anxiety and she was very understanding. She winks at me and peers around my back. "Would you like Daddy to come watch you for the first ten minutes?"

I squint over at the reception desk to the wall-mounted clock directly above. Amber and Freja will be here any minute. I know the second Freja turns up Ellie will be okay.

There's a small crowd around the desk as parents sign their children in. My eyes bounce from head to head. No sign of Amber and no sign of Freja.

Fantastic. I was hoping to go sit in the parents' room.

Ellie tugs my hand. "Please, Daddy."

She sticks her bottom lip out and attempts puppy-dog eyes. My heart melts seeing her look so cute.

You big softie, Seth.

I suppress a smile and give my best serious expression. "Ten minutes, not a second more."

I follow Miss Kavanagh into the studio. Ellie follows closely behind. Occasionally her ballet shoes crash into my heels. This is what I didn't want because she'll expect it every week. She starts school in a few weeks. I need to build her confidence as much as I can between now and then.

"Ellie, would you like to stand by Esme?" Miss Kavanagh asks, pointing to a girl near the front. Ellie doesn't move from my side.

I crouch down in the corner of the room, hoping Ellie will join in with the other children. She doesn't. Her tutu looks like a damn marshmallow stuck to her butt as she sits on my knee.

"Positions, please," Miss Kavanagh singsongs, clapping her hands.

The music starts, and the children stand in lines. Three dance teachers are standing at the head of the studio facing us. The children copy as the women run through the moves. I give Ellie's butt a little nudge, which only makes her fall back into me.

Well, as the saying goes, you can only lead a horse to water. Feeling like I have nothing to lose, I stand. With Ellie by my side, I copy the dance teachers' leg work and Ellie slowly starts to copy me. As the song progresses, the space between me and Ellie increases. I watch as she slowly moves toward the other children whilst I move closer to the door. My hand makes contact with the metal handle when it moves down of its own accord. It swings open and as Freja runs in, I slip out. On the other side I peer through the glass viewing window and see that Freja and Ellie are holding hands and Ellie is joining in.

When I turn, I spot Amber standing at reception. Her back is toward me and I can see her pointing at the clock, shaking her head at the lady standing behind the desk. I don't wait, I figure she doesn't need an audience. I walk along the corridor a little until I reach the parents' room. It's as I'd expected, a small rectangular room crammed with mums sitting on high-backed chairs. Small children squeal, weaving between legs, and older children sit quietly on iPads. Spotting a few empty chairs at the back, I make my way past the small huddles and sit down.

I can't miss the glances my way. To say I feel like the elephant in the room is an understatement. Within a second of sitting down I have three mums pulling their chairs up to my side. Fluttering their lashes, they introduce themselves. Introductions over, Nadine, Emma, and Julia start firing questions at me. I sneak a glance at their ring fingers, and they're bare—of course they are. I'm not here to pick a woman up after Lizzie broke my heart, but as hurt as she's left me, she's shown me that I can love again.

"So, is Mum around?" Julia asks, leaning forward, her knees touching mine.

No, Mum is fucking someone else, next question.

I look up into the vivid green of Julia's eyes. "No." I hope she gets the hint and stops interrogating me.

Curiosity skates over her round face, and she offers me a wide-mouthed smile. Christ, she looks like a Cheshire cat. Sure, she's attractive, but there's nothing more unattractive than someone who's desperate.

"A lady friend?" she continues, her finger slowly tracing the neckline of her top. I guess her hope is that my interest follows her finger and I look straight at her breasts, which I do, but quickly look away. My gaze meets hers. *Smooth, real smooth.*

She leans closer still. Her knee sandwiches itself between my thighs. "A lady friend?" she repeats.

Lizzie pops into my mind. There's not a moment I haven't thought about her, haven't wondered what she's doing, haven't wanted to go around there and demand answers. Problem is I'm too chicken to look in her eyes and make her tell me it's over. Hearing it over the phone is one thing, seeing it will destroy me.

The chair legs squeak underneath me as I push the chair back, releasing Julia's knee. I don't answer her question. Why? Because it's none of her goddamn business.

I try not to be rude, so casually slide my phone out of my trouser pocket and tell the ladies I have business to take care of. I thought they'd take the hint and fuck off. I thought wrong. It's as though they're waiting for me to finish what I'm doing so they can grill me some more, like I'm their shiny new toy or something. I don't do small talk. Crossing one leg over the other, I angle my phone in my lap so the women can't see the screen. I have nothing better to do other than sign onto social media. My profile is blank. I don't share my life with the world. I only keep my account open so that I can post on our business page and occasionally look at what Lizzie's been up to.

Her last post was made five nights ago. She posted a picture of the sea with the caption, 'In the sea I see everything, in the land I see nothing.' I get the feeling the breakup is eating her up, and it confuses the fuck out of me why she ended things. I suspect Cole played a part and wonder if he offered her money. It makes sense, I guess, for her to take it. She's young and money would make her life so much simpler.

I jump when my arm is pushed aside and my phone almost falls out of my hand. I look up to see a shapely ass bending down in front of me, sitting down on my lap. With fire racing in my gut, I'm about to tell whoever it is to kindly remove themselves. That is until I see the Barbie-blonde hair, the bright red nails. "Amber, what the—"

She leans her chin on her shoulder, blowing a bubble of gum inches from my face. "I'm sorry, baby, there were no other seats."

Frowning, I glance up into her blue eyes and that's when I notice my three admirers have left.

Amber winks and leans into me. "It's like feeding time at the zoo here and you're fresh meat. If they think you're taken they'll leave you alone."

I nod, kind of grateful. "Thanks, but did you have to sit on me?"

She shrugs nonchalantly. "There were no more chairs."

I nod my head in the direction of Julia's chair. She picks up on my cue and moves to an empty seat.

She begins finger-combing her hair. Damn, she's beautiful, and I know I'm not wrong when I say that she knows it. She looks almost pixie-like with her long blonde hair, tiny features and small upturned nose.

Her nose twitches before she turns and looks down at me. "So, how's tricks?"

I shrug. "Same old."

I'm lying. Things haven't been the same since Lizzie and I split. Darcy finished working her notice at the hospital and has committed her time to watching Ellie whilst I've been at work. Good job, really, as Cole made sure my next job was a five-hour round trip away. I leave the house at five am and get home after eight pm. The only good thing that came out of my long hours is that Ellie is falling asleep in her own bed. I feel as though very slowly she's making progress.

Amber nudges me with her foot. "You know what I mean."

"I'm great. Did I tell you my ex-wife is moving to Australia?"

She raises a brow. I know what she's asking—how I

am after Lizzie—but I can't do this feelings shit. I'd rather get my balls waxed than open up to someone.

She scrapes her shoe along the floor. "Okay, if you're not going to tell me how you are, will you tell me how Ellie's doing?"

"Dig, dig, dig, is that all you can do?"

Her eyes go wide and the bubble she blows pops and sticks to her chin and nose, which she begins picking off.

"Sorry, Amber, I didn't mean that." I sigh. "Ellie misses Lizzie a lot. She thinks it's somehow her fault that Lizzie is no longer around, which of course I said it isn't, but what the hell do I say?"

Amber shakes her head. "I have no idea. Something's seriously up with Lizzie though, I know she isn't happy."

That makes two of us.

"Sucks to be her. Me, on the other hand, me and my baby are going to Disney World in two days."

"Two days doesn't give me much time."

"Much time?" I quiz.

"To giftwrap your canvas, silly."

I rub my hands over the back of my neck. "Shit, I'd completely forgot about the photoshoot and the photo. When can I pick it up?"

She sucks in her lips. "If you're not fussed about the giftwrapping, how about after the girls finish ballet?"

"Sounds good." The moment the words leave my lips, it occurs to me that I didn't see the photo Ellie selected. "Is Lizzie in the picture?" I ask, my tone sharper than I intended it to be.

Amber's gaze shifts into her lap. "Yes."

"Then I can't take it. I'll pay you to have another made up without Lizzie in the picture and I'll pick it up after we get back from Disney World."

She pauses for a beat. "What do you want me to do with the original canvas?"

I shrug. "The hell should I know? Burn it for all I care."

Amber smiles. "No, I have a better idea."

With Darcy helping Ellie pack her suitcase, I make myself scarce. I pop to the shop to pick up some cigarettes. I've smoked half a dozen whilst parked outside Cole's house. Cole lives in an affluent area, large red-brick houses with beautiful, landscaped gardens. The estate is old money—the houses have been passed down in families for years and most of the residents are over sixty. Cole is new money and is a hit with the blue-rinsers.

I need to stop filling my lungs with this shit and knock on the door already. I've been sat here for over an hour. I'm surprised the neighbourhood watch hasn't called the police on my ass. Several curtains already twitch from nosey neighbours. I take a deep breath and head towards the front door. I'm not nervous about seeing Cole, I'm nervous of what tomorrow will bring. I made some life-changing decisions, and now it's time to face the music.

My shoes crunch against the coarse shingle as I walk to the front door. Curling my hand into a fist, I tap on the wood.

The door opens within seconds. Cole's blue eyes narrow. "What took you so long?"

I force a smile. "You saw me in the van, eh?"

"The whole street did. I had Brenda, Florence and Bertha, God love them, all call to tell me about a strange van parked outside my house. I assume you're wanting your money and have come to sign the contract agreeing to leave my sister be?" Cole steps aside to let me enter.

I fish out my wallet from my trouser pocket and pull out the cheque he gave me. "Not quite." I place the folded paper in the breast pocket of his shirt, which I tap for good measure.

I'm not rich like Cole. I don't have a flash car, or a big house, but I feel one hundred times the man he is. I feel it's fitting that I return his gesture, so bowing my head, I don my imaginary cap. "Give my regards to…" I pause. Cole has no one. "Give my regards to your bank balance. May the many zeros bring you a lifetime of happiness." I turn my back on him and head to my van.

"I don't understand," he calls after me.

"It's simple, really." I pull my house keys from my trouser pocket and toss them in his direction. "I don't want your money, and I don't need your house. I want nothing from you."

"Only my sister?"

His words slice into me like a knife. I mustn't let them. I've got to look forward, not back.

Shingle crunches underfoot, and Cole's breaths draw nearer. "Mate, I'm not going to kick you and Ellie out of the house. I was angry, I didn't mean—"

With narrowed eyes, I turn and meet his stare. "I'm not your mate, not anymore. A true friend wouldn't have acted how you did."

"Seth." Cole attempts to place the house keys back into my hand, I let them fall to the ground.

"I tried to call you several times when you decided to go MIA. Which reminds me, how did you find out about us?"

Cole looks skyward. "I bumped into your sister at the petrol station."

Darcy, of course.

"I should have heard it from you." His tone is harsh.

"Oh, yeah? And how was I supposed to do that? Every time I called your phone went to voicemail. I tried to tell you about Lizzie. I'm sorry, I truly am. I didn't count on liking the girl, I didn't count on falling in love with her."

"We all know you're not over Anna. I know it, Darcy knows it, and deep down you know it, too. My sister will not be your revenge fuck or your rebound."

"I never slept with Lizzie out of revenge. She was never a rebound."

Cole's jaw clenches. "Please come inside so we can talk—"

I laugh. "There's nothing left to say." I feel as though we've taken a jackhammer to all our years of friendship and smashed them to nothing but rubble. It's kind of sad, it's very final, but at least we both know where we stand.

He takes my forearm. "Seth—"

I look down with disgust and remove his hand. "Some other time maybe, or maybe not. I've got a suitcase to pack, and a little girl to read a bedtime story to." I take a long, satisfying breath in. "Goodbye, Cole."

Chapter Thirty-Two

Lizzie

The sound of the doorbell wakes me. Hugging the quilt into my chest, I roll over and squint at the digital clock on my bedside table.

Seth and Ellie flash in my mind. My pulse quickens; they'll be on their way to the airport now. I wonder if Ellie will have one of those little suitcases on wheels she can ride on. I wonder if she's wearing one of her cute summer dresses, or her smiley face t-shirt. I close my eyes on the tears that are threatening to fall. My heart aches and yearns for what's missing. God, I miss them so much it hurts.

The doorbell rings again.

Six am. Who could possibly want me at this hour? I rub sleep and tears out of my eyes.

The doorbell rings for a third time without pause. Whoever is outside is holding their finger on the button. I unhook my robe from a hook on the door and make my way downstairs. "I'm coming," I yell.

I make my way into the lounge and grab the curtain,

squeezing the heavy material between my fingers. The fantasist inside me is hoping it's Seth and Ellie on a white horse about to whisk me away. The realist knows it isn't them. Releasing the breath I'm holding, I pull the curtain aside and peer out at the doorstep.

No Seth. No Ellie. No white horse. My shoulders drop when I see Cole standing there. I'm about to close the curtain and return to bed when he looks straight at me and waves. I've not spoken to my brother since finding out from Darcy he was blackmailing Seth.

I feel as though a volcano has erupted inside me. With clenched teeth I hurry to the front door, unlock it. I don't open it to welcome him in, instead I turn my back on him and storm into the lounge.

"Whoa, sis. Nice to see you too."

I don't hear the words that follow. I hear his threats to Seth, threatening to make him homeless, threatening to take his livelihood from him.

My nails dig into my palms as I squeeze my hands into tight balls. I can hear Cole behind me, so spin around and start pummelling my fists on his chest. He doesn't stop me, doesn't grab my wrists like I was expecting, he stands tall and waits. When pummelling his chest has little effect, I scream in his face and start shoving him.

He withstands my shoves and it angers me when his face is stoic and his body remains perfectly still. I start slapping his cheeks. I want him to say something, I need him to ask me why I'm lashing out.

He yawns, as if growing bored, which only ignites my anger. Making a fist with my left hand, I reel back, prepared to throw a punch. I've never punched anyone before. My actions are fuelled by adrenaline. I'm about to catapult my fist into his face when he grabs my wrist.

"Lizzie, stop."

His words snap me out of my craze. My legs quake and give way underneath me and I collapse to the floor, where I curl up into a ball and sob. I sob for Seth, I sob for what I've lost, I sob for the brother I thought I knew, not the stranger I'm breaking down in front of. My whole world has shattered around me and there's nothing I can do to fix it. My brother has orchestrated everything, it's all his fault.

I can feel his hands under my arms as he attempts to lift me. "Get up, we've not got time for this."

I push him away and through sore eyes and wet lashes I glower at him. "Fuck off."

His eyes go wide and his mouth falls open. "What did you say?"

I have never been a believer in vulgarity. I believe such words are more effective when they're not the main source of one's vocabulary. Cole has never heard me swear before. He must know how angry I am, if not from my actions, then my words alone.

"You heard me," I seethe. "Fuck off."

"Whoa, what happened to my sweet and innocent sister?"

His words are like a red rag to a bull. I stumble in my attempt to stand and then charge at him. His large hand spans over my forehead, stopping me in my tracks. He takes my shoulders and pushes me back until my legs hit the settee and I fall back on my ass onto the cushion.

I jump to my feet. Cole gives me a little nudge and I fall down. We repeat this a few times until I finally give up and sit staring up at him. "What do you want, Cole?"

He eyes the space besides me. "If I sit next to you, will you promise not to hit me?" He attempts to smile and starts to lower himself down at my side.

"I will make no such promise."

He freezes and flashes me a glance. My resting bitch face has been amplified. If I look as angry as I feel, he would know better than to sit at my side.

Clearing his throat, he makes his way to the easy chair opposite and sits. "So," he begins, crossing one leg over the other. "I take it Seth told you about our little conversation?"

I look at the wall space directly behind him, where I hung the canvas Amber brought around. Me, Seth, Ellie and Freja are standing underwater. Nemo and Dory swim between Seth and I, and a school of fish have circled the girls. The perfect family photo, except they're not my family and they never will be.

The leather squeaks under Cole as he turns and looks up. When I finally meet my brother's gaze, I can see regret staring back. "Lizzie, I—"

I lift my hand. "Seth didn't say a word to me, it was Darcy. She told me you threatened to take his home, his livelihood away, everything. Did you know his ex was blackmailing him? She was going to take Ellie to Australia if he didn't pay her ten thousand pounds."

"Darcy may have filled me in."

"Of course she did. Well, I hope he's taken every damn penny of the fifteen thousand pounds you offered him."

Again, Cole shakes his head. "He didn't take a penny."

I lean my elbows on my knees. "What?"

"He came to see me last night. He returned the cheque I'd given him, along with the keys to the house."

"What? Why?" The keys to his house? Where's he going to live? I blink several times, trying to process what he's told me.

Cole shrugs. "You'll have to ask him in person."

"Yeah, like that's going to happen."

Cole stands, makes his way towards me, leans over the settee and retrieves my suitcase, which was still stored in the space behind. "Pack your suitcase, Lizzie." He reaches into his trouser pocket and retrieves a ticket and a wad of notes—not sterling, dollars.

I look from him to the suitcase. "I don't understand."

"What's not to understand? I'm giving you five thousand dollars and a plane ticket. Go pack, grab your passport. You're going to Disney World." He turns, looking at the clock on the mantel. "Now, Lizzie."

I sit like I've been shot with a stun gun. I don't say a word, I just stare. The thought of setting foot on a plane sends my head spinning. I feel sick. I try to push the nausea aside. I need answers. "I need to understand, why? Why did you blackmail Seth? Why didn't you want me to be happy?"

Cole glances out of the window, taking long seconds to contemplate his words, but I don't want a rehearsed speech, I want real.

"Cole—"

Tentatively, he makes his way toward me and sits at my side. "I had to know Seth was worthy of you."

"Worthy of me, are you for real? He's a good man and you know that. The guy's your best friend."

"And you're my little sister, damn it. He crossed a line."

I shake my head. "Boys and their stupid egos."

"Will you hear me out already?" He pauses for a beat, only carrying on when I agree to listen. "You're all I have left in this godforsaken world. I have plenty of money, but only one sister."

"I'm sorry, but that isn't reason enough to behave how you have."

"When I bumped into Darcy, she started going on about how Seth wasn't over Anna and how you were just a bit of fun. Something inside me snapped. I couldn't bear to see Seth hurt you the way Dad used to hurt Mum." Cole slaps his hand to his mouth, as though that piece of information was not meant to leave his lips. "Sorry, I shouldn't have said that."

"No, go on," I prompt.

Silence.

"Cole!"

"Okay, okay, but you're not going to like it."

"I can handle it."

After a long pause he sighs, focusing on the floor. "Dad had a woman in every port." His stare meets mine, and he waits for me to nod before continuing. "Mum was sick of being made a laughing stock. She finally said enough was enough. Their divorce was going through when she found out she was pregnant with you."

I fall silent. All this time, Mum only stayed with Dad for me. As the years passed by, Dad's health decreased, and so she became his full-time carer. I don't know if that makes me feel happy or sad—a little of both, I guess.

Cole's gaze dances over the underwater canvas of us

298

all together. "I thought if I offered him the money Anna was asking for, and a little extra for good measure, that he'd break things off with you. I was wrong, I can see how much you love each other, you can't fake that, and I'd never stand in the way. I'm sorry. Please, take the ticket, go to Disney with him and Ellie, go be happy."

A tear rolls down my cheek. I raise my arms and lunge for my brother. Initially he holds his arms up for protection, but when he realises I'm hugging him, he relaxes and hugs me back.

"Am I forgiven?" he asks rather sheepishly.

"Not by a long shot," I snap, "but it's a start."

He tenses a little in my embrace. "I've always thought as you like a daughter. Shit, I practically brought you up when our grandparents died and I moved home."

He's right. Mum had me late in life, and she and Dad retired when I was in single figures. Although they looked after me in every sense of the word, they never loved me. Mum never hugged me or tucked me in at night, Cole did. Cole was my everything, which is why his betrayal hurts so much.

"As extreme as my actions have been, I've only ever had your best interest at heart. I love you, Lizzie."

"I love you."

There's a moment we share that I don't think we'll ever share again in our lifetime. A moment full of emotion that completely consumes us. Love is happiness, sadness, excitement, sorrow, hate, anger—the list is endless, it's every emotion crammed into one.

I'm sure Seth hates me now. I've got to win him back.

My gaze shoots over the clock on the mantel. Although I'm petrified of flying, the thought of losing Seth scares me more. "How long have I got to pack?"

"Ten minutes."

I can feel my eyes go wide. "Are you kidding me? You expect me to pack for a seven-day holiday in ten minutes?"

"If you don't want to miss the check-in time, then, yes."

I don't think I've ever moved so quickly. I race up the stairs and throw whatever I can grab into my suitcase. Hangers come down as well as clothes from my wardrobe. I haven't got time to separate them, just shove them in and hope for the best. Underwear, swimsuits, shoes, my toothbrush. I cram as much as I can in, sitting on the lid so I can zip it shut. I race downstairs.

The airport is half an hour away by car. Cole isn't someone I'd describe as a slow driver. As soon as we hit the motorway, he glides across into the fast lane and puts his foot down.

Once at the airport, Cole drops me off in a taxi bay. I push my nerves at the idea of flying to the back of my mind and focus on Seth, what I'm going to say to him.

"Tickets, passport, money," Cole says as I shuffle said items in my hand.

I draw ticks in the air with my finger. "Check, check and check."

Cole gets out of the car and opens the boot, making a face when he lugs my case out. "My God, have you packed the kitchen sink?"

"Oh, shoot, do you think it's too heavy?"

Cole nods. "Little bit, Liz. Right, stop stalling and go." We share a look, and he ruffles my hair. "Go."

I drag my suitcase into the busy terminal. Once inside I find the screen with my gate number, number seven. The queue is slow-moving, and glancing at all the heads, I wonder if I'll see Seth and Ellie. Cole didn't say we were on the same flight. Damn, he didn't tell me where I'm stopping when I get there. I stay back, pull my phone out of my pocket and call my brother. The call goes straight to voice mail. Of course it does, he's driving. Scrolling through my contacts to Seth's name, I take a deep breath, wondering if I should call him or not. I count to three and press his name. Looking over the queue, I hold the phone to my ear. It rings eight times before he picks up.

"Yes."

It's so good to hear his voice. He doesn't say my name. I guess he doesn't want Ellie to know who's on the other end. Standing on tiptoes, I try to see over heads in front of me, hoping to see Seth and Ellie.

"Where are you?"

The phone goes quiet. He's cut the call. My eyes instantly fill with tears. I'm wasting my time. He'll never forgive me. I take my phone from my ear and glance down at the screen.

"Behind you, apparently."

I turn. Seth and Ellie are standing right behind me. I don't meet Seth's eyes, I can't, so instead I glance down at Ellie. As I thought, she's riding a child's suitcase on wheels. The suitcase has been designed to look like a giant fish. She's wearing her sailor's summer dress and her brown hair is matted. Rubbing her bloodshot eyes, she squints up at me. The sleepy expression she harboured seconds ago is replaced by a toothy smile. She lunges off her case and wraps her arms around my waist. My heart melts as she squeezes my legs with all the strength she has.

Seth clears his throat. "What are you doing here?"

My attention leaves the little girl and I meet Seth's cold gaze. He looks down at his phone and back up at me. Damn, he looks good. He's wearing a blue t-shirt and grey pair of shorts, his hair is a sexy kind of mess and his beard looks longer than the last time I saw him. In all honesty, he looks as though he's overslept and got dressed in the dark, but the just-got-out-of-bed look looks good on him.

My heartbeat speeds up and I hold my breath. I'm expecting a scene out of the movies where the guy runs to the girl, sweeps her up in his arms and spins her around, but Seth doesn't smile, he doesn't hold me, he doesn't do anything. He looks down at me and down at my suitcase and repeats his question. "What are you doing here?"

I scuff my shoe on the marble floor. "I thought that was obvious."

His eyes go wide when he sees the gate number I'm standing in front of. His expression hardens. "No way," he says, taking hold of Ellie's arm. "Say goodbye to Lizzie."

Ellie only squeezes my legs firmer. When it dawns on Seth that he can't dislodge her, he rears back up at me, his jaw ticking. "Why are you here?"

Because I love you are the words I want to yell, but don't. Telling someone I love them in public isn't something I'm capable of doing. I'm not good with expressing my feelings openly. Me being here, about to step on a plane and face my fears for him speaks volumes. Except I didn't tell Seth about my fear of flying. He has no idea that in my mind I'm putting my life on the line for him. I'm petrified the plane will hit an air pocket and fall thousands of feet or worse. The thought of being trapped in a metal tube and not being able to escape has my heart pounding in my chest.

"Well?" His tone is terse, and it pulls me out of my thoughts.

"Cole—"

Seth's head shoots round. "You're here with Cole?"

"No, I—"

"Whatever game you're both playing, it stops now. This isn't fair. Ellie's been really looking forward to our holiday and—"

"Will you shut up and let me talk?" I snap. Seth's eyebrows rise, his forehead creasing. I don't recall telling anyone to shut up and meaning it. I've always been nice, predictable Lizzie, but no more. I'm so sick of being told what to do, sick of being too polite to put me first. Well, no more. "Cole isn't here. He bought my plane tickets. He gave me five thousand dollars' spending money." Standing on tiptoes, I wave the notes in his face.

"Okay, you're going to Disney, where are you staying when you get there?"

My mouth forms an O. "I... I don't know."

I'm about to call Cole again when Seth grunts. He shakes his head vehemently. "Well don't be under any illusion that you're topping and tailing with us."

I frown. "I wasn't for one second suggesting I was staying with you two." My eyes narrow at him, and I scowl. "Why are you being like this?"

My heart's beating faster and faster. Adrenaline and fear pump rapidly around my body. The words I've been dying to say are on the tip of my tongue. I just need to find the courage to say them aloud.

Chapter Thirty-Three

Seth

Why am I being like this? Is she joking? What answer does she want? How about 'You broke my heart and it hurts like hell to be around you'?

"I love you, you jerk!" Heads turn as she hollers so loudly her voice echoes in the large terminal. Her face turns bright red, though her eyes never leaving me. I know she's trying to prove a point, to make things right between us, but unfortunately her words alone don't cut it.

"Leave." I can't help the anger bubbling in the pit of my stomach, and I can't help my reaction to her. She has her arms wrapped around my daughter, the same daughter she didn't want to know. I'm a big boy, I can handle a breakup, but when someone walks out of my daughter's life without so much as an explanation, well, that person can go fuck herself.

I haven't got time for this bullshit. If she wants to go to Disney World alone, fine. I glance past Lizzie and at our gate. The queue for gate seven has got noticeably smaller. Picking Ellie's small suitcase up, I squeeze the handle of mine. "Come on, Ellie, we've got to get checked in."

I force a smile and attempt to pass Lizzie, who steps to the side, blocking my way.

"Where are your manners? I was here first. Therefore, you wait behind me."

My jaw tightens. Lizzie takes Ellie's hand and joins the queue.

I look down at my side and frown, knowing something is missing—my daughter. "Ellie, come."

Lizzie's eyes narrow as she glowers at me. "She's not a dog."

She's pissed. I'm pissed. There's a huge wall of tension between us and I don't know how to break that wall down.

We stand in silence as people in front of us hand their tickets in and pass their luggage over. Before I know it, Lizzie's having her case weighed. The lady behind the kiosk shakes her head and sticks tape on the handle that says 'heavy'. I smile inwardly when Lizzie gets a fine. I try not to laugh out loud but can't help it. Tossing her hair over her shoulders, Lizzie frowns at me before paying the fee.

Lizzie and Ellie stand together and wait for me. I pass the woman my flight tickets and she informs me that I've been upgraded to first class. I don't argue with her. First class beats economy any day.

I lift Ellie's little case on the conveyor belt. The woman nods, and it's taken away to join the rest of the luggage. Smiling smugly at Lizzie, I toss my case up to be weighed. The woman rolls her eyes and proceeds to label my case as 'heavy'.

"No way, I weighed it last night."

The woman's face hardens. The last thing I want to do is cause a scene. My smile dissolves, and I also pay the fine. I can feel Lizzie's smugness before I look at her. She doesn't say a word, she doesn't have to.

"Touché," I spit out.

Biting her lower lip, she looks up at me. Goddamn it, she has no idea how my body is reacting to her. My heart wants to open up and pull her inside, but my head won't allow it.

We make our way to airport security. None of us have hand luggage, so it's just a case of putting anything metal and our phones into a plastic box to be scanned and walking through a metal detector. I don't attempt to push in front. I stand back and let Lizzie go first. The alarm goes off the second she walks under the metal detector.

I flip her the finger when she's stopped. I take Ellie's hand and we walk straight through. I'm tempted to rush ahead and lose Lizzie in the crowd, though part of me thinks it's funny she needs to be frisked. Another part of me wants to see exactly where the security guard is putting his hands.

I stand with my arms folded across my chest and watch as Lizzie is taken to the other side of the metal detector. Once there she removes her belt. The moment her belt comes off, her jeans slide down and I get a glimpse of her black lacy underwear. Damn. I adjust the waistband of my shorts.

The guard points at her shoes, which she takes off and puts in a plastic box along with her belt. The guard glides the metal detector over her one final time. It buzzes when he holds it over her breasts. I step forward, about to rip the man's damn head off if he so much as suggests she removes her bra. She's wearing a white t-shirt, which will be completely see-through if she de-bras.

I take Ellie's hand, storm through the walk-through metal detector and stand at Lizzie's side. I eye up the security guard, placing a possessive arm around Lizzie's shoulders. "What seems to be the problem?"

The guard's dark eyes meet mine and he hits his hand-held metal detector a few times, indicating that it isn't working properly. "Nothing, sir. Would you mind stepping aside?"

Doing as he asks, I clench my teeth as he runs his hands over Lizzie's body. It makes me uncomfortable seeing another man with his hands on her, but at least standing this close I can see exactly where he is touching.

He nods, clearly satisfied. "You can go."

One at a time, we pass under the walk-through metal detector without a problem. Lizzie grabs her belt, shoes and mobile phone from a plastic box, and we head into the departures lounge.

I follow Lizzie into a duty-free shop and she picks up a bottle of perfume, which I pay for. When she reaches for my hand I take her hand in mine and hold it so tightly that I never want to let go of her.

And just like that we melt back into our old way of normal. I'm holding Lizzie's hand, and she's holding Ellie's. The illusion of the perfect family to the outside world, but it's a lie. A war is raging in my mind, and part of me wants to tear our hands apart, grab Ellie, and run. The other part of me wants to stay and disappear into the illusion.

Having four hours to kill, we head to a small café. We

sit on a ranch-style table and chairs and order breakfast. There's a small amusement area next to the café, and Ellie rushes over to play on a virtual driving game. I turn my chair so that I can see my daughter, thus offering Lizzie my profile.

When the silence between us is too much to bear, I finally speak. "Why?"

The word I've been dying to ask her. One small word, so many questions. *Why did you go? Why did you break my heart? Why didn't you come back? Why—*

She takes a deep breath, reaches for my hand across the table, and I pull away. Before we get too comfortable with one another, I have to know why she did what she did. I need to know.

She moves seats so she's sitting at my side. I guess the closeness helps her somehow, but it's destroying me. To be so close to the person you want more than anything, but know they're poison.

"I did it for you." Her voice cracks. She grabs my t-shirt, buries her head into my chest and starts sobbing. She tells me how Darcy went round to see her and told her I was being blackmailed. She tells me she didn't want me to lose Ellie and that she's never stopped loving me.

Her tears wet my t-shirt, the material cooling my chest. I wrap my arms around her head and pull her into me. Sometimes the most painful words are delivered with love. Everything she did was for me, for Ellie, she sacrificed her own happiness for me.

She pulls away, but I don't let her go. I don't think I'll let her go ever again.

"Cole bought me the plane tickets; Cole wants us to be happy." Her words are muffled as her face is still

FINDING OUR FOREVER

pressed against my chest, but I heard every word.

I don't know whether to believe that or not. If it's true, I feel the need to punch him in the face, and then bro-hug it out after.

"You gave him the keys back to your house. Where are you going to live?" She pulls away, and this time I release her.

I rub my hand over the back of my neck. "I'm going to move in with Darcy for a little bit, get some money behind me. I used all of my savings to pay Anna off. It wasn't enough, so I had to get a loan to cover the rest. After Cole's threats to take the house off me, I decided it was time to get on my feet."

"You can still live there."

I can, but don't want to. "No, Cole was right, I'm paying peanuts for rent, and it's not right. He helped me out a lot when Anna and I split up, but I can't use him as a crutch."

A waitress brings our drinks over and informs us our breakfasts will be with us shortly.

Lizzie reaches for my hand, which this time I allow. "So, where does this leave us?"

I pull her fingers up to my mouth, placing a kiss on them. "I don't know, honestly, I don't."

She breathes out, as do I. I take my attention off Ellie for a split second to look at Lizzie.

"I meant it when I said I love you, Lizzie, but you should have spoken to me instead of ending things over the phone. I know why you did it, but it doesn't make it right."

"I know." She sniffs. Her gaze leaves mine and she watches Ellie. I know it's too painful for her to look at me, it's killing me to look at her, but I can't take my eyes off her. She's so damn perfect. Losing her made me realise how shitty my life was without her in it.

"I would like to give things another go, give us another go, but Ellie can't know we're more than just friends. She has to be my number one priority, and if you get cold feet or decide this isn't for you, walking out of her life isn't an option."

"I would never."

I release her hand, and her arm falls onto the table. "But you did, Lizzie, you walked out of our lives without so much as a backward glance. You can't do that again, and we have to build some trust between us before we take our relationship to the next level."

After breakfast we make our way to the viewing area and watch planes board and take off. Ellie's back is toward us, her little nose pressed against the glass window. Lizzie sits back in her seat, and apart from smiling when Ellie looks her way, her face is straight and she rubs her palms up and down on her jeans. Switching chairs, I sit at Lizzie's side and take her hand in mine. She's shaking.

I raise a brow. "Nervous?"

She shakes her head, then nods when she sees my 'don't bullshit me' face. "A little," she croaks.

If I didn't know better, I'd say she's beyond nervous. She's as white as a ghost.

I glance up at the screen that displays flight times.

Amazing.

I scuff my shoe on the floor. "You can relax, our flight has been delayed."

"You're joking." Lizzie's gaze leaves her lap and she turns to look at the display screen. She exhales, rubbing her hand over her jeans, and sits taller. "Okay, I can do this."

I laugh. I don't know who she's trying to convince, because she isn't convincing me and I doubt she's convincing herself. My heart swells in my chest knowing how much of a big deal this is to her, she's clearly petrified.

In the seven hours we spend in departures we end up looking around every duty-free shop, twice, and we buy a shitload of things we don't need. We return to the ranch-style café for lunch. Lizzie joins Ellie on the virtual cars. Lizzie is so much more relaxed—she's laughing and joking, that is until it's time to board. I've never seen a human impersonate a robot so well as when Lizzie gets her ass on the plane.

Lucky for Lizzie, our seats are all next to each other, which is coincidental considering Ellie and I were upgraded last minute. Then it hits me. Cole upgraded our seats.

Lizzie cries or sleeps for the duration of the flight. Ellie and I take it in turns to comfort her, and it works until we hit turbulence. I've never heard a twenty-five-year-old yell "fudge," "fiddlesticks" and "love a duck" so many times. She's so damn cute. She divides first class—the miserable fuckers cluck their tongues, and the ones who don't have a stick up their asses laugh.

It's eleven pm our time when we land, five pm local time. With Ellie asleep in my arms, we collect our luggage and make our way through the relevant checks before leaving the airport.

The heat hits us immediately when we step outside. Even late evening it's a scorcher. We're walking along the pavement, but to where, I don't know. I still have no idea where Lizzie is staying. Neither does she. We've both attempted to contact Cole, though our calls have been diverted to voicemail, and his social media account is inactive.

We stop at a taxi bay. Lizzie looks lost. Her brother flew her all the way out here, alone, with nowhere to stay.

Nice move, dipshit.

I booked the cheapest hotel I could get last-minute. It's open-plan and only accommodates two people. "Well, shit, looks like you'll be topping and tailing with us after all."

She pulls the wad of notes out of her pocket and begins waving them in the air. "It's okay, I'm sure I can get a room with this."

My hotel is fully booked. I managed to scoop a last-minute booking. I'm about to insist she stays with us when someone clears their throat. We turn. A man is standing feet away. He's holding a sign with the names 'Lizzy', 'Beth', and 'Ellie' handwritten on it.

"You?" he asks, pointing to the names.

Lizzie and I glance at one another and she snickers. "If 'Beth' is meant to say 'Seth', then it's us."

The man turns the sign around and shakes his head. "Not Beth?"

I can't miss the man's accent. Eastern European, at a guess. By the look of confusion on his face I'd guess his English isn't the best. He opens his jacket, retrieves his phone, scrolls down and stops. Turning the phone around, he shows us a picture of Lizzie.

"Lizzie?" he questions.

I don't know how I feel about some random guy having her photo on his phone.

"This you, no?"

"Yes, that's her," I say, taking the phone out of his hand and deleting the image. Another image appears in its place. It's a picture of me wearing a mankini.

Motherfucker.

Cole took this picture at Patrick's stag weekend. There were twelve of us in total. We each had to choose our outfits for the evening out of a hat. Cole was an adult baby, Rick was a giant penis, and I had to wear a fluorescent green mankini. It left very little to the imagination and was wedged in my ass all night.

The man takes his phone from my hands and turns it around so we can see. "This Beth, no?"

I attempt to grab the phone for a second time when Lizzie captures his hand. I swear her pupils dilate at the same time as she bursts into laughter.

Note to self: dig up all of Cole's old photos to show his next bird.

"Beth, Lizzie, Ellie. I drive you to hotel."

Still laughing, Lizzie follows behind the man. "Come on, Beth," she teases.

The man shows us to a limousine. I glance at Lizzie. "Did you know about this?"

She shakes her head. "No, I had no idea."

Far too tired to argue, I let the man take our luggage and we slide into the back seat.

Ellie wakes up just in time for me to strap her into the seat nearest the window. I sit next to Ellie, and Lizzie next to me. The aircon is lush, and the drive is so smooth. Ellie slouches, her little head in my lap as she sleeps, and it isn't long before Lizzie's leaning against me. Feeling my eyes grow heavy, I lean my head back and rest my eyes.

"Beth, we here."

A hand shakes me and I wake up to see the driver bent down, his face inches away from my face.

I attempt to sit further back in the seat. "Yeah, thanks."

The driver nods, getting closer still. He's all up in my face. The guy's a damn space invader. I can feel his hands moving around next to my ass. Ellie and Lizzie aren't anywhere to be seen. I'm starting to worry, that is until Lizzie pokes her head through the open door.

"Have you found it?" she asks.

I glance down. The guy's head is nearly in my lap. "Dude, do you mind?"

"Got it." He moves away from me, an earring in his hand. Of course, Lizzie lost an earring. I unbuckle my seatbelt and get out of the limo.

The car is parked in front of the Orlando Paradiso. The hotel is ginormous, a curved white building with at least twenty floors. If I remember correctly, this is one of the most expensive hotels in Florida. I shake my head. "This is the wrong hotel."

He retrieves his phone and again starts scrolling. "No, Beth, this right."

Fucking Beth.

I'm about to correct him when Lizzie tips the man and he returns to his limo and goes on his way.

I lift my hands up in the air. "What the fuck? We're at the wrong hotel."

Ellie tugs at my t-shirt. I look down. "Yes?"

"You said a naughty word."

I rake my fingers though my hair. "You're right, Daddy's sorry."

She yawns. "I'm tired."

"If we were at the right hotel, you could go to bed."

Lizzie clucks her tongue. "Cole messaged me in the car. We're at the right hotel."

This is the most expensive hotel in Florida. *This has got to be a joke*. "We're wasting time here. The Mango Hotel I booked isn't far away. Let's get a taxi and go."

Lizzie grabs the handle of her suitcase, the little wheel squeaking as she pulls it behind her. It's obvious she isn't going to listen, so I follow her in. We are met by porters who take our luggage from us, stacking them in silver trolleys.

I'm about to make Lizzie look very silly.

"Seth Stevens," I say to the woman behind the desk. She presses a few buttons on her keypad, shaking her head. *I told you* is on the tip of my tongue when Lizzie steps beside me.

"Elizabeth Crowley."

Again, the woman starts tapping away at the keypad. "Ah, I see you have booked a room for two adults and one child. Welcome to Orlando Paradiso." She opens a drawer underneath her and retrieves a room card. "You're in room seven hundred and nine, one of our penthouse suites."

Penthouse suites? Is she kidding me?

"Please take full advantage of the minibar and room service." She smiles a pearly white smile. "Enjoy your stay."

Chapter Thirty-Four

Lizzie

The penthouse suite is breathtaking. It consists of a spacious sitting area, three large bedrooms, all with en suites, and a balcony with its own infinity pool.

I run from room to room, snapping pictures on my phone and uploading them on social media. In the master suite I find Seth lowering Ellie onto the super-king-sized bed. He places his pointer finger over his lips and we tip-toe out of the room.

"I don't know about you, but I'm starving."

I nod. "Room service?"

Seth wraps his arms around my waist. "I'm not hungry for food."

Laughing, I twiddle the ends of my hair. "Tell me, Seth, what are you hungry for?"

My heartbeat quickens when he tugs at my t-shirt, pulling it up and over my head. "You," he whispers.

Our lips lock and he walks forward, giving me no

other choice but to walk back.

"I've missed this," he says, unclasping my bra and tossing it to the floor. He sucks one of my nipples into his mouth, kisses his way across my chest and sucks my other nipple into his mouth. "I've also missed this."

Squealing, I turn, and Seth slaps my ass.

"Bed. Now," he commands.

I run into one of the bedrooms, Seth on my heels. I automatically flick the light switch off. He flicks it on.

"I want to see you, Lizzie, every inch."

"Then it's only fair that I see you, every inch."

Seth doesn't waste a second. He unbuckles his shorts, drops them and his boxers to the floor, and stands before me, fully erect.

Taking a deep breath, I unfasten my shorts and lower them along with my panties to the floor.

"Turn around, bend over, and spread your legs."

Biting my lip, I do as he requests. He approaches.

"Wider."

I hear him open the condom packet and sheath up. I can feel the head of his cock around my sex. He dips the head of his cock inside of me. I moan. It feels so good. Pushing into me, he cups my breasts in his hands. Long, slow, delicious thrusts, in and out. He pulls out and gives me a little nudge, guiding me onto the bed, where I get on all fours.

"God, I could eat your pussy right here and now."

I turn to see him jerking himself off whilst admiring the sight of me bent over. Oh, my God, I've never felt so naked as I do in this moment. Embarrassed, I fall onto the bed. Seth grabs my shoulders and flips me over. He nods his head in the direction of the bed. "Get in."

Doing as he requested, I laugh when he stands at the bottom of the bed. He pulls the quilt up and crawls his way to me. He stops briefly to tease my clit with his tongue.

"Will you stop teasing me already?" Fisting his hair, I yank his head up.

"Fuck, Lizzie." He rises above me, rubbing his head. "I like it when you're feisty." He grabs my hips and rolls us over. "Ride my cock."

It doesn't bother me I've never done this position before. Lowering myself onto him, I begin grinding myself forward and back. It doesn't take long for him to grab my hips and he ups the pace.

The sex isn't fast, it isn't ferocious like the times before, it's different. He isn't fucking me, he's making love to me. In this moment we are one, joined body and soul.

He kisses my hand, my arm, pulling me down. His lips dance as he kisses my neck. When our lips finally meet it's as though they've never been apart. We make love, savouring every moment as though it could be our very last.

"I love you, Lizzie."

I glance down at him, into eyes I want to be the last thing I see before I go to sleep at night and the first thing I wake up to. I love the guy with everything I am, everything I'll ever be.

"I love you too."

I lean forward, towel-drying my hair. I drop the towel and my robe to the floor and get dressed in a pair of denim shorts and a blue t-shirt.

I look around at the vast space. I can't stop thinking about how much money this would have cost Cole, not that I'm complaining. Revelling in luxury, I prance into the lounge and open the blinds. I gaze out of the window and my mouth drops open. I don't think I've ever seen anything as beautiful—a panoramic view of lawned gardens and Disney theme parks with Cinderella Castle standing tall in the distance. The blue sea and its white sandy beach lie beyond.

There's a knock at the door. "Room service."

Seth and I went through the breakfast menu last night. We called down to reception after midnight and placed our order.

I rub my hands together. "Come in."

A waiter dressed in a dark suit pushes a silver serving trolley towards the far end of the room. He stops in front of the white marble dining table and begins laying out the plates from the trolley. I breathe in and smell the sweet essence of fresh fruit.

The moment he leaves, I run over to the table. I've never seen such a variety of food—yogurts, hazelnut granola, assorted cereals, Marshall's Farm honey, and every fruit imaginable arranged in glass dishes. I pour myself a glass of fresh orange juice, admiring the crystal centrepiece.

I stop before taking a sip. Seth and Ellie's voices come from the bedroom. The door to the master suite swings open and Ellie parades out wearing a green summer dress.

I smile. "You look very pretty, Ellie."

Bending down, she pulls the skirt of her dress taut

around her legs. "I'm going to see *The Little Mermaid*'s grotto, so I want to look just like Ariel."

"And that's your mermaid tail?"

She nods. I have to bite back a smile. Her face is so serious. Her attention is drawn to the large window, where she stands looking at her faint reflection. Seth joins me at the table, wrapping his arms around my shoulders. He gazes down at the same time as I gaze up. As cheesy as it sounds, I just know that our story is going to be a happily ever after.

I need to be patient. As much as I want everything to happen overnight, we both agreed to move our relationship along slowly for Ellie's sake. Seth needs to know his daughter is happy and there's room in her life for me.

I picture the three of us like a jigsaw, the pieces almost fitting together, but still having small gaps between them. I don't think it will be long before we fit together perfectly.

"I'm starving," Seth says, reaching across the table and grabs a slice of watermelon. We tuck into breakfast, though Ellie refuses to eat. She bounces up and down on the chair nearest to the window.

"I'm not hungry. I want to see Beauty and the Beast, and Donald Duck, and…" She reels off one Disney character after another, having to stop to breathe.

Seth lowers his spoon and gives Ellie the 'don't mess with me' face. "It's going to be a long day. You're not leaving until you've eaten."

Slurping milk from her spoon, she finishes a bowl of cereal. "Okay, I'm done."

After breakfast Seth covers Ellie in sunscreen, tweaking her nose between his pointer finger and thumb. "Can't have my baby burning, now can we?"

She hops from one foot to the other, pulling on his arm. "Can we go now?"

Seth smiles. "We sure can."

We leave the hotel and make our way to Disney's Magic Kingdom. Ellie skips between me and Seth, exhilaration shining in her eyes. I don't think I've ever seen her so happy.

Ellie lifts her arms in the air, flapping her hands for us to hold. I take her right, Seth her left. It feels as though we're swinging our little girl between us as we head to the theme park.

After a short walk from our hotel we enter a very new world, the magical world of Walt Disney.

We stop as a parade makes its way down the long winding street towards us. The street is transformed into a musical show, and theme tunes from Disney movies blast out of speakers attached to large floats.

Ellie starts jumping up and down. "Pluto, Mickey Mouse."

People gather around and we stand together, lining the street. Ellie turns to Seth with her arms in the air and he lifts her onto his shoulders.

A horn blasts. Ellie squeals and reaches for Pluto, who parades past on tall stilts. Mickey, dressed in his striking red tunic, follows closely behind, waving his white gloved hands.

Ellie screams, waving to get their attention. Mickey passes and appears to look straight at us. She blows him a kiss. "I love you, Mickey."

Seth takes a sideward step, closing the small distance between us. I glance at Ellie and Seth. I can't believe we're here together, that something so broken only days ago can feel so perfect.

The next float to drive towards us is *The Little Mermaid*. The song *Under the Sea* blasts from the speakers and Ellie sways from side to side in time to the music. She watches in awe as one float after another follows, finishing on *Beauty and the Beast*.

The parade passes and people move on. Seth crouches down and Ellie hops off his shoulders. Red-faced, she throws her arms round my waist. I smile down and hug her tightly. Looking between us, Seth winks. "My girls."

I smile big. A warm feeling swirls around my stomach. Those jigsaw pieces are starting to fit together so naturally. Seth joins us for a group hug, placing a soft kiss on my temple.

We carry on through the park, weaving between colourful castles, ornate palaces and crooked houses. I can't get over how visual everything is. With Ellie's focus elsewhere, my and Seth's hands manage to find their way together and our lips share the odd kiss.

The next attraction we visit is *The Little Mermaid*'s coastal retreat. We're greeted by Ariel and her friends in her magical grotto. After, we have a ride on Aladdin's magic carpet.

At five pm we make our way to the Mad Hatter's Tea Party for something to eat. Alice, the White Rabbit and the Cheshire Cat are waiting on the tables. The Mad Hatter appears and shakes Ellie's hand.

She crinkles her nose. "You look funny."

He straightens his tall hat. White hair springs out from either side. "I am funny," he says, leading us to an empty table.

We enjoy our dinner surrounded by all of the Wonderland characters. When it's time to leave they stand and wave us off.

With the rides and shops starting to close, we head towards Cinderella's palace for the night-time extravaganza. Wide-eyed, we stand and watch as fireworks explode into the night sky. A vibrant array of colours sprinkle through the dark clouds like a beautiful fountain. Spellbinding lasers come to life, making Cinderella's palace look even more magical.

I turn to see Ellie's little face. She's in Seth's arms, her head resting on his shoulder, her eyes closed tight. "How can she be asleep through this?"

He grins. "I know, right?"

He wraps his arms around me. We stand and watch the remainder of the show. Today feels like the first day of the rest of my life. It's the moment I realise that Seth and Ellie complete me. The moment I realise Seth and I are for keeps.

Epilogue

Lizzie
Six months later

Amber, Chelsea and I have spent the last two hours in the kitchen. I've been preparing sandwiches whilst Amber has been cooking finger foods. Chelsea's job is to arrange the games for my and Seth's gender reveal party. Chelsea has been somewhat inventive, from nappies filled with Nutella and baby dummies dipped in a range of sauces.

"We make a good team," Chelsea says while filling the last nappy with chocolate sauce and wrapping it up as though it were a present.

"We certainly do," agrees Amber while arranging sausage rolls onto a white ceramic serving dish.

The three of us step back and take a look at our preparations. Blue and pink balloons are secured on each of the ladder-backed chairs. The food is prepped and arranged perfectly on the breakfast bar, and I smile big, taking in a deep breath. The food smells amazing, in fact the fragrances are stronger than they ever have been. Then the scent of marzipan twists my insides and I feel sick, physically sick. Clasping my hand over my mouth, I make a beeline for the bathroom.

I pass Seth on the stairs—he's on his way down but, seeing me, turns around and follows me up. Like the gentleman he is, he pushes the bathroom door open for me. I run inside and dry-heave into the toilet. It physically hurts my insides and my eyes water from the force with which my body is trying to be sick.

Seth brushes the side of my face as he moves my hair out of the way. "Are you okay, sweetheart?"

When the awful mouth-watering has stopped, and the feeling of needing to vomit subsides, I sit straight. "I'm fine, thank you."

His hand moves from my neck and down to my stomach, which he slowly rubs. "You two are giving Mummy a hard time."

I place my hand over his. "They certainly are."

We share a glance and his eyes crease in the corners. "Bernard and Rupert."

I elbow him playfully. "You are not calling our son Bernard. Anyway, we could be having two girls. Nora and Jazlyn."

Seth pulls a face. I'm not sure if it's my names or the fact he could be sharing a house with four women.

It's official though, we will find out the sex of our babies today. Cole is bringing the balloons filled with colourful confetti with him when he arrives.

Seth stands and grabs a flannel from the sink, which he wets and places on my forehead. "Or a boy and a girl. Bernard and Nora?"

I snatch the flannel. "Bernard isn't happening."

He sits behind me, and I lean back into his chest. He wraps his arms around me and forms a heart with his hands over my baby bump. "We have a few more months of quiet time, we should really make the most of it."

We jump, hearing a loud bang from upstairs, the loft room. Ellie and Freja have been making tents in Ellie's bedroom all morning. All my bedlinen and sheets have been draped over her cupboards and headboard.

Another bang, followed by the girls' raised voices. Sounds like they're arguing. It's not surprising. Since starting school they've become best friends and are together more than they're apart. Since Darcy no longer minds Ellie, Amber and I have split the childcare between our jobs, and it's been working really well.

"Quiet time?" I tease. The bathroom door is closed, so I take this moment to reach behind me and rub my hand over the crotch of his trousers. "I'd like that."

I'm not going to pretend this pregnancy has been easy so far. It hasn't. One thing being pregnant has done in our favour is crank up our sex life. I've never felt so horny as I do right now.

He hardens in my palm as I begin rubbing him faster. He laughs, nudging my hand away. "Later."

Another bang, and this time Ellie starts crying. Seth shuffles his way out from behind me. I smile as he pulls down his black t-shirt and adjusts the waistband of his trousers.

I crawl on all fours towards him. "Do you want me to help you with those?"

He shakes his head. "No, you stay there, unless you want me to have blue balls all afternoon."

I get up onto my knees, gripping his jeans. "Who said anything about blue balls?"

He pauses for a second, as if considering my offer, but when Ellie's crying gets louder his gaze leaves me and fixes on the door.

I toss the flannel at him. "Go."

He winks at me before slipping out of the bathroom.

The last six months have been a blur. It's like every broken facet of our lives has fallen into place and fitted together.

Ellie and Seth moved in with me when we returned from Disney World. Seth and Darcy had a huge argument when she discovered we had gone on holiday together. Their argument resulted in her kicking him out. Being the charitable person, I am, I offered them a room. It was the right thing to do.

By trying to split us up, Darcy only pushed us closer together. Irony at its finest.

Seth and Ellie slept in the spare room for a few months. Of course, he paid me some late-night visits. Our little living arrangement was working out nicely, that was until I found out I was pregnant. The pregnancy threw us a curveball for sure. We could no longer pretend to be 'just friends.'

We sat down as a family and had the talk with Ellie. It was decided that Seth would move into my bedroom, the spare bedroom would be the nursery and the loft room would be Ellie's new bedroom. Seth has since built an aquarium into her wall, which is home to several clown-fish. I transformed the boring blue walls into the magical world of *The Little Mermaid*. It wasn't complete without the addition of Nemo and Dory, who are playing with

327

Flounder and Sebastian. Funny thing about love, you sacrifice what you love for the people you love more. I gave up my art room, my dream of drawing with the sea as my backdrop. My house is no longer bricks and mortar, but my home, with the people I love most inside.

I jump as a foot or an elbow presses into me hard. I tap my bump softly. "I know, I know. I have a gender reveal party to get ready for."

Hearing voices downstairs, I head to my room to change and freshen up. I opt for a long flowing red t-shirt and a pair of my maternity jeans. I stand in front of the full-length mirror, focused on my baby bump. This is real. I'm having twins with the man I love, the man I've been obsessed with since I was a child.

"Lizzie, your parents are here," Amber calls.

"Showtime." Smiling at my reflection, I run my hand down my t-shirt. Seth often asks how the hell he got so lucky, but I feel like the lucky one. I didn't realise how incomplete I was until he came into my life. Having Ellie and the babies in our lives only cements what I already know. We're a unit. I'm complete.

I make my way downstairs; my parents are standing in the doorway. My mum is holding a large bag bursting with gifts.

I kiss her on the cheek. "Thanks, Mum." I take the bag from her and she helps my dad into the kitchen, where I can see other guests mingling.

Cole, with two helium balloons in his hand, is the next to arrive, followed by Seth's parents, his sister Imogen, and finally Darcy.

Seth has no idea I invited her, but I figure I'm carrying her nieces or nephews, it's about time we put the past behind us. She stands on the welcome mat, I guess unsure if she is indeed welcome. She doesn't back off, nor does she advance forward. She's waiting for me to invite her in. When the silence is too much to bear, she flashes a glance behind her at her car. "I don't think—"

I don't let her finish. I throw my arms around her shoulders and I hug her. She doesn't hug me back. One small, solitary tear spills from the corner of her eye, which she quickly wipes away. Well, well, so the ice queen does have a heart.

"Thank you for inviting me." Her words are forced, but she's trying. I had to swallow my pride to ask her to come in the first place, but actually turning up is huge for someone as proud as Darcy. I'm serving her a large slice of humble pie, which I know she'll eat crumb by crumb.

"I owe you an explanation," she says.

I lift my hand. "It's forgotten."

"No, Lizzie. I have to get this off my chest once and for all." She takes a deep breath before continuing. "I don't know if Seth told you, but Dwight and I struggled to have a family of our own. After years of unsuccessful IVF we simply stopped trying. Just before Anna fell pregnant with Ellie, I found out I was expecting. Dwight insisted we wait until the twelve-week scan before we told our families, so I waited. Dwight met me on his lunch hour. Jennifer, the sonographer, rubbed the gel on my stomach, and then we watched the screen as she glided the probe over my skin."

My heart is pounding. I feel sick as I know what she's about to tell me. As I place my hand over my stomach, Darcy places hers over mine. "I didn't get to see the tiny flicker of its heartbeat. I didn't get to see my baby turning

329

somersaults in my womb. I was the only mum to be leaving that room without a picture of my baby, without a baby."

The hold she had on my hands moments ago is gone, and she drops her hands to her side. She miscarried. I can't even begin to imagine what she went through. A tear makes its way down my cheek. So this is why she acted the way she did with Ellie. I want to speak but have no idea what to say. "Darcy—"

She shakes her head vehemently. "I don't want your pity, and this doesn't change anything with us. I still don't trust you, not yet."

I guess the bitch persona is easier for her to deal with than the pain she carries daily.

"Just let me in, Lizzie."

It's funny the ambiguity her statement carries. Let her into my house? Let her into my life? I'll concentrate on the latter later.

I move aside and let her enter. She hurries past me and joins her sister and parents through the kitchen's open door.

"You didn't have to do that." Seth speaks from the bottom step of the stairs as he pulls ear buds from his ears.

"I wanted to," I say, trying to add conviction to my voice. I don't think his sister and I will ever be the best of friends, but I'll make sure she knows I'm here for her, if and when she wants to talk.

He takes slow, calculated steps towards me. "Did I tell you that I love you?"

I place my hands in his and we lace our fingers together. "All the time."

He bends down and crashes his lips into mine. Our

lips don't just meet, they make love. Our tongues dance to a silent melody, one to which only we know the tune.

"Ewwww." Hearing Ellie's voice, we break the kiss. She and Freja are standing on the stairs. They're wearing matching blue sailor dresses—cute. Both girls are giggling, though Ellie looks more repulsed than entertained. She's at the age she thinks all boys are gross, and she gets awfully embarrassed seeing me and her dad kissing.

I take a step towards them. "Have you come downstairs to play some games?"

Ellie glances at Seth, and they share a conspiratorial look. I narrow my eyes at them, but Seth merely shrugs. He takes my hand. "She just wants to see if she's having brothers or sisters."

"Or one of each," I'm quick to correct.

We make our way into the kitchen. Everyone appears to be having a good time eating the food we've prepared and participating in at least one of the games. It's somewhat satisfying watching Darcy eat out of a nappy filled with chocolate sauce.

An hour of small talk is drying up. Everyone's focus turns to the two balloons tied to the ladder-backed chairs. Two balloons that Cole hasn't moved from and has guarded with his life.

Seth takes my hand. "Pink or blue?"

I reach my hand out for Ellie, which she takes. "I want two sisters."

I smile down at her. "We're about to find out."

As a family, we make our way to the balloons. Seth clears his throat and addresses our guests. "So, the moment you're all waiting for."

"Here, sis," Cole says, passing me a Swiss Army

LAURA RILEY

knife. He shakes Seth's hand and steps aside. I know Cole
has struggled with me and Seth being together, but he and
Seth have managed to put aside their differences and re-
build their friendship.

I glance up at the first balloon. Closing my eyes, I
push the knife up. The knife doesn't pierce the balloon,
and instead it bobs from side to side.

Seth grabs the balloon between his hands and I push
the knife up. Blue confetti rains to the ground, along with
something else.

"A boy," I squeal, and jump into Seth's arms.

"We're having a boy!" Seth yells. I look around the
room and everyone is clapping and hugging one another.
Rick hugs my mum and Amber hugs Chelsea. Rick and
Amber's relationship ended as quickly as it began, which
is a shame, but I don't miss the way they look at one another from across the room.

"What's that on the floor?" Seth says, pointing to the
confetti. I bend down and push the confetti aside to reveal
not a key but a gold ring. I turn to Seth, who's down on
one knee.

My heart's racing in my chest, and in this moment I
don't see anyone else in the room, only Seth.

"Lizzie, I love you more than you'll ever know. I love
you. Ellie loves you. You complete our crazy. You and our
children are it for me. Make me the happiest man alive and
be my wife."

Tears spill from my eyes, and I'm shaking. I jump into his arms. "Yes, yes, yes."

I hold out my left hand for him to slide the ring onto
my finger. Seth slides the ring down my finger, it gets
stuck on my knuckle. He attempts to wriggle it from side

to side, but it doesn't move. "Damn it."

My ring is perfect. An ocean-blue gem glistens up. "Nothing a trip to the jewellers can't fix." I quickly slide the ring onto my little finger and ball my hand into a fist so I don't lose it.

One by one, people come to congratulate us. Cole is the last person to hug me. He holds me so softly, as though he's scared of hurting the babies. I'm so happy I could explode; I wrap my arms around him and squeeze him.

"Don't worry about the cost, sis, I'll pay for everything."

I smile but know I won't take him up off his offer. Truth is, as well as my job, I'm making a decent amount of money from artwork. When my studio became Ellie's bedroom, Seth built me a summer house in the back garden— my new studio where I while away the hours lost in pastel, watercolour and chalk. Seth encouraged me to showcase some of my work at the art gallery in town. Roger, the gallery owner suggested setting up an online store, so I did. My latest piece sold for five hundred pounds and is to be sent all the way to Japan. I'm making money the right way, the honest way, which makes me question Cole's sudden windfall.

Loosening my hold on him, I gaze up into his eyes. "How? How can you pay for everything?"

I've often asked him how he could afford to buy me the house and upgrade us to the penthouse suite in Disney World. His answer has always been the same.

"I promise, I'll tell you when the time is right," Cole says, pulling away. "Now you have one more balloon to pop. I want to see if I have another niece or another nephew."

I love that Cole refers to Ellie as his niece. She won't call him uncle yet, but she will talk to him now. Her separation anxiety has improved greatly since she started school, though she regressed slightly when Anna visited. Anna came to say goodbye and tell Ellie she'd got a one-way ticket to Australia. The whole time Ellie clung to me like I was her anchor and Anna was the storm. Although Ellie was quiet for the meeting, I think it sank in after what Anna said to her. Ellie was being abandoned all over again, and it took Seth and I weeks to undo the damage that one meeting had caused.

"Lizzie, the balloon," Seth calls.

With the knife in my hand, I smile and look up at the balloon. I won't miss this time; I push the blade hard and the balloon pops on impact. Blue confetti rains down on us, along with something else that falls to the floor.

"Another boy," we all call, jumping up and down.

"Nice," Cole says, high-fiving Seth. "Now, to get them to wear the blue football shirt like their uncle Cole."

Seth shakes his head. "No chance."

Whilst everyone celebrates, I fish through the confetti and pull out a tiny necklace locket. I flip open the clasp and look at two small hearts. One of the hearts has a photo of me inside, the other has Ellie. I look around the small group of people and locate the little girl peering up at me.

I crouch down. "Come here, sweetie."

She walks over to me and peers into the locket. "Do you like it, Mummy?"

Mummy? My heart's bursting with pride. It's the first time she's called me Mummy, but it feels good, it feels right. We've had the conversation that I'll never replace her real mum, but that's okay. I'm going to be the best mum, the best stepmum, the best wife I can be.

"Here, let me help you with that," Seth says.

I pass him the necklace, my engagement ring sliding off my little finger and into his palm.

"Don't lose this," he warns, a playful smile tugging his lips. I watch as he unfastens the tiny clasp. "Turn around."

I do as he says. I move my hair to the side, his fingers brushing against my collarbone.

"There," he whispers.

The small locket and my engagement ring are held in place by the thin gold chain. Both are resting over my heart—incidentally, the place Ellie and Seth will always reside.

I spin around and face the two people I love most in this world. Ellie attempts to wrap her arms around my stomach, around her brothers. Seth wraps his arms around me, and poor Ellie is sandwiched between us.

"I love you guys," I say into the hug. My insides twist. The babies are particularly active today.

Ellie taps my stomach, then glances up at me. "Mummy, Bernard just kicked me."

I narrow my eyes at Seth. "Bernard is not—"

My words are stolen as Seth's lips crash against mine.

Moments are like stepping stones. They form unique paths. Once started these paths cannot be erased, nor can you stop the journey, no matter how hard you fight it.

Our future is in front of us. I can see the stones laid

out, and all we need to do is continue our journey.

Nobody said the path to love would be easy, and I'd be lying if I said it was. Nothing in life is guaranteed. You need to grab love, life and happiness with both hands. Treasure every moment. I've found my king and my little princess, and we're waiting for our princes to complete us.

This is it for me. I've found my forever.

Thank you for reading *Finding Our Forever*.
I hope you loved Lizzie and Seth's story.

If you'd be so kind,
please leave a review for me on Amazon.

Next is Rick's story, *Yours to Keep*.

Sign up to my newsletter and never miss a release!
http://eepurl.com/ds_fXj

Books by Laura Riley
British Billionaire Romances:

Charmed (co-written with April Wilson)
Captivated (coming soon)

Romances:

Finding Our Forever
Yours to Keep (coming soon)

Acknowledgements

Laura Riley is the pen name for Laura Williams. *Finding Our Forever* has been co-written with Judith Brimble. I want to thank my co-author Judith—this was a fun project.

To my besties, April Wilson and Vi Carter—you've always been there cheering me on, always pushed me to be a better author, always helped me believe in myself. This book wouldn't be here if it weren't for you both. You both are fantastic authors and my very dear friends. I'm blessed to have you in my life.

RJ for a fantastic job proofreading and editing my book. ME Kusel for my amazing cover. Wander, for our amazing cover image, and not forgetting model Dane.

CONTACT ME

Join Laura Riley's mailing list for news
and exclusive material.
(http://eepurl.com/ds_fXj)

READING GROUP
(https://www.facebook.com/groups/1116820285338874)

FACEBOOK
(https://www.facebook.com/authorlaurariley)

WEBSITE
(https://www.authorlaurariley.com/)

INSTAGRAM
(https://www.instagram.com/author_laura_riley/?hl=en)

Printed in Great Britain
by Amazon